RB

ADDITIONAL P
THE BARKERY & BISC

Bite the Biscuit

"Recipes for both dogs and people ad ... cozy that will taste just right to fans of both foodie and pet mysteries."

—*Booklist*

"Kicking off a cozy new series, prolific Johnston blends mystery and romantic intrigue."

—*Kirkus Reviews*

"An enjoyable mystery."

—*RT Book Reviews*

OTHER BOOKS BY LINDA O. JOHNSTON

PET RESCUE MYSTERIES, BERKLEY PRIME CRIME

Beaglemania

The More the Terrier

Hounds Abound

Oodles of Poodles

Teacup Turbulence

KENDRA BALLANTYNE, PET-SITTER MYSTERIES, BERKLEY PRIME CRIME

Sit, Stay, Slay

Nothing to Fear but Ferrets

Fine-Feathered Death

Meow is for Murder

The Fright of the Iguana

Double Dog Dare

Never Say Sty

Howl Deadly

Feline Fatale

HARLEQUIN NOCTURNE

Back to Life

The Alpha Force miniseries

HARLEQUIN ROMANTIC SUSPENSE

Undercover Soldier

Covert Attraction

Covert Alliance

SUPERSTITION MYSTERIES, MIDNIGHT INK

Lost Under a Ladder

Knock on Wood

Unlucky Charms

BARKERY & BISCUITS MYSTERIES, MIDNIGHT INK

Bite the Biscuit

To Catch a Treat

— A Barkery & Biscuits Mystery —

LINDA O. JOHNSTON

Midnight Ink
Woodbury, Minnesota

First Edition
First Printing, 2017

Book format by Bob Gaul
Cover design by Ellen Lawson
Cover illustration by Christina Hess

Midnight Ink, an imprint of Llewellyn Worldwide Ltd.

Library of Congress Cataloging-in-Publication Data
Names: Johnston, Linda O., author.
Title: Bad to the bone / Linda O. Johnston.
Description: First edition. | Woodbury, Minnesota: Midnight Ink, [2017] | Series: A Barkery & Biscuits mystery; #3
Identifiers: LCCN 2016056335 (print) | LCCN 2017002875 (ebook) | ISBN 9780738746289 | ISBN 9780738751825
Subjects: LCSH: Dog owners—Fiction. | Murder—Investigation—Fiction. | GSAFD: Mystery fiction
Classification: LCC PS3610.O387 B34 2017 (print) | LCC PS3610.O387 (ebook) | DDC 813/.6—dc23
LC record available at https://lccn.loc.gov/2016056335

Midnight Ink
Llewellyn Worldwide Ltd.
2143 Wooddale Drive
Woodbury, MN 55125-2989
www.midnightinkbooks.com

Printed in the United States of America

Bad to the Bone is dedicated to people who love their pets, most especially dogs—as are the other books in this series and nearly everything I write! Our pets are family and we all want to feed them well, including with tasty, healthy treats.

It's also dedicated to people with a sweet tooth and mystery readers who enjoy stories involving pets and food—especially those who read the Barkery & Biscuits Mysteries.

And, no surprise to those of you who read my books: I dedicate this one, too, to my dear husband Fred, who brainstorms with me and tastes the treats—the human ones—that I bake.

Plus, it's dedicated to my beloved Cavalier King Charles Spaniels: Lexie, who's no longer with us; Mystie, her "sister," who loves tasting the treats; and Cari, the newest member of our family.

ONE

"How about another dozen chocolate chip cookies?" I asked Sissy. The grinning middle-aged lady stood across the counter from me at Icing on the Cake, the people-treats portion of my two adjoining bakeries. Sissy, dressed in a loose red jacket over jeans, was a regular here, and she was planning a party for her poker club this weekend.

"Why not?" she replied. "And … well, let's go for another dozen of my favorites, too."

I knew what her favorites were. Sissy adored red velvet cupcakes. She had adored them far longer than I had owned Icing and its counterpart next door, Barkery and Biscuits, where I baked and sold healthy treats for dogs. Previously, the connected spaces had been one store, called Icing on the Cake. I'd bought the business from my friend Brenda Anesco when she'd had to leave Knobcone Heights to care for her ailing mother, and I'd split it into two shops. Brenda had specialized in the red velvet cupcakes, and I'd gotten the recipe from her.

"Absolutely," I told Sissy. I used fresh tissue paper to add cookies to the partly filled box I held, then grabbed another red box with the Icing logo on it from the shelves behind me and put the cupcakes into it.

I inhaled the delightfully sweet aroma emanating from the bakery's kitchen as I started tallying up Sissy's order. One of my part-time assistants, Vicky Valdez, was in there, baking today's final batch of treats for Icing. It was late afternoon now.

Before I finished totaling Sissy's bill, my only full-time employee, Dinah Greeley, entered through the door from the Barkery. I'd inherited Dinah along with Icing, and she was wonderful: a slightly overweight, young-looking college graduate who loved to help—and to write.

"Carrie, can you come over to the Barkery?" she asked, approaching me with a smile and a wave toward Sissy. "A friend of yours is here asking for you."

I knew who it was: Jack Loroco. He'd called me earlier.

"Sure, as soon as I'm done here."

"Oh, I'd be glad to finish helping Sissy." Dinah's smile widened. So did Sissy's.

Mine, too. "Great," I said. "Thanks." Once Dinah had reached my side behind the counter, I quickly showed her what I'd been up to, then said a quick and warm goodbye to Sissy, wished her luck at poker and with her party, and headed toward the door that Dinah had just come through.

As much as I loved Icing, I was about to enter my very own, very special creation, Barkery and Biscuits. As soon as I opened the door, I inhaled the meatier aroma and glanced across the blue tile floor—with its beige dog biscuit decoration in the center—to see my own adorable Biscuit, a golden toy poodle–terrier mix, in her large open-air crate at the far side of the room. She was trading nose sniffs through the mesh with Rigsley, Jack's large gray mixed-breed dog who was several times Biscuit's size.

Jack, holding the end of Rigsley's leash, was standing at the Barkery's glass display case, a mirror image of the one in Icing. It contained dog biscuits that were round or shaped like bones or even spaniel faces—every one of them my own creation or created specially for me.

"Hi, Carrie." Jack had obviously been watching for me. When I'd first met him months ago, he was tan and wore light-colored, sometimes-casual clothing, but it was October now, chilly in the San Bernardino Mountains. Jack was visiting our resort town, Knobcone Heights, more frequently than in the past, and now tended to wear long-sleeved shirts and dark trousers. Today, his shirt was beige, his trousers black.

I joined him at the display case. "Hi to you, too."

Jack was a good-looking guy, and at times I'd thought we might start sharing some kind of romantic connection, but that had never materialized. Instead, we had a business relationship—or, Jack wanted us to have one. And I was considering it more seriously now.

I'd developed healthy treats for the patients at the Knobcone Veterinary Clinic, where I still worked part-time as a veterinary technician. I loved working there. But I'd always wanted to be my own boss, so here I was, baking and selling my treats. And that was why Jack was in town so much. He worked for VimPets, the large pet food manufacturer, and he'd been trying since I'd opened to get me to sell to his company some of my best-loved and healthiest dog treat recipes. At first his company hadn't been interested. And even when things changed on that front, I'd remained reluctant. Now, though, Jack and I seemed to be headed toward a mutual agreement. He had convinced me—maybe—that the promotional advantage and public credit I'd get by selling VimPets a recipe might be worth it. And recently he'd told me he was fine with my idea of coming up with a brand-new recipe or two just for VimPets, rather than providing one I'd already created and used to bake products sold here. He wanted to promote his company's credibility in selling healthy and unique pet foods by showcasing me, and my Barkery, as an example. So now I was more receptive to the possibility.

Moving closer to the dogs, I started petting Rigsley. "I was wondering when you'd be back in town, Jack." After commuting for months to his home in Los Angeles, stopping to market VimPets products along the way, last month he'd actually rented an apartment in Knobcone Heights. His new relationship with my friend Billi Matlock, one of our City Councilwomen, might have been one reason why. Although Billi claimed it wasn't, she smiled a lot whenever I brought up the subject.

"So which treats look best to you today?" I asked Jack, teasing him in a way. The biscuits now in the case were the same kinds that were always there, and included carob-and-peanut-butter dog treats, pumpkin-and-yam biscuits, and small, crunchy training rewards that contained beef and yams.

The kinds of recipes I'd been waffling about selling to Jack.

"They all look good to me," he said. "You know that. And we can talk later about your ideas for the new recipes you're developing for me. You are doing that, aren't you?"

"Still thinking about it," I said as noncommittally as I could.

"Great. I'll be in town for a while and I hope we can work something out." He stopped looking into the case, straightened, and glanced down at me. He was about six feet tall, and his hazel eyes sparkled. "Anyhow, I just stopped in to say hello. Although—" He stopped, the expression on his face somewhat pleased, as if he'd just come up with a good idea. "How about if you and Reed and your dogs join Rigsley and me for dinner tonight? Since I just got back into town, I'm hungry for a meal at the resort."

Dr. Reed Storme was one of my bosses at the vet clinic. He and I were dating, and things had started to get a bit hotter and heavier between us, though for fun, not commitment. I never refused a possible evening out with Reed if I could help it, and dinner at the Knobcone Heights Resort, one of the nicest venues in town, was always fine with me. It's also where my brother Neal worked.

In fact… "Would you mind if I also invited Neal and Janelle to join us?" I asked. Janelle was one of my part-time assistants, as well as Neal's girlfriend.

"Fine," Jack said. "The more the merrier." He bent down to pat Rigsley's head, since his dog had come over and begun rubbing against Jack's leg.

"I assume Billi will be there, too." I walked toward the crate that held my little Biscuit, who looked a bit forlorn since Rigsley had stopped trading nose sniffs with her.

I was surprised not to immediately hear an "of course," and turned to face Jack just as the bell at the Barkery's door rang and some customers walked in. I'd installed this type of bell in both shops to alert my assistants and me when someone entered, in case we were all in another room.

This time, the visitors were a couple I didn't know, with a black miniature poodle ensconced in the woman's arms.

After aiming another quizzical look at Jack, I headed in their direction. "Welcome," I said. "Have you been to the Barkery before? Would you like me to give your pup a sample dog treat to help you decide what to buy for him—her?"

"Him," the twenty-something woman said. "He's named Vespa. And, yes, I know he'd love a sample." She knelt and put her dog on the ground, where Rigsley sniffed him and Biscuit wriggled behind her fence, obviously hoping to meet Vespa.

I walked behind the sales counter, to the back of the display case, where I could pick out a treat for little Vespa. When I turned around, Jack was watching me.

"Gotta go," he said, shortening Rigsley's leash. "And, sure, I'll call Billi and invite her to join us."

Why hadn't he said that before? Maybe the dinner was really an unplanned idea. Still, his reaction to my question sounded off.

"How's seven o'clock?" he added.

It was fine, since my shops both closed at six. I'd invite Reed and Neal when I had a moment to get on the phone. "Sounds good," I said, and got one of the carob-and-peanut-butter biscuits out of the case. As I walked around the counter, I heard the bell sound as Jack and Rigsley left.

I handed the woman the biscuit and she gave it to Vespa. As I started describing the ingredients in it, and the other wonderful biscuits the couple could buy, I couldn't stop wondering why Jack hadn't invited Billi to dinner until I'd asked.

I saw my friend fairly frequently, since in addition to being a City Councilwoman and owning a day spa, she ran Mountaintop Rescue, the local no-kill animal shelter. I always took leftover treats from the Barkery there, as well as to my vet clinic, before they got stale.

Was the relationship between Jack and Billi getting stale already? Surely she'd have told me…

I was overthinking this, I decided. I directed my concentration fully toward my customers. Tonight, I'd learn anything there was to know about Jack and Billi's relationship.

It was quarter till seven, and I was waiting for Reed to pick Biscuit and me up at our house. I'd changed from my usual shirt promoting one shop or the other, or both—the Barkery today—into a frilly white blouse and black skirt, with low-heeled black shoes that were pretty, I thought, but comfortable.

With no hesitation, Reed had accepted the invitation to have dinner with us at the resort. Of course, I'd assured him we'd eat outside under the heating gadgets, so that Hugo, his Belgian Malinois, could join us, too.

My house was in a nice residential neighborhood without a lot of traffic, so I had no problem hearing Reed's arrival. Biscuit woofed as I opened the door. I smiled at the handsome guy standing there and figured he must have taken time to shave, since usually, by this hour, he had a dark shadow of beard that complemented his thick, wavy black hair.

He smiled back and bent so we could share a kiss before heading to his car, where Hugo was waiting.

The drive to the Knobcone Heights Resort didn't take long, mostly because the town was fairly compact, not because my neighborhood was among the posh ones in that area. The resort was off Summit Street, on the shore of Knobcone Lake. It consisted of several sprawling buildings, each a couple of stories high, with sloping slate roofs over thick white walls and dark wood-framed windows. Reed found a spot right away in the parking lot—which would not be a cheap undertaking, and I doubted Neal would be able to validate our parking tonight. But I anticipated a fun evening.

As we exited the car with our dogs, I noticed Billi off to our right in the busy lot. I nudged Reed, and we headed in her direction. She saw us and stopped to wait.

Billi was a member of one of Knobcone Heights' most elite families, but she was sweet and down-to-earth and constantly busy with her three careers. She was lovely and trim, with long, highlighted dark hair and a face I was sure any man would notice, with high cheekbones, full lips, and smiling deep brown eyes. Tonight she wore a silvery shirt-dress and carried a small matching bag. She hadn't brought her dogs, Fanny and Flip, so she was alone.

"Hi, Carrie and Reed," she said as we reached her. "Biscuit and Hugo, too." She bent to give both dogs a pat on their heads.

"How are things at Mountaintop Rescue?" I asked as we headed for the door of the main reception building, past rows of parked cars and people heading into and out of the parking lot.

"Fine, as always. In fact, some guys who work at a technology company in San Bernardino came by today to check out a couple of pit bulls they saw on our website. Can you guess the rest?"

"Those pit bulls are now in their forever homes?"

"Yep." Billi's smile grew even wider, and I matched it.

We reached the door quickly. While the resort's two other buildings contained mostly hotel rooms, this one held the reception desk, restaurant, bar, and spa, and also provided access to the stairway that led to the lakefront.

Inside, the ceilings were tall and slanted. I turned right, toward the reception counter, and stood in front of it just long enough to wave at Neal to let him know we were here. Then I joined Reed and Billi again.

The resort's main restaurant was at the rear of the building, facing the lake, which provided a wonderful view. There was a substantial patio behind the restaurant, overlooking the beach. We headed there with the dogs.

Reed held the door open for all of us. Jack had already arrived, and sat at the head of a couple of tables he'd pushed together to accommodate the group he expected. An outdoor heater on a tall post stood at each end of the table, and I could feel the warmth the nearest one generated. Rigsley sat at his feet.

We weren't the only ones outside, despite the chill. In fact, the patio was fairly crowded. I glanced toward the nearby window and noted that the inside lights glowed on an even larger crowd. To get seated faster, a bunch of people must have decided to sit outside.

"Hi." Jack stood as we joined him, as did Rigsley. Out of curiosity, I observed the initial interaction between Jack and Billi. It was what I would have expected before sensing his hesitation earlier. She approached him quickly, and they shared smiles and a brief kiss.

I hadn't lost my curiosity about his earlier behavior, but apparently Jack and Billi remained an item. I still wasn't sure whether or not it was what I wished for my friend, but if it was what she wanted, then I was fine with it.

"Good to see you, Reed," Jack said. "And Carrie, thanks for helping me put this group together. I take it that Neal will be joining us?"

"Yes, and Janelle, too."

We sat in the seats Jack indicated. Our dogs took their places on the ground beside us. Billi sat beside Jack, and I sat next to her with Reed on my other side. The opposite side of the table remained empty for now, but two of the chairs would eventually be occupied by my brother and his girlfriend.

That still left one seat. Would someone else be joining us?

I didn't ask, since I knew I'd find out one way or another as the evening progressed.

A server soon came over to take our drink orders. It was Gwen Orway, whom Neal had romantically pursued before he met Janelle a few months ago. I'd gotten the impression that Neal had genuinely cared for Gwen, but that she wasn't as interested in him. She had, after all, told Neal she had a boyfriend, one who didn't live in Knobcone Heights.

She greeted us all warmly. I wondered briefly if she was still dating the guy down the mountains.

All the drama in relationships. I'd had some of my own in the past, too, and a failed relationship had been part of the impetus that sent me to Knobcone Heights once I'd qualified as a veterinary technician. I was glad about it all now, but, despite my growing feelings for Reed, I still felt hesitant about getting too deeply involved in a relationship, after my own experience and seeing those of others.

If I decided to open up, though, I could do a lot worse than Reed.

"Hi, Gwen," I said after she had taken the others' orders. "I'd like a glass of the house merlot to start with, plus a glass of water."

"Sure, Carrie." A note in her voice made me look up at her. Had Neal just walked out with Janelle? But when I glanced in the direction she was staring, I saw that she was looking at Jack. "I'll bring your beer soon, Jack," she called to him.

Had he demanded that she serve him before taking the orders? No matter. Jack could wait like the rest of us. As I continued looking toward him, Neal and Janelle did in fact appear.

People always remark on the strong resemblance between my brother and me, thanks to our similar Kennersly characteristics. I'm not sure whether these characteristics are more masculine or feminine, but I consider my blond brother handsome and myself okay-looking. And Janelle was pretty that night, as always.

They joined us at our table—and the seats Jack asked them to occupy left one chair empty on his other side, the side opposite Billi. This meant we must indeed be expecting someone else, and I wondered even more who it was.

Gwen took Neal and Janelle's drink orders, then hurried inside. I noted no drama between them.

Jack started the conversation by asking Neal if he had any hikes scheduled soon. He was aware that my brother's passion was his work as a local tour guide. Neal took tourists, and locals, too, on hikes as often as he could get a group together.

Neal answered affirmatively. He had several dates in mind, and even hoped to lead a hike the evening of Halloween. "Not to collect candy like the trick-or-treaters, though," he assured everyone.

We all started discussing whether we intended to wear any Halloween costumes, and I let people know I'd be baking special people treats at Icing on the Cake for the holiday. Janelle promised to take lots of pictures of all of us, since in addition to working for me, she was a great professional photographer.

As we spoke, I noticed a woman stand briefly in the doorway, then head in our direction, grinning broadly and seeming to stare at Jack. Was she the person who'd be sitting with us?

"Hey, Jack," she called effusively as she reached his side. She was short, pretty, and dressed all in black, with a mop of curly blond hair. I wondered who she was.

Jack rose. "Everyone, this is Wanda Addler. She works with me at VimPets, and I've brought her along on this trip to see how I promote our products—and how I look for new opportunities." He glanced down and winked at me.

"That's right. Hi, everyone." Wanda looked around the table. Her glance seemed to stop on Billi. Did they know each other?

Before I could figure anything out, Wanda turned back to Jack. She pulled his head down toward her, apparently knocking him a little off balance, since he grabbed the back of his chair.

A moment later, Wanda's mouth was on Jack's, and that kiss looked like one sexy act. It lasted for a while, too. Jack appeared to try to pull away at first, but remained pressed up against Wanda for several long seconds.

When he finally succeeded in pulling back, his eyes were open wide and he seemed to swallow hard.

Before he could say anything, though, Wanda's gaze swept the table once more, landing finally on Billi. And if I was any judge of what she was doing, she sure appeared to be sending a smug and challenging look toward our huge-eyed, frowning City Councilwoman.

TWO

I SHOT A LOOK at Billi, too—one both curious and sympathetic. Had she known Jack was seeing someone else, a coworker who was with him on this trip?

I guessed not, since although the expression she leveled on Jack looked calculatedly neutral, her mouth curved downward at the corners. If I had to guess, I'd believe she felt somewhat crushed.

"Well, well," Billi said after we all were silent for a moment. "Who knew? And you work together? You must see each other a lot, and how convenient. How lucky—although I thought it was generally frowned on for coworkers to see each other socially."

I swallowed a bit at that and glanced toward Reed, beside me. He only smiled, although I figured he knew why I was looking at him. I supposed some people at our veterinary hospital might be frowning at us now and then. We didn't publicize the fact that we were seeing each other socially, but neither did we hide it—not that we kissed or anything like that at our clinic. At least not much. He was a vet, I was a vet tech, and we worked—and played—well together.

In fact, the clinic's main vet, Dr. Arvus Kline, was aware of it, and Arvie always seemed to encourage it. He was a good friend of mine, after all, as well as to Reed, and wanted the best for us—which, I assumed, meant he could see us developing a real relationship someday.

"Well, we don't exactly advertise it," Wanda said, her arm still around Jack's shoulders as she stood beside him, an expression of triumph still on her face. "But yeah, we're lucky."

Physically, she appeared to me to be the antithesis of slender and lovely Billi. Oh, she was pretty enough, but shorter and plumper than my friend, who worked out often in her spa. Wanda's blond hair was a golden cap around her full face. She wore slacks, and her tight sweater appeared to have been chosen to highlight her generous curves.

Jack turned, in effect shrugging off Wanda's embrace. If I read his expression as well as I believed I'd interpreted Wanda's, he was embarrassed but wanted to appear fully unemotional.

Was she the reason he hadn't invited Billi at first? I'd have bet on it.

Rigsley stood up then, and so did Biscuit and Hugo. Jack bent to pat each of them briefly. Wanda ignored them.

"Sure, we're friends, and we work together," Jack said. "I like that. But… well, let's not get carried away." This, of course, was addressed to Wanda, whose triumphant smile turned into an irritated glare.

"Oh, I'm not carried away," she said, blinking her bright blue eyes—again, very different from Billi's brown ones. "Unless you want to carry me over the threshold of your apartment." She grinned at his shocked look, then turned her smile toward Billi. "I'm staying there with him, you know."

Her smile appeared challenging, as if she was daring Billi to ask if she was taking full advantage of nighttimes spent in the same apartment as Jack. Whether she was or not, I figured I knew what Wanda would say—and didn't really want to know.

Instead, ignoring her—and Jack, too—I gently pulled Biscuit and Hugo's leashes and got them to settle down again, then turned to Reed as Rigsley also joined his master. "I heard rumors of a really wonderful lifesaving situation you were involved in at the clinic the other day. I want to hear all about it."

If the rest of our tablemates didn't, too bad. At least it would change the subject.

"Well, it started when Billi called us from Mountaintop Rescue," Reed began, looking over my shoulder toward where Billi sat. She was now facing us, ignoring Jack and the woman who claimed to have all his attention now. Good. I didn't want to look at him at this moment either. Although to see my friend, I did have to look in Jack's direction.

Billi recounted her part in the very moving tale, about how a sixteen-year-old boy who sometimes volunteered at Mountaintop Rescue had burst into the shelter a couple of days ago, crying that he had a dog in his car who'd jumped out of the woods when he was on the way up the mountain toward Knobcone Heights. He didn't see the dog until it was too late, and had hit it. He made sure the dog was still alive and put it in his car, driving to the shelter as fast as he dared.

When Billi and her staff went out to the car, they found a very injured dog who appeared to be a Golden Retriever mix. They borrowed the kid's keys and drove the damaged pup immediately to the Knobcone Veterinary Clinic. There, Reed had been the first vet to hurry out to the vehicle, and he got staff who brought the dog in on a gurney.

It had all happened at a time when I wasn't working there, so I'd only heard part of the story.

"I don't want to go into the gory details," Reed said, and I turned back toward him. "But there were a lot of injuries we needed to deal with. It was touch and go ... but fortunately mostly go. He's still with us at the hospital, and it looks like he'll survive."

"That's so wonderful." Billi's smile was now genuine-looking, for the first time since Wanda had appeared.

"Absolutely," I said.

"Well, gee, that is a happy ending," Wanda broke in. "Looks like there's another dog that could be fed with VimPet products soon."

Maybe so, but it was a weird thing to say. Having the poor dog heal from his injuries didn't have a huge amount to do with what he ate, as long as his food was nutritious.

But *keeping* this dog, and others, in good health could have a lot to do with their food—or treats. In fact, Jack had told me when we'd first met that he loved the idea of purchasing recipes created specifically to keep dogs in good health, or to help them become healthier. And his superiors now agreed with him. What better promotion was there for their company than to be able to say a vet tech had created some of their products to help her clinic's patients? My recipes were unlike many other treat recipes that were put together carefully yet somewhat randomly, without having a specific health goal in mind.

In other words, my recipes were the best, since they'd nearly all been developed by me, at home, while I worked at the vet clinic. I had a nutritional purpose for each treat, a particular type of sensitivity or illness to deal with. So far, all my treats had seemed to work well for whatever issue I approached. And I'd do the same thing with any recipes I created for VimPets.

VimPets marketed its products nationally. All of its products contained supposedly healthy ingredients, or at least they were promoted that way. Adding any of my treats to their inventory and promoting how they were created could only help the company's reputation. I somewhat liked the idea, especially on behalf of promoting the Barkery, but hadn't been too eager to actually get started on it.

And now, seeing this Wanda woman, who also worked for VimPets—well, I wasn't at all sure I wanted to do anything to aid a company that hired people like her.

Jack had sometimes brought other VimPets personnel on his many trips, and I'd had no reason—before—to dislike any of them. But that was before.

Gwen brought our drinks and stayed to take our food orders then, and I appreciated the timing. After she left, I pondered how to again direct the conversation in a way that wouldn't ruin this gathering any more than it already had been, but just then I heard some music, presumably a phone's ring.

Wanda pulled a phone from her purse, which was hung over the back of her chair. Making no apologies as she glanced at the screen, she stood up and walked away.

Good. We could hope it would be a nice, long call.

"So glad your rescue story had a happy ending." I smiled first at Reed at my left, then toward Billi at my right.

"Absolutely," Billi said and took a sip of her wine.

Conversations at the table began again. They were general and seemed somewhat uncomfortable, even in Wanda's absence. We all thanked Gwen when she brought out delicious wheat rolls and butter.

After I'd taken my first bite, though, Billi said quietly, "I'd like a potty break. Care to join me?"

I heard an undercurrent there, as if she had something she wanted to discuss with me, so I said, "Good idea."

I asked Reed to keep an eye on Biscuit. I could have asked Neal or Janelle, too. They all liked my beautiful and adorable little dog —especially Neal, who always called her "Bug."

The restroom was relatively roomy. Before we entered the stalls, I continued the conversation I'd begun with Billi on the way over, speaking softly.

"You know Jack's one giant flirt," I said quietly. "Remember, you even asked if I was okay with you dating him, since he'd flirted with me for a while, and—"

"Yes, I remember all that, of course. Even so, he was being somewhat serious with me, though I still saw how he acted with nearly every woman he had a conversation with. And now—well, I'll have to get over it. I did think we were heading toward something special. He made it look that way. I was beginning to really—"

Before she could finish, a stall door opened. Wanda walked out. She just stood there and smiled. "Well, fancy seeing both of you here. And it's a good thing you're backing away from him, Councilwoman." She turned to face only Billi. "You see, the thing is, I know Jack and who and what he is. He's a great asset to VimPets—and to me. And now that I've set my sights on him, you can be sure he'll be all mine."

She turned her back on us, then, as if we weren't there—or if we were, we didn't matter—and washed her hands.

I aimed a glance at Billi, whose expression appeared livid. Hey, she was a City Councilperson. She'd run for office, which meant she was used to competing for what she wanted.

Would she want to compete with this nasty witch for Jack? Wouldn't it be better just to dump him?

I wasn't about to ask while we were still in Wanda's presence. Instead, I pursed my lips, shook my head, and headed for one of the stalls. Billi chose the stall next to mine, both of us pretending to ignore Wanda even as she pretended to ignore us.

When I came out, Wanda was no longer there. The door to Billi's stall remained closed. "She's gone," I said.

"Good." Billi's door slammed open, as if she'd been waiting for me to give her the green light to exit.

Though Billi and I were good friends, I wasn't sure what to say to her. I began with the obvious. "Whatever Jack thinks of her, she knows you and he have something going and is trying to push you apart. The question is—do you care enough about Jack to jump into her little game? My opinion is that, if you do want a genuine relationship with Jack, and he wants it too, let him be the one to tell her where to go."

"Yeah. Back to LA, fast. Before I really decide to kick her butt." Billi was muttering as she finished washing her hands.

"It's easy enough for me to say," I said as I reached for a paper towel from the dispenser next to the sinks, "but I think this is Jack's situation to fix. And if he doesn't, then that tells you who he really is."

Billi aimed her angry brown eyes at me. "You're right. I know it. But just in case he doesn't tell her to buzz off—or at least buzz off anything personal, since they work together—I would absolutely hate to have her think she's winning this situation."

"If he doesn't tell her to buzz off," I said quietly, not moving my gaze from hers, "then she does win. But that also would tell you that Jack's not worth the tiniest bit of effort to fight over."

That apparently got to her. She'd been standing tall and stiff near the sinks, but now her shoulders lowered and her position loosened. "Hey, Carrie Kennersly, has anyone ever told you that you're a good judge of people, not just pets?"

I smiled broadly. "I think someone just did. Thanks. Now, let's go back and show both of them that you're in charge of your own life and feelings."

We returned to the table just in time for Gwen to serve our meals. All the dogs with us sat up and started wagging their tails, and I appreciated their greeting.

I half expected Wanda to be sitting on Jack's lap, or leaning beside him nibbling his ear, or something else equally yucky. Instead, there was an interesting conversation going on about dogs and taking care of them, both from a veterinary and feeding perspective, which was appropriate to this group though not exactly neutral, as it turned out.

Reed caught my eye as I took my seat again and tossed me a sympathetic look.

"Then you do think all dogs should be saved when possible, Dr. Storme?" That was Wanda, and she stared across the table toward Reed.

"Of course," he said, turning toward her.

"But some are known to be aggressive. And others—well, there are a lot who will never live with people but are stuck at shelters to live out every minute of their sorry lives." Wanda's look now was straight on Billi, as if challenging her to come up with something that made all dogs' lives worthwhile, even if they remained unhomed and unloved.

"Mountaintop Rescue, and many other first-rate shelters, have workers and volunteers who do everything possible to show love to the residents while we have them, as well as find them new homes." That was Billi speaking, the ultimate pet rescue organization representative. She sounded matter-of-fact, as if in educator mode, even though I suspected she spoke through gritted teeth toward this woman. "If any dog is poorly trained or homeless, you can blame the people who should have taken care of him, or at least had his parents spayed and neutered."

"But that would mean fewer dogs around to eat VimPets food—although I realize most shelters can't afford our premium products." Wanda smiled at Billi, then at Jack. "I have a feeling, though, that Mountaintop Rescue has been feeding its wards some of our goods. And, hopefully, paying for it, since I've seen no files about donating to the shelter here."

She was now baiting both of them—Jack, in case he'd donated food to the shelter run by the woman he was dating, since in some way that was inappropriate to VimPets policies; and Billi, in case she'd used donations to the shelter to pay the premium prices charged for VimPets products.

I noticed that everyone else around the table—Neal, Janelle, and even Reed, for this moment—were eating, trying to act as if all was fine. I took a couple bites of my own chicken Kiev and rice.

"Don't get me wrong," Wanda continued. "I understand what you're saying. I love dogs. And I really hope we can get some good, healthy recipes from you, Carrie, ones we can brag to the world about since they were developed by a skilled veterinary technician as over-the-top healthy treats for all our customers' dogs. But just like I wonder about whether Mountaintop Rescue is all it's professed to be, I want to make sure that any recipes we get from you really are healthy and unique, and not just something anyone can find online."

The smug smile she shot at me made me want to stand and confront her. Or take the position right now that she, and VimPets, would never get me to sell any recipes to them at all.

In fact, I moved my glare toward Jack with that message in my eyes. I figured he'd be able to read it.

He did. Maybe he was expecting it. Suddenly he stood. He took Wanda's arm and made her stand, too, facing him.

"Back down, Wanda," he growled at her. "I'm not sure what you're trying to accomplish, but if it's supposed to be helpful somehow, I don't see it. And some of our higher-up execs might be interested in hearing what's happening here."

"I'm sure they would. That's what I'm saying. One in particular would be interested in hearing what's happening between us." Since she was across the table from me, I saw her expression, which appeared both joyous and challenging.

I didn't understand what was going on between Jack and her, but her next words confused me even more.

"Oh, don't worry, my dear Jack. My report to our bosses will be about what a great job you're doing here, as we discussed. And how you're doing such a great job wooing the veterinary technician, whose new Barkery is gaining such a following in Knobcone Heights and beyond, to sell you some very special recipes." She paused. "Or, at least, that's what I'll tell them if it leads to your saying nice things about me, too. I'm ready for a promotion, just like you are. And of course, if we keep seeing each other, I'll tell them all the stuff that they'll like."

I didn't understand what this woman was really trying to accomplish. What she was saying seemed almost contradictory. Did she like Jack romantically? Did she want him to work with her, and would she help him achieve what he supposedly was looking for here in Knobcone Heights? Or was she threatening him in case he didn't bend to her wishes and give her lots of kudos and recommendations to their bosses?

I wasn't sure which way Jack was interpreting it either, but apparently not the way Wanda wanted.

He again took her arm, perhaps harder this time since she seemed to wince and try to pull away.

"I don't know what you're up to, Wanda. We've been working together for a while, and I've liked it—till now. You seem to be trying to undermine what I want to accomplish, for your own purposes and not for the good of the company. And this personal stuff? We've talked, yes, and you're staying in my apartment, but not—"

"Let's not talk about it in front of all these people, Jack." Wanda's tone was harsher now than I'd heard it. "And if you think you're going to get away with breaking things off with me to—"

It was Jack's turn to interrupt. "There's nothing to break off with you."

"Not that you want anyone to know. But we know. And I'll make sure you pay big for anything you do that's not good for me."

"Ditto," Jack yelled. "And who's more senior, with the higher position within the company? Not you. You can be sure you'll pay for this nonsense. And—"

"Forget it. That's enough, you pig. I'll make sure you're the one who'll pay. Believe me." She pulled away from him, shot a glare toward everyone at the table, and stomped away from the patio.

THREE

For a long moment, all of us were quiet, even the dogs.

I felt both stunned and confused. What was really going on?

Who was that woman, and what was actually on her mind? She worked for a company that was all about taking good care of dogs, and she claimed to love them, yet I wasn't certain she even liked them. She'd seemed to taunt Reed for trying to save the lives of all dogs, not only aggressive ones but the poor, sweet ones who were housed in shelters. She'd taunted Billi about that, too. Her attitude was definitely upsetting to a dog lover like me.

Then there was Jack. She claimed to care about him, even sleep with him, yet she'd just threatened his career at VimPets. But Jack was higher up in management, wasn't he? He told her that. How could she harm him—except by telling lies?

And why?

I couldn't help myself. I had to ask.

Turning to Jack, who'd just sat down again, I said, "What was that all about?"

He glared at me initially, as if his hope had been to just let Wanda leave and pretend nothing unusual had happened.

Then his shoulders sagged.

"I'd like to say that woman is just nuts, but—well, she's actually pretty smart. And conniving. She's trying to work her way up the Vim-Pets corporate ladder by any means she can." He smiled grimly. "*Any* means, including sleeping with one of the highest executives—and I certainly don't mean me. But she's threatening to tell him that I've come on to her, so he'll fire me." He shook his head.

"Then she's not staying in your apartment?" That was Billi, who remained seated. Her tone was cold enough to make Biscuit stir at my feet.

"No, actually, she is—mainly because that same executive knows I have a place here and that she wanted to come and check out what I was doing. He essentially tied me to her, here, so she could observe me and report back to him. She intends to use her position to do her damnedest to get rid of me, since the next rung on her ladder to the top is currently occupied by me."

I was surprised when my brother was next to dive into this conversation, since he and Janelle were the most remote observers in this group. But Neal, his light eyebrows raised as if he felt sympathy for Jack, said, "Then there's nothing at all—well, intimate in your relationship?"

"No, there's not." Jack sounded furious that someone would even ask. This time it was Rigsley who moved, standing and rubbing his back against his owner's leg as if trying to comfort him—without success. "Wanda is staying in the extra bedroom in my apartment, just like my boss and I discussed. But she slipped into my room last night and tried—well, that's too much information. And now she's making it clear she'll try to use the fact we're in the same apartment, and the lie that there's more to it, that I tried to initiate something, to control me. The b—" He didn't finish but seemed to sag again.

I glanced at Billi. Was she buying this?

Did she care?

I thought I read a momentary look of sympathy in her dark brown eyes, but then her expression hardened. "You could have said no, even if it was your boss who asked you to let her stay there," she said. "It sounds fairly obvious it could lead to trouble."

"Sure, I could have. But you don't know the personalities involved. I might have been canned on the spot for daring to disobey the guy."

The two of them traded glares, but their expressions both softened simultaneously. Maybe Jack and Billi really did care about one another. If so, Wanda was definitely an intruder.

Of course, if Jack did care for Billi, couldn't he have found a way to deal with this in advance—maybe by not coming to town right now? Or by subletting his apartment, so he wouldn't have someplace for Wanda to stay? Or…

Okay. I was getting too wrapped up in this situation, maybe because I cared about Billi and her feelings, and I'd started viewing Jack as something of a friend, too. After all, I had fun jousting with him in our negotiations about selling him recipes. But now he sounded like a weakling within his organization, nervous about being booted out. Who knew whether he'd be able to make good on any promises about how my recipes would be promoted, even without this extra Wanda twist to the situation?

I decided this might be a good time to change the subject. "Hey," I said, "my chicken Kiev tonight is really good but I'm letting it get cold. Anyone else enjoying their dinner?"

A couple pairs of eyes—Jack's and Billi's—seemed to regard me as if I'd just solved all of the world's problems, and both began describing their own food: Jack's T-bone steak and Billi's lemon pepper chicken salad. As this discussion continued, I managed to look at our other tablemates, Reed and Neal and Janelle, and couldn't help grinning at the relief and amusement on all their faces. Reed even took the opportunity to slip a piece of his own steak to Hugo.

The worst of the evening was over.

Reed drove me home, with both dogs in the backseat again. We soon pulled into the driveway and parked. "Would you and Hugo like to come in?" I asked.

I'd checked with Neal beforehand. My brother lived with me, but he was spending the night with Janelle at her place, so Biscuit and I would be alone.

"Sure," Reed said.

We took our dogs for a short walk in the cool night along the sidewalk of the slightly curving street, the streetlights sufficient for us to see our path easily. I had a fenced dog run for Biscuit but tended to walk her as often as I could. It certainly made sense for us to walk both dogs this evening. It wasn't extremely late, only eight thirty. Plus, it was enjoyable to stroll past my neighbors' houses. They were similar to my single-story home, most covered in attractive wood siding, stained a cedar shade, with several small wings with sloped roofs—but all had their individuality, too.

Soon we returned to my place and went inside. "Would you like some beer?" I asked Reed. I was keyed up enough after all the emotional overtones of our miserable dinner to figure that coffee would keep me up all night. Alcohol might help me sleep.

"Sure." Reed followed me from my entry down the hall and into the kitchen.

First thing, I made sure that the dog bowl on the wood-grained floor was filled with adequate water for Biscuit and Hugo. Then I strode to the metal fridge and brought out two bottles of beer imported from Ireland—part of Neal's supply, but I'd replenish them.

Neither of us needed a glass, and we sat side by side at my round kitchen table sipping beer and rehashing some of the nonsense.

Until I stopped it.

"I know I've got lots to think about regarding whether to sell VimPets some of my recipes, new or existing," I said, looking into Reed's dark eyes.

There was definite concern and sympathy in his expression. "I gather you had some interest in it, though, to help promote your Barkery. But I also gather your business is pretty good, so getting extra publicity would be ... well, icing on the cake."

I laughed aloud as he smiled at his own joke. "You're right," I agreed. "My interest in selling recipes to them has gone back and forth over time, and the VimPets management wasn't particularly interested at first anyway. Jack wasn't great at following up, either. He came to town often, though, for his work and even for recreation, since he likes to go boating. Now that he's being even pushier about it—well, I gather from everything we just saw that he's hoping that buying recipes from me will somehow help his position against Wanda at VimPets, but I don't really see how. And now my answer is no. I certainly don't want any part of his company's politics, let alone to do anything that would bring Wanda back here again."

"I'll drink to that." Reed lifted his bottle of beer.

We clinked our bottles, and as we did so we began looking deeply into each other's eyes.

I had a feeling we were drinking to more than staying out of VimPets politics.

And when Reed rose, and I rose, and I found myself in his arms kissing him deeply, I was sure of it.

He knew where my bedroom was, down the hall. In fact, I let him lead me there.

I woke up earlier than Reed the next morning, earlier than I needed to rise to get ready to run off to my shops and start baking for the day. I even preceded Biscuit and Hugo, who both slept on the floor in my bedroom.

As I lay there, I couldn't help thinking about the most enjoyable parts of our bedroom antics last night. Then I thought more about who I'd done them with.

I'd started dating Reed a few months ago, soon after he joined the Knobcone Heights Veterinary Clinic in the spring. At first it was just fun, since I really liked him and admired his attitude about saving animals. But I also didn't like the idea of settling down with one guy, so I'd dated others, too—including Jack when he was in town. As time went on, I'd still had some interest in seeing other men, but that had started to wane.

And now? Well, now we were exclusive. And, clearly, more. In fact, I'd really come to care about this guy despite constantly reminding myself that we really weren't in a relationship.

Joining him in bed was one thing. Making a commitment was something else.

I believed he cared about me, though. And if I was honest with myself, well … I was potentially really falling for him.

So why was I hesitating? Because of my last relationship, the one that had gone so sour more than five years ago—which was when I moved to Knobcone Heights.

I tried not to think about it much, but I'd once believed I'd found the love of my life, John—a lawyer around my age who appeared to love animals. Or so he claimed, and I believed him since he had a sweet pit bull named Rambo. But then he decided, in order to further his career, to move into an upscale condo where dogs weren't allowed. Without telling me, he dumped poor Rambo at a high-kill shelter.

I'd saved Rambo and dumped John, half wishing I could leave *him* in a high-kill shelter.

Well, there was no possibility of that happening with Reed, who spent his life saving as many animals as he could and ensuring that those he couldn't save didn't suffer.

If he hurt me at some point, animals wouldn't be the cause.

So did I dare, after all this time, to consider some kind of commitment?

"Are you awake, Carrie?" asked a deep, husky voice from beside me. Since both dogs suddenly stood at attention, I would have been awakened even if I hadn't been before.

"Yes," I said. "Thanks. It's about time for me to start getting ready."

Reed knew my timing, so it wasn't a surprise to either of us that it was only four thirty in the morning. In fact, he thought he was helping me by waking me. Which he was.

And I appreciated it.

I turned onto my side and pulled him tightly against me, and, well, things began to happen again. Enjoyable things. But all good things come to an end, and eventually I gave him the last kiss I'd be able to give him in bed this time. Too bad.

I finally got up then, and so did he. I put on a robe and let both dogs into my fenced dog run, then got dressed.

"Do you have a session at the clinic today?" Reed asked as I walked him and Hugo to my front door.

"Happily, yes. A couple of hours this afternoon."

"Great. I'll see you then and we can talk about getting together for a private dinner, just the two of us, tonight. Sound okay?"

"It sure does," I said and gave him a goodbye kiss.

Of course, at that time, I didn't know what would happen at my shops that day.

FOUR

THE DAY STARTED OUT differently than usual on several counts. One difference was my delightful overnight visit from Reed. That led to the second, since I was almost never late to my stores. I always aimed to get there at five a.m. to start baking, and often had one of my assistants get there at that time, too.

Today it was a good thing that I'd asked Frida Grainger to come in first thing. Frida lived in Knobcone Heights because her fiancé did. She'd graduated from the Art Institute of California and occasionally worked as a chef before moving to Knobcone Heights, and now she created her own gourmet people food in her off hours.

Frida was a great asset to both Icing and the Barkery. And today I considered her extra special for arriving before me and starting the day's Icing treats.

I parked in the lot behind the stores, then walked Biscuit around to the front to let her perform any necessary duties, and also to avoid the kitchen. Biscuit was always permitted in the Barkery and

Biscuits sales area, but not any other parts of the shops, in accordance with local law.

As we reached Summit Avenue, I looked up and down the street, where streetlights provided most of the illumination in this early morning hour. A few cars cruised by but things were still pretty quiet. I didn't see anyone across the street in the dimly lit town square.

Despite being about a quarter-hour late, I didn't have to worry this early about people lining up in front of my stores, about to protest that they couldn't yet buy any of my pet or people treats.

"Good girl," I said to my little golden Biscuit as she sat down on the sidewalk in front of the Barkery while I fished my keys out of my purse. In a few moments we were inside.

So was Zorro, Frida's beagle mix. She didn't always bring him, but she had today. He came over to greet us, sniffing first Biscuit, then me.

I left Biscuit loose after locking the door behind me. When we opened for business, I'd confine both dogs in the fenced area, but no need to do so now.

I had to flick the lights on in the Barkery, but I saw light at the bottom of the door into the kitchen and smiled. Frida was in there, of course, diligently baking.

"Stay," I told Biscuit, then slipped through the door into the kitchen. Sure enough, there was Frida, stirring up some really delightful cinnamon and other aromas that went with a people bakery.

"Good morning," she said. Though her hands were covered in dough, she managed to steal a glance toward the watch on her left wrist as if she was reminding me of the time.

"Good morning," I repeated. "And I appreciate your taking over my earliest duties so I could sleep an extra fifteen minutes."

"Is that what you were doing?" She grinned mischievously, as if she guessed why I really was late. Well, people around here knew I was dating Reed, but I never discussed what any of those dates involved. She was just guessing, or having the fun of teasing, or both.

Today she wore a loose-fitting green Icing on the Cake T-shirt over khaki slacks. As always when she worked here, she'd pulled her medium-shade brown hair back into a ponytail. She seemed to love both parts of her career, my shop as well as creating her own gourmet recipes at home. Her fiancé ran a grocery store in town, so she never lacked for ingredients. She wasn't exactly svelte, either, so I knew she enjoyed sampling all she made. She was definitely an asset to both my stores, especially since I rarely saw her without a smile.

"I'll never tell," I said with a smile of my own. We then got into discussing the Icing items she'd started, and what I should begin baking for the Barkery.

I jumped right in, partly because I had to and mostly because I loved what I did. An hour, then more, passed while we put trays of products in the respective ovens for each shop and then got them out and into their display cases.

Opening time for both shops was at seven, and at six forty-five Dinah came in to start her day, too. She would be working till closing time. Frida would leave in the early afternoon and my other part-timers, Vicky and Janelle, would join us.

A couple of minutes before our official opening that day, I entered the Barkery, looked at how the trays of our wonderful doggy treats were laid out behind the glass in our display case, and then went around to the back of that case and took out two small liver biscuits. I used them to lure Biscuit and Zorro into the open-air crate that kept them from slipping out the door when customers came in, and paid them off by giving them each a biscuit.

It was opening time.

Frida was in charge of Icing and Dinah took care of the Barkery, and I slipped between them making certain all was well. Given my choice, I'd have spent more time in the shop catering to dogs, but this early in the morning there were more Icing customers, choosing scones and croissants and other treats to start off their days.

About mid-morning, when things were a little slower in Icing but picking up in the Barkery, I took the opportunity to go into my small office, which was located at the rear of the Icing side of the kitchen, to go over some finances. Fortunately, all seemed well. Better than well, in fact. I checked on some bills that were paid automatically—including the loan I'd received to buy and remodel the stores, from my wonderful boss Arvie at the vet clinic. My shops had only been open a few months, so not much of the loan had been paid back yet, but I felt certain it would all work out over time.

As I finished staring at my computer screen, I heard a knock on my open door. I looked up. Dinah stood there. Her sweet and pudgy face held an expression I couldn't read: Amused? Confused? Challenging? Maybe all three, and maybe something altogether different.

"Hi," I said. "What's up?"

"A very strange customer in the Barkery is what's up," she said. "She hasn't offered to buy anything. She didn't bring a pet along, and all she's been doing is asking questions about each product in the display case, and about you and this shop. I tried to answer her at first, but she kept throwing questions at me even when I started helping another customer who'd just walked in."

I felt my stomach churn, but gagging wouldn't help. I had a fair idea of who this "customer" was.

"So you decided to come get me?" I said. "Good plan."

"No, she finally interrupted my discussion with the other customer and demanded that I bring you into her august presence."

"She used those words?"

"No, just that attitude."

I didn't know too many people who'd describe a confrontation that way, but of course Dinah was a writer in her spare time. She'd recently published some online articles on choosing a pet and feeding dogs, but she preferred writing fiction. I liked what I'd seen of her stories and I knew she had aspirations for a lot more.

"Well, my august presence will follow you," I said. Turning off the computer screen, I stood and headed toward the office door.

As we walked through the kitchen, I made a mental note to check on all our supplies in both stores' display cases. That felt better than what my mind kept hinting awaited me in the Barkery.

But sure enough, when I entered the shop I saw Wanda standing near the door, arms crossed and her irritatingly pretty face looking aggravated, as if I'd promised to join her there hours ago.

Was she here to annoy me, as she had our whole crowd at the resort?

Where was Jack—and had she spent last night in his apartment despite their argument?

"Well, hi, Carrie," she gushed, loud enough for me to hear her clear across the shop despite the conversations going on among two sets of customers with their dogs. "How good to see you."

That's not what I'd expected her to say after the expression she'd leveled on me. But, heck, I'd only met this woman once before and I certainly didn't understand anything about her except that she worked for VimPets and seemed to be more than a thorn—a giant spike?—in Jack's side. Were they actually lovers, or had she really just made that up as a threat to Jack, as he'd indicated?

Today Wanda wore a very short cocoa-colored dress, and matching stockings that emphasized how long and surprisingly slim her legs were despite her short height. As before, I had to admit she was a highly attractive lady—physically, at least.

I'd seen no other aspect about her that seemed appealing or even tolerable.

"Hello, Wanda." I crossed the Barkery's blue tile floor, sorry I had to ignore Biscuit and Zorro as they stood and wagged their tails in their confined area. I made no attempt to welcome her or ask if I could sell her any of our products. I didn't know why she was here but figured it was for a reason I wouldn't like.

She opened her arms as I got closer and I had a horrible feeling she was about to hug me. I didn't get near enough for that but just stood there, trying not to compare what I must look like in my blue knit top, blue slacks, and low-heeled shoes with Wanda's dressy appearance.

Hey, I liked what I wore—a top different today from the T-shirts my assistants wore. I'd designed the logo on the pocket of the shirt but so far had only worn it myself. It was a heart, with lettering on the top that said *Barkery*, with *Bakery* at the bottom.

I might not be as glamorous as Wanda, but I wasn't bad looking. My hair is light blond with some added highlights. I have the Kennersly longish nose and blunt chin as well as fairly sharp cheekbones, part of the look I share with my brother Neal.

"So aren't you going to ask why I'm here?" Wanda lowered her arms but raised her head.

"Sure," I said as casually as I could muster. "Why are you here?"

"Hey, I'll tell you." She bent her head in the direction of the door to the kitchen. "Do you have an office in there, or someplace else we can talk privately?"

I didn't want her to enter my kitchen, let alone my office. I had an odd vision of her emitting invisible smells or vibrations that would ruin everything. Unreal, yes, but I was developing a genuine antipathy toward this woman.

"You know, I planned to take Biscuit for a walk now." I tilted my head toward the two dogs without saying which was which. "You can come along if you'd like."

"I guess that's good enough." But her words came out in a sigh and her bottom lip moved into a pout.

"I know you love dogs," I said before turning to go fetch Biscuit and her leash. "Or at least that's what you said last night." Not a claim I actually believed, of course.

"Absolutely." But her tone sounded as false as everything else I'd noted so far about Wanda.

Zorro didn't seem happy about being left alone, but I gave him one of our treats in consolation. Dinah had again taken control of running the Barkery and I told her I'd be back shortly. I had a shift scheduled at the veterinary hospital that afternoon, but this morning I could take the time to talk to Wanda—not that I wanted to.

We were soon outside on the fairly busy sidewalk. I decided the best place for our little chat that I didn't look forward to was in the town square. We could keep strolling there among the visitors and people walking dogs, or we could sit on one of the many benches.

"How about if we go over there?" I asked Wanda, pointing across the street.

She shrugged one of her narrow shoulders. "Why not?"

We crossed at the corner, then started meandering along the bench-lined sidewalk surrounding the square, which was a park-like setting of grass-covered hills and knobcone pine trees. The air was crisp, and a slight aroma of pine and potential precipitation hung around us.

I let Biscuit do her thing, of sniffing and more, without looking at Wanda to see whether she was okay with it or impatient. I didn't really care.

"Okay, so here's the thing," Wanda said after a few minutes. "I know Jack has been after you for a while to sell some of your recipes to us at VimPets, but he hasn't been very organized or dynamic about it. But me? I happen to know what our bosses really want."

Including the executive you've been sleeping with? I wondered, but didn't ask. "What do they want?" I asked instead.

"Well, there are so many ingredients and recipes in the world that whatever you've put together here is unlikely to be completely original. But here's my take on it, which I'll push with our execs. Knobcone Heights has a reputation for being an elite community, so what's created here is already pretty highly respected. That includes the town's pets and veterinary clinic, so recipes developed and sold in this town as particularly healthful can be promoted as being quite special. That's why we'd buy some recipes from you, Carrie. Even if Jack isn't as assertive about it as he should be."

"But you'll be assertive," I said with no question behind it. Nor did I contradict her about how Jack had been communicating with me.

"Exactly. And we'll really make it worth your while." She took my arm and led me to an empty bench near where we'd been walking. Then she proceeded to lay out some of the incentives Jack had already offered, including lots of recognition for me and, more importantly, my Barkery and Biscuits shop. She added some new ones, too, including a sweetening of the financial offer Jack had suggested, to include a potential stake in VimPets. Altogether, it was a fantastic incentive, with the possibility of my being really well compensated.

I'd become a bit tempted before. I was a lot more so now.

If only I could set aside my mistrust and dislike of this woman.

"Very appealing," I said when she was done. "But I'll have to think about it."

"Of course. Meantime, I've got the connection to get a company lawyer to write up the offer."

"Meaning, you can contact the executive who's your particular friend," I said. I figured that somehow in all this, she'd get compensated well, too—possibly in bed as well as in the bank.

But what about Jack, if I agreed to what Wanda had offered? Would she lie about their relationship, as she apparently had last night—to get him fired? Or would my cooperation with her save Jack's job?

Or none of the above?

"That's right." Wanda's grin as she stared at me from across the bench was almost wicked. Then she stood up. "You get the drift of what's going on, and how VimPets can do great things for you. I'll be in town for a few more days and we can talk some more. In fact, we *will* talk some more. You can be sure of it. And let me know if you think of any questions."

I already had—about Jack.

And about my friend Billi, who cared about Jack—or at least she had, for a while. In any event, I did like the guy as a person, and now even as a friend.

I didn't get into that, though. Instead, I gently pulled on Biscuit's leash. "Okay," I said. "I will."

"I can tell you're intrigued," she asserted as we headed back toward the street crossing.

"Yes," I acknowledged, without suggesting anything more.

"In case you're free, Jack and I are having dinner again tonight at the Knobcone Heights Resort. Inside, this time, without dogs. We've scheduled a date."

A *date* date, or a business meeting, or something else altogether? I didn't ask.

"We'd love for you to join us," she added.

As a buffer between them, or would they both discuss the offer to buy recipes from me and their respective ideas about why and what? Or, again, something else altogether? I didn't see either of my first two guesses as logical. Plus, I wondered if they would remain civil enough to each other to have a pleasant meal.

Still, I was curious. And, if I was honest with myself, I was intrigued by what Wanda had said. I didn't have to like the woman to do business with her, assuming she had all the authority she claimed.

Impulsively, I said, "Sure. I'll join you for dinner tonight."

And wondered if I should wear some kind of armor to protect myself from the slings and arrows of corporate conflict that were likely to be shot between Wanda and Jack.

FIVE

Dinner that night wouldn't exactly be the private date with Reed I'd anticipated, but I knew it would at least be different from the night before—despite the location being nearly the same, and some of the participants, too.

For the rest of the day after Wanda left, I pondered what I was doing to Jack by even speaking with her.

Well, heck. Jack was supposed to join us for dinner. It couldn't hurt him—probably—if I just continued to listen, and then charted my course after that. Maybe it would even work out well for him if I helped him find a way to acquire healthy recipes from me while downplaying any involvement of Wanda and the exec she supposedly had some kind of relationship with.

Eventually it was time to close my shops and take Biscuit home—I gave her food, drink, and some extra loving and treats. I arrived at the resort a bit before six thirty, our scheduled time, and headed straight through the arched doorway from the lobby into the restaurant. I'd already told Neal what I was up to, but since he wasn't invited to this dinner I chose not to wave hello to him. I'd see him later that night anyway, or so he'd said during our phone call.

The restaurant was quite busy, as usual. Lots of diners, many as nicely dressed as I was, sat at tables of various sizes bedecked in pristine white tablecloths. The noise level suggested a myriad of conversations, and quite a few servers strode between the tables, often with plates of food in their hands.

I'd chosen to wear a suit that evening, a cobalt gray one of a fabric that shimmered. My blouse was a lighter shade of gray, and I wore a small blue pendant around my neck. My black heels were high but fell short of stiletto.

As soon as I entered, I spotted Wanda at a table right in the center. It would hold four diners, but as far as I knew, there would just be three of us.

However, I found I was wrong shortly after I'd walked over to greet her and she, despite my taking a step back, managed to give me a hug. "Thanks for coming, Carrie," she gushed.

She, too, was dressed up, although of course I expected that of her. Her dress was short, as before, but a shade of pale yellow, and flowing this time so that her slight plumpness was hidden in its plentiful material. Her slim legs showed once again, and unlike me she did wear stilettos, in gold.

Her short blond hair was unchanged, a curly golden cap. Mine was lighter and highlighted, somewhat longer, and, I believed, more of a frame around my face.

But our hair and clothes wouldn't be what was important. What we planned to talk about, and how it went, was the reason I'd come.

"So glad you're joining me here tonight," Wanda said. "I think we'll both have a very good evening."

“I hope so.” I looked around as I sat down. I’d never known Jack to be anything but prompt, but he wasn’t here yet.

“Hi, Carrie,” said Gwen, coming over to our table and handing us menus. I was pleased she was working inside this evening rather than on the patio. “Welcome to both of you. May I bring you drinks?”

“Someone else is joining us,” I said, “but, yes, I’d love a drink now.”

I needed a small boost, so I ordered a glass of merlot again. Wanda asked for a martini.

I glanced around once more for Jack—and was surprised to see Billi making her way through the restaurant. I was even more surprised when she joined us at our table. She was dressed as if she had just attended a City Council meeting, and maybe she had. Her suit was dark, her blouse tailored … and the expression on her usually lovely face suggested she was steaming inside. “Hi, Carrie,” she said, then looked at Wanda. “So why am I here?” she asked as she took a seat at Wanda’s other side.

“Oh, I think you’ll like our conversation—or at least there’s a good possibility you will.” Wanda’s grin appeared sly, and I wished I knew what she was thinking. Better yet, what she was planning.

I was sure I’d find out soon, since, as Gwen brought our drinks and some menus, Jack joined us.

He didn’t sit down immediately, though. He stood behind the chair that remained empty for him, leaning forward with his arms crossed on its back. His gaze stopped on Billi first, and I thought I caught a hint of confusion as well as caring in it. Its next stop was on me, where I gleaned an emotion I couldn’t completely interpret, although I guessed it was asking whether I was with him—or a traitor.

Finally, it stopped on Wanda, where it definitely hardened. “I thought just the two of us were meeting tonight over dinner, to discuss our differences and find a better way to deal with them.”

"That's why I invited Carrie and Billi." Wanda leveled a catlike smile on him. "They both play roles in our differences, so I figured they could also be part of our working things out."

"Don't count on that," Billi said slowly. She appeared to stare daggers toward Jack, as if she'd managed to transform any hurt she'd felt when learning of his possible affair with his coworker into fury.

Too bad I couldn't somehow bottle up those expressions and find a way to sell them, maybe to actors since they conveyed so many different thoughts and feelings. I realized, though, that I was allowing my own thoughts to wander as a way of pulling back from all the emotions surrounding me.

As to my emotions? I was interested. Curious. And sympathetic, first to Billi and also, somewhat, to Jack.

I was also very irritated at Wanda and the harm she appeared able to bring to people I considered friends.

"Actually, I do count on that," Wanda finally said to Billi. But before she could give any further explanation, Gwen came by to take the additional drink orders.

Unsurprisingly, both also contained alcohol: a beer for Jack and a glass of white wine for Billi.

"Okay, then," Wanda said after she and I clinked glasses while our tablemates waited for their drinks—ironic, of course, as if we wished each other good luck. "There was a good reason for me to invite each of you here tonight, and I'll tell you why." She moved her sly grin to each of us, one at a time, and I almost shuddered when she got to me. This should be interesting, I nevertheless thought. I'd figured she just wanted to get more anger flowing, but maybe there was more to it than that.

"I'll start with you, Billi." Wanda planted her gaze on Billi, whose face now appeared cool and unemotional—though I was certain she felt the opposite inside. "I know you're interested in Jack. He'd have stayed interested in you, too, if I hadn't stepped into this picture."

Neither Billi nor Wanda looked toward Jack, but I did. Instead of matching the indifference of Billi's expression, his was now furious as he trained it on Wanda. He remained silent, though, clearly waiting for her to continue.

"Now, despite how much I care for Jack," Wanda said, "I'll let you have him if everything I suggest tonight can be arranged."

At that, Jack nearly rose. I could see him clench his fists on the table as if he intended to use them as leverage, but he caught himself. He stayed still, but he did dare to cast a glance at me that suggested his rage.

"But what if I—" Billi began, and I was sure she intended to say she wanted nothing to do with Jack … now.

Wanda interrupted. "Oh, I know you may be a little miffed at him now, but just wait. I think the two of you could become a good item."

Before she continued, Gwen arrived with the other drinks and to take our food orders. I wasn't hungry after all this but ordered a salad anyway. I gathered from what my companions asked for—a bowl of soup for Billi and a BLT for Jack—that they weren't exactly starving now, either.

Wanda, on the other hand, ordered a full steak dinner. Clearly her plans for us must require energy on her part. She was the only one evincing much of an appetite.

After Gwen left, Wanda turned to me. "You're next, Carrie. We've already discussed how much I want you to sell some excellent, healthy dog recipes to VimPets, and how I'll make sure the company gives you lots of good profit in return. All I'm asking from you, on top of this, is that you confirm with our executives that I'm now your primary contact." When Jack, between us, opened his mouth in apparent protest, she continued, "And before we're through here, I'll be your only contact."

"Forget that, you bitch," Jack said, actually standing this time.

Wanda remained seated, shooting an unruffled, almost sympathetic gaze up at him. "Oh, I won't forget it. And you'd better not call me names. Not if you want me to make sure you get anything positive out of this."

"You're not in charge," he shot back, although he sat back down. "I can take this idiocy back to the company and have you—"

"Have me what? Fired? I don't think so. You know I have the ear of one of our highest-up execs, and you probably suspect his ear is not all I have. In fact—"

She turned and unhooked her small and shiny purse from the back of her chair, then whipped out her cell phone. She leveled a smug smile at Jack as she quickly pushed a button on it and brought it up to her ear.

"Hi, Marv," she purred after the person on the other end apparently answered. She waited for a moment, then said, "Yes, I'm still in Knobcone Heights. That really nice vet tech and store owner Carrie Kennersly and I have been talking, and I think I've nearly convinced her to sell us some of her best recipes. Of course, I've promised her the extra compensation you and I discussed."

Her eyes shot to mine and she smiled. I didn't smile back, but I admitted, only to myself, that I had liked the extras—like shares in the company—that she'd suggested. That didn't mean I'd accept them, though, to Jack's detriment.

Maybe.

"Yes. Right," she said. "But the thing is, Jack is here too, and he keeps insisting that Ms. Kennersly is his find and only his to deal with. He's been giving me such a hard time." Her voice now sounded sad and frustrated.

Jack had risen again. His expression clearly reflected his anger—and indecision. I figured he was trying to determine whether or not to yell at her, since it would only confirm he was giving her a hard time.

"Don't you have someone above this guy you can talk to?" I whispered to him, but he didn't look at me. I assumed the answer was no, or he at least didn't believe it would help.

"No, no, that's okay. Let me try to get things settled down with him first. You don't have to fire him ... although I might suggest that he quit. I think we'd all be happier that way."

Jack's eyes were huge and furious by then. I saw him clench his fists even harder.

But Wanda soon made some lovey-dovey comments and hung up. Then she looked at Jack. "So you see how things are. And that's your part in my plan—leaving. I really do think you'd be happier if you quit. I'll bet you could find a job here in Knobcone Heights so you could be with your sweetie Billi. Maybe Carrie could hire you, or the people with that pet boutique, or some other business altogether. Or you could start your own shop—though I don't know what you'd sell. I'll bet I could ensure you get a nice package for leaving."

That was when our meals arrived. Everyone just sat there staring at each other while Gwen placed the food in front of us. She looked puzzled, aiming her gaze at me.

I simply shrugged.

And that appeared to be that. As we ate, Wanda steered the conversation toward how Billi rescued and rehomed animals. Billi seemed to lighten up a bit as she talked about her favorite topic.

"I'll bet Jack would love helping you with that, wouldn't you, Jack?" Wanda asked. "You two could do it together."

Then she asked me about being a veterinary technician and the animal illnesses and allergies that had led me to develop some of my treats.

In fact, the rest of the meal seemed to go quite smoothly, as if Wanda had never made her odd threats and suggestions.

But when we were finally done eating, she said, "Now, I don't expect any decisions right away, much as I'd like them. Think about what I said—overnight. We can all talk again, one on one, tomorrow."

"And if we say no to any of your suggestions?" Billi's tone iced up again as she stared at Wanda. When she glanced briefly toward Jack she appeared slightly warmer, but only for an instant.

"A no from any of you could make things quite difficult for all of you," Wanda said. "Now, here's my contribution toward our bill." She whipped fifty dollars out of her wallet and placed it on the table. "I'll talk to each of you tomorrow." She grinned yet again, in a way that looked almost evil. "You might want to discuss it before you leave here. Have a great night."

And then she left.

The only discussion that went on afterward consisted of things Wanda clearly wouldn't like. None of us were interested in coming up with ways to accommodate her demands.

Jack tried to solicit Billi's attention. For a short while I thought he was succeeding, but she finally faced him and said, "I don't want to talk about this. I thought we had something going, but I'm not about to try to save it because your buddy said I should want you to quit your job and then help you feel better about it."

"I'm not quitting anything," Jack growled, glaring at her. "And we did have something going, as far as I was concerned, but not now. I'm not going to continue to see you because Wanda said we should."

"Fine," Billi said.

"Fine," Jack repeated.

My thought was that they should aim their anger in the direction it belonged, toward Wanda, but I didn't say so.

All I said was, "Jack, I don't want to encourage Wanda either. But she did offer me more compensation for any recipes I provide than you seemed able to. I'd much rather do business with you if I form a relationship with VimPets, but I wouldn't mind the additional incentive. Any possibility you could match it?"

"I'll see what I can do." But his expression was a bit bleak, as if he wasn't sure he could do anything at the moment with VimPets.

We each paid a third of what was left after contributing Wanda's fifty dollars toward the bill, as well as a generous tip to Gwen, who'd put up with us ignoring her now and then as we argued.

When we left, I believed we all intended to head in different directions. I certainly didn't want to remain in the company of either of the others just then, not even Billi—although I suspected she might need some cheering up. But at the moment I could have used some, too.

In fact, I called Reed as I reached my car, and he sounded glad to meet me for a drink at the resort bar. I found myself smiling as I went back inside the lobby and headed to the rear, but this time to the right side, toward the bar, rather than the left and the restaurant. I grabbed a table for two in the crowded and noisy establishment, one at the back where there was a wonderful view of the lake during the daytime. At this hour, though, there was mostly darkness punctuated by the glow of buildings on the cliffside overlooking the water, their lights gleaming on the pulsing lake surface below.

I ordered another glass of merlot and sipped it slowly, looking at it rather than at any of the patrons—especially since there were a couple of guys at a nearby table who seemed interested in getting my attention. I'd have played along if they'd had dogs with them, to get them to visit the Barkery sometime—but not now.

Fortunately, Reed arrived fairly quickly, which made me smile. So did the hello kiss we shared. He sat down and ordered a beer, and I told him what had gone on that evening in his absence at the restaurant.

"No wonder you look so glum." He came around the small table to kiss me once more.

I felt my glumness slipping away.

As we talked, my mind relaxed, even as my body tensed a bit with the good feeling of being with the right company at the right time.

In fact, when we'd finished our drinks, I called Neal. He was home that night and told me he'd been caring for Biscuit and would continue to. That left me free to visit Reed and Hugo at their house for an hour or two.

Reed lived south of downtown Knobcone Heights, in a very nice area. It wasn't a neighborhood where the town's richest residents lived, but I enjoyed driving and walking through its pleasant streets.

I later returned home to sleep, though, since, as always, I had to rise early the next morning to start my day.

The next morning, I was quite surprised to receive a call from Jack as I reached my shops.

"I need your advice, Carrie." There was something in his voice that made him sound like someone else—a squeakiness, a fear, a lack of the usual sureness that he evinced.

"What's going on?" I asked.

"I... I took Rigsley out early this morning, since he was restless and demanding, and... Carrie, he led me behind the apartment building, near its parking lot. I found... Wanda is there. She's apparently been stabbed. I've called 911 for paramedics and cops and all, but I think she's dead."

SIX

I'd just walked Biscuit in front of the stores. Now, she was on her leash beside me. I managed to open the door into the Barkery, phone in hand. I closed it behind us and began shaking, an image of a bloody Wanda forming in my mind.

I shook it off, kneeling to release Biscuit from her leash as I stumbled for something to say to Jack. As it turned out, there wasn't much time. I heard sirens behind his voice over the phone.

"I don't know what to say," I began.

"Just promise you'll do your usual thing and help figure out who did this," he said. "I've got a good idea who they'll want to blame."

Him. Of course. He'd been arguing with Wanda. She'd threatened his career, as well as the relationship he'd been attempting to establish with Billi.

"Maybe not," I said hopefully, without believing it. "For now, just remember all the stuff you see on TV. Don't touch anything." I hesitated. "You haven't, have you?"

"No. Of course not. It's so … well, you don't need to hear how awful it looks. How awful she looks."

But I could imagine. He said she'd been stabbed. With what? I didn't ask. But there would be blood. Maybe a lot …

He wasn't certain she was dead. Might she survive? But in any case it sounded grim.

I pulled my concentration away from the ugly vision in my mind. "Okay, then make sure you don't answer questions without a lawyer. I can refer you to someone locally, if you'd like."

"I'd like," he said.

I'd been accused of murdering someone in the spring. That was probably why Jack had asked me for help—and said it was my "usual thing." I'd figured out who the killer really was, and I'd done this a second time when there was another local murder and the cops thought Janelle was responsible. Neal and Janelle had just started their relationship and I believed her to be innocent, so I'd helped her, too.

Now, there was Jack.

"Try Ted Culbert," I said. Ted had advised me when I was a suspect, and I'd referred Janelle to him. Ted and I had even flirted a bit for a while. I considered him a friend, in addition to a good and competent lawyer.

Only …

This time things were different, I realized, as Jack said the EMTs had arrived and he needed to hang up.

I stuck my phone in the pocket of my dark slacks, slowly approached the counter beside the glass-fronted display case, and leaned against it. Maybe I shouldn't have mentioned Ted.

I'd been innocent. I'd felt certain Janelle was, too.

But Jack?

He'd actually had reason to hurt—to kill—Wanda. She'd already put a dent in his new relationship with Billi.

She'd threatened his job. His career. His livelihood.

If that wasn't a good motive, what was?

Jack had said he'd found Wanda's body behind his apartment building that morning, thanks to Rigsley. What if he'd encouraged Rigsley to go toward the parking lot so that he could blame his dog for helping to "discover" Wanda?

As I closed my eyes and continued to lean against the counter, Biscuit came over. Adorable, sweet little girl that she was, she clearly knew that her mommy was upset and she tried to help me, nuzzling my leg. I knelt beside her on the blue tile floor and hugged her warm, furry body.

But my mind was still engaged in what was going on.

Jack. He had motive. Maybe opportunity, too, since it was outside where he lived. What had Wanda been doing there? Was she still staying in Jack's apartment despite their argument?

I knew someone else with motive, too: Billi. Could she have run into Wanda outside Jack's apartment and stabbed her?

If I had to choose one of them to be guilty, I preferred Jack over Billi. But she'd already appeared to pull back from liking Jack, so her motive would be sketchy—except that Wanda appeared to be the reason she'd distanced herself from him.

Well, I didn't know the full story. Maybe it had even been someone else. After all, Wanda wasn't the nicest person. She probably had other enemies, too.

Or so I hoped.

I realized that I was starting to blame myself a little, too. Hadn't I thought, after dinner last night, that Jack and Billi shouldn't aim their anger toward each other but toward Wanda?

Maybe one of them had done just that.

Could they even be accomplices, both playing a role in trying to kill Wanda? I hated to think that. But I also hated to think it could be either one of them.

I wondered if Jack was already being approached by my detective non-buddies, Bridget Morana and Wayne Crunoll. If so, would they attempt to interrogate him as ceaselessly as they'd latched on to me?

Maybe Jack would get the opportunity to meet Wayne's dachshunds, Blade and Magnum, or Bridget's cat, Butterball—all patients now and then at the vet clinic.

Or—was I going nuts? My thoughts were leaping all over the place, maybe to avoid thinking about Wanda. I might not have liked her, and I'd somewhat wished her far away from Knobcone Heights, but not via death.

I hugged Biscuit even closer, then jumped as I heard a noise behind us.

The door from the kitchen had opened and Dinah walked into the Barkery.

"Carrie? What's wrong?" My wonderful assistant was suddenly kneeling on the floor beside us. Her youthful face appeared furrowed with concern.

I let out one brief and hysterical laugh. "I'm not sure yet, but there may be something going on that you'll want to write about."

She stared at me, her bright blue eyes wide. "Not another murder."

"I hope not," I replied, even as I felt certain that tiny hope would be quickly dashed.

But Dinah's presence did help. Biscuit's, too. Between them, they reminded me where I was, and when. It was time to start baking. To begin getting both shops ready for a day I hoped would be busy.

Too busy to think about what had happened to Wanda, and how. And why.

Only the thought was always, inevitably, there, especially since I could tell that Dinah really wanted me to talk about whatever was bothering me, even though she didn't say anything about it in the kitchen once I'd left Biscuit in the Barkery and come in to bake. At the long stainless steel utility counter, which ran down the kitchen's middle, she stood on the Icing side preparing dough for the people goodies, and I faced her on the Barkery side. We were, as always, careful not to combine ingredients, since some human stuff, like chocolate, is poisonous to dogs. Huge ovens lined the respective walls behind us. Dinah's yellow T-shirt promoted the kinds of products she was preparing; it said Icing on the Cake.

As Dinah mixed and kneaded dough, she glanced up at me often. I remained quiet at first, working on the dog treats dough. Eventually, though, I said, "Okay. You're right. I'm not sure of her condition, but I gather that someone was stabbed last night."

"Her who?" That wasn't Dinah who asked. I turned quickly toward the sound of the voice to see that Janelle had just walked through the rear kitchen door from the parking lot.

I suspected that Neal's girlfriend wouldn't be surprised at the answer, after the dinner she'd attended a couple of nights ago. I didn't want to turn it into a game, yet I found myself facing her briefly and saying, "Guess."

Her blue eyes narrowed. Today Janelle was wearing a blue Barkery and Biscuits T-shirt over beige jeans, since she would work more on that side of the shops than Icing. She also had on purple athletic shoes, her usual.

"Since you're asking me, I assume it's someone I've met," she said. "And the person who most deserves it, if anyone, is Wanda."

The smile I trained on her felt lopsided, maybe more like a sad frown. "You got it."

Both Dinah and Janelle began asking questions, and I held up my dough-covered hands.

"Here's all I know," I told them, and I briefly described Jack's phone call. "I don't know if Wanda is dead, and certainly hope she isn't." I didn't wish death on anyone, but neither did I wish anyone serious injury.

"I can guess why Jack called you." The grin on Dinah's face suggested her mind was already at work on whodunit and whether she could write something about it.

"I can, too, but I really don't want to get involved this time," I said—even as I realized that it was inevitable, and that, in some ways, I already was involved.

I felt even more involved later that morning. Both shops had been open for a while by then and we were delightfully busy, which kept me from dwelling—much—on what had happened to Wanda. I felt sure I'd learn more about it later, from local media like KnobTV and the small weekly paper, the *Knobcone News*, as well as gossip and social media.

I didn't want to contact Jack, even though I figured he would eventually get in touch with me again. When he could. If he could.

Had he been arrested?

Maybe he'd been wrong about what had happened to Wanda. Maybe she'd been injured in some kind of car accident. After all, he did say he'd found her near his apartment parking lot. A hit and run?

"Tell me again," said the older lady I'd been helping at the Barkery, right at the glass case displaying our most scrumptious doggy treats. "Which ones have carob? Which have yams?" The little Yorkie in her arms seemed interested in all of them, considering the way he kept raising his nose in the air and wagging his tail.

I'd already told her the ingredients of nearly everything on display but patiently went through it again—effectively moving my mind away from Jack and Wanda… for a few minutes, at least. Until I'd placed half a dozen of nearly everything in a box for the delighted customer and started ringing her up.

I still had several more people patiently waiting for me, since both assistants were over in Icing at the moment. But the bell on the door chimed.

Detective Wayne Crunoll had just entered. He was alone. His colleague and superior officer, Detective Bridget Morana, wasn't with him. That was okay. But the fact that he was in the Barkery without either of his doxies told me he most likely hadn't come just to buy them some treats.

He was probably here on official police business.

"So that's all you know about it?" Wayne stared dubiously at me across the narrow desk in my small back office.

I was barely aware of the light cinnamon odor wafting from the kitchen outside the door. Dinah must have baked some additional Icing cupcakes or scones. But sweetness wasn't really on my mind.

I'd succumbed to the inevitable when Wayne said he wanted to talk to me. I asked Dinah to take over helping customers in the Barkery without explaining why, especially since I didn't want to get

Janelle, who remained in Icing, stirred up about it. Janelle had already tried calling Neal, but my brother was busy at the front desk of the resort and said he'd call her back.

He would know about the situation eventually if he didn't already. And just then, I needed to create a bit of time to talk to the detective without my assistants or brother tugging at my attention, too.

"Yes, that's all I know," I said to Wayne. "The call from Jack came just as I arrived here, before I started baking this morning. He was clearly upset, said he'd found Wanda Addler on the ground at the back of his apartment building. She'd been injured and he wasn't sure whether she was alive." I was relating pretty much what Jack had said. I didn't need to add my own thoughts and concerns about who'd hurt Wanda, or whether it had been intentional … or whether Jack was the guilty one.

"Did he say how she'd been injured?" Just injured, I hoped, and not dead?

My interrogator was relatively young, perhaps only in his mid-twenties—several years younger than my thirty-two years. He kept his dark hair short, and although I'd seen him with a dark beard-shadow on his round face later in the day, he was clean-shaven now. As a detective, he didn't wear an official police uniform, but was clad in a white shirt and black trousers.

"I'm not sure he knew how, although he did mention a wound of some kind, and that everything looked awful." Okay, I shaded the truth a little bit there. Jack said Wanda had "apparently" been stabbed. But he didn't describe what he saw, so what I said was close enough.

"Did he mention any kind of weapon around there? Or anything else that might help us determine the origin of her wounds?"

Wounds. Not wound, singular. Had Wanda been stabbed more than once? Even if it had been some kind of hit-and-run, she could have been injured in more than one location.

"That's pretty much all he said," I replied.

"'Pretty much'?" There was a glint in Wayne's eyes that suggested he not only wanted more from me, but he was hoping I'd make some kind of false statement that he could pounce on. Why? Surely he didn't consider me a suspect this time.

Even so, I quickly went back over the timing in my mind. I hadn't awakened Neal that morning, so unfortunately he couldn't vouch that I'd been home at the time Wanda was attacked. Dinah had arrived at the shops before I did, so she could attest to that, but maybe I'd theoretically had time to stab Wanda and hurry here.

I hadn't, of course, but I still figured that Wayne would just love to consider me a suspect again. Or maybe this was his way of encouraging me to blurt all I could against Jack to clear myself.

Maybe I shouldn't have suggested that Jack hire Ted Culbert, in case I needed a lawyer myself.

No. Ridiculous. I had no reason to hurt Wanda. In fact, since she'd been trying to do business with me at Jack's expense—to bolster my own potential profit—I had more reason to protect than attack her.

Even so, I wouldn't accuse Jack. I couldn't eliminate him as a suspect in my own mind—not yet, at least—but that didn't mean I had to encourage Wayne to arrest him.

Unless, of course, there was evidence I didn't know about.

"Detective." I leaned forward on my desk chair, as if to impart something important to him. He in turn drew closer to me over my desk, and I had to prevent myself from pulling back once more.

"Yes, Ms. Kennersly?"

"I'm not sure what you want from me. I've told you about the phone call I got from Jack and what he said. I wasn't anywhere near Wanda, if that's what you want to know. Nor did I have any reason to harm her."

"Oh, I just want the truth, Carrie, and anything you know that you can tell me. I don't suspect you of anything."

I didn't trust him not to arrest me if he found it expedient, though.

"I'm glad to hear that," I said anyway. "And if you're asking me to implicate Jack or anyone else in whatever happened to Wanda, I can't. Yes, Jack and Wanda had disagreements at dinner the past two nights. I'm sure he'll tell you all that himself." Or at least if he was smart he would, since others had overheard it. "But I don't think Jack would have hurt her. And I'm not even sure what *did* happen to her."

I looked at him with my eyes wide, as if asking him to tell me.

"That's still under investigation," he said, "so I can't discuss it other than to say she was injured."

And was she now in the hospital, or was her body being examined by the local coroner? I suspected the latter but chose not to mention it.

"I understand," I said. "But let me repeat that I really don't know anything except that I received that phone call from Jack Loroco. He sounded upset, of course. He told me he'd found Wanda that way." In other words, he hadn't confessed that he'd been the one to put her in that condition.

"Fine." Wayne stood. "We may have additional questions. If so, we'll contact you again. But thanks for your time, Carrie. Oh, and by the way, while I'm here I'd like to buy a few treats for Magnum and Blade."

I considered offering them to him for free but thought that might look too much like a bribe for his finally leaving me alone. I suspected that was what he was hoping for.

Instead, I said, "What a great idea. I've got a new liver-flavored biscuit that they couldn't have tried before. I'll give you a sample for each of them in addition to whatever you decide to buy."

There. That was just being nice, not bribing him.

Though if I believed that giving him a whole boxful of treats would prevent him, or his colleague, from returning and questioning me, I probably would have done it.

SEVEN

DESPITE WISHING I HAD the time to go there daily, I hadn't been at Cuppa-Joe's for nearly a week.

I was on my way to my shift that afternoon at the Knobcone Veterinary Clinic. I needed someone to talk to after this morning, someone I felt close enough to that I could say all that was on my mind.

That would include Reed, who'd be working at the clinic. Head vet Arvie, too—of the three veterinarians who owned the Knobcone Heights Veterinary Clinic, Dr. Arvus Kline was far and away my favorite. But I figured things were as busy at the hospital as usual, the staff focused on caring for animals and saving their lives. There might be no time for my bit of craziness, or my need to spill it to seek catharsis.

I could talk to them both later.

Meanwhile, I had a good set of assistants on duty at the shops, since Vicky had also come in. She was the one who was best at scheduling everyone, so I'd asked her to put together next week's hours as soon as she had some spare time.

In any case, I felt comfortable leaving a bit early with Biscuit. I even brought along a bag of leftover dog treats to give to patients at the clinic—and to dogs at Mountaintop Rescue, if I had time to head there after my shift.

Cuppa-Joe's, the coffee shop and more, was owned by my pseudo parents, Joe and Irma Nash. Or *the Joes*, in keeping with the coffee theme. They'd lived in Knobcone Heights forever. From what I'd gathered, Joe's parents had started the shop when they were younger than I was now, and Joe had helped them as he grew up. Eventually, Irma had fit right in. Now their daughter worked with them, although their son had become a lawyer and moved away.

And when I'd come to town as a vet tech, they'd welcomed me with arms so open that I fit right in, and I considered them family right away.

Gina, their daughter, mostly worked in the Cuppa-Joe's office, so I didn't see her much, but she was always friendly to me. And the family's love of dogs had recently been proven by their adoption of Sweetie from Mountaintop Rescue—an adorable little dog who resembled Biscuit.

My walk didn't take much time, since Cuppa-Joe's was on Peak Road, on the far side of the town square from my shops. I eschewed its very nice inside area for the equally pleasant patio at the far end, where Biscuit would be welcome.

As soon as I took a seat at a metal table beneath one of the heating units, server Kit came over, a young girl with a toothy smile. Biscuit stood and wagged her tail, and Kit stooped to gently touch her with a paper towel she'd been holding—a good thing, since that way she wouldn't have to immediately wash her hands. Like the rest of the Cuppa wait staff, Kit wore a knit shirt with buttons and a collar and a steaming coffee cup logo on the pocket. Today's shirt was green.

"The usual?" she asked.

"Yes, please." I was looking forward to some nice, strong, tasty coffee—with unlimited refills.

Kit had barely walked away when Irma joined Biscuit and me, motioning me to stand up for a hug. Then she knelt to pat Biscuit. I knew she kept Sweetie in a fenced area just outside the door, and I promised myself I'd go say hi before we left.

Irma took the seat across from me at the small table. She was in her sixties but looked a lot younger. Her brown hair was cut stylishly and highlighted, and it framed a face with relatively few lines and made up as well as any model's.

"Glad to see you, Carrie." Irma had brought a cup of coffee from inside. The Joes both appeared to really enjoy their own products. "Okay, tell me what's wrong."

As I said, they were like parents to me. They seemed to have an intuitive grasp of what I was thinking. Sometimes I found it hard to deal with.

Today, I appreciated it.

"Who said anything was wrong?" I asked nevertheless.

"Those little lines beside your eyes and the way you're holding your mouth said so."

I immediately opened my eyes wide, concerned that my worry was aging me, or at least wrinkling my face. I also made myself smile despite knowing she would see right through it.

"Well, you're right," I said. "Sort of. Something is wrong but I don't know the extent of it, not yet at least. And I'm not exactly involved with it, but even so—"

"There hasn't been another murder in Knobcone Heights, has there?"

Irma was one perceptive lady—although I hadn't said or done anything to bring murder to mind. Except be a little upset about something I hadn't yet explained.

"Honestly? I don't know, but—"

I was glad at the interruption, so I didn't have to finish … yet. Joe had come over carrying two coffee cups. I assumed one was his and the other mine, and he confirmed it by placing the one in his left hand on the table in front of me.

He put the other one down on our table, then pulled a chair from nearby and sat down. Joe was probably about Irma's age, but unlike her, he looked it. What hair he had left beyond his receding hairline was gray, and he had deep divots at the sides of his mouth that always emphasized his smiles.

Joe was smiling as he joined us, but he must have caught the concerned expression on his wife's face and the unhappy and resigned look on mine. He trained his deep brown eyes on me and asked, "So what's wrong?"

"That sounds familiar," I said with a sigh, reaching for the cup in front of me. I took a sip while deciding how to respond.

With the truth, of course. After all, their sympathy was one of the primary reasons I was here.

"I don't want to go into a lot of detail," I continued, "but someone I know has been at least injured and maybe more." I kept my description brief, but I told them about Wanda and her relationship with VimPets and Jack and her offer to me that had appeared to trump Jack's. Then I told them briefly about Jack's phone call. Had that only been a few hours ago?

"You poor kid." Irma came over to me and knelt to give me a hug. Biscuit wriggled over to get another hug from her, too.

Meantime, Joe had whipped out his smart phone. After a minute stroking and studying it, his expression turned grim. "Yep," he said. "Another murder in Knobcone Heights."

Then it was confirmed. Wanda was dead. The media, or at least online sites, had said so.

Joe looked at me. "How do you find a way to get connected to all of these murders, Carrie?"

"I wish I knew," I said with a sigh, "so I could find a way to stay far away from them."

I couldn't hang out with the Joes for long, since my shift at the clinic was about to start. Even so, having them with me, shrouding me in their sympathy, helped my mood a bit.

Soon, Biscuit and I said goodbye. After I stopped to say a brief hi to Sweetie and Biscuit traded nose sniffs with her, we started toward the animal hospital. We turned the corner onto Pacific Street and headed to Hill Street, a little north of it. I still carried my bag of dog treats. The sky was overcast, the air was cool, but after all it was October. The weather forecast suggested rain, but more likely tomorrow than today.

Like Joe, I'd read the sparse accounts of Wanda's death on my phone. No details were given, which was probably a good thing.

Biscuit and I reached the vet clinic and went around to the back so we could enter the doggy daycare part from the parking lot. I always liked bringing Biscuit here when I was at work, partly because she got lots of playtime and attention at daycare.

The single large room had a shiny beige linoleum floor that could easily be cleaned in case of accidents. Crates of different sizes sat along the walls. Most visitors played well with others, but if they didn't, or needed a time-out, that was taken care of.

We had a special staff dedicated strictly to the daycare. They didn't just watch the dogs, but also got groups of them together for learning and playing and having as great a time as possible.

Right now, several staff members, including Faye, who was in charge, stood behind the check-in counter. This was clearly the right job for the thin, fortyish pet lover, and her part-time assistants seemed to enjoy it, too. Faye was talking with someone I assumed was a pet owner, but she immediately caught my eye. In moments, she was walking toward me, even as one of the assistants, Charlie, came from a corner where a pack of dogs of different sizes were playing and took over Biscuit's care, unhooking her from her leash.

Charlie was one of a couple of college students who worked at the daycare to help determine if they wanted to study to become vets. As always, he wore a bright red T-shirt that said *Knobcone Vets Rock* over jeans.

"How are you today?" I asked him.

"Real good, Carrie," he replied.

Faye joined us. "Hi, Carrie," she said. "I need to talk to you."

That sounded worrisome, but I smiled at Charlie anyway and reached into my bag to hand him the small plastic-wrapped bunch of treats for the dogs here. I bent down to give Biscuit a farewell hug, then joined Faye as she headed toward the door to the hospital.

"What's up?" I asked when we were alone in the hallway.

Instead of answering, she nodded down the hall. The busy corridor was uncharacteristically empty at that moment, given that it was one of the main ways that doctors, techs, patients, and their owners slipped between the examination rooms. I only saw one person at that moment: Reed.

"He wants to meet with you right away," Faye said, and immediately slipped back inside the daycare facility.

I was glad, as always, to see Reed. He looked good in his white veterinarian scrubs that contrasted nicely with his dark wavy hair. Plus, it was late enough in the day for him to have a bit of beard-shadow.

As I started to say hi, I saw the expression on his face: challenging? Concerned? Upset?

"What's wrong?" I asked immediately. Before he could respond, another of the techs, Kayle, appeared, leading a woman carrying a Maltese down the hall.

Reed grabbed my arm and led me to an examination room. "I just heard the news of another murder in town. I gather it's that nasty woman, Wanda. You're not involved with this one, are you?"

Was I? I wasn't about to lie to Reed. "Maybe," I admitted. "Jack told me he found her, and he was concerned he'd be a suspect."

"That's no surprise, and I wouldn't be surprised if he actually did it." Reed peered down at me, his brown eyes appraising but also a bit teasing. "If you don't want to ruin your record of solving all the murders you look into, don't take this one on, especially if you hope to clear your pal Jack."

"Well, I'm two for two," I said as lightly as I could. But then I grew more serious. "And if I do start trying to figure this one out, it might be to help Jack, but it could also be to help Billi. She's a potential suspect too."

Reed's expression became pensive. "I hadn't considered that. I only heard about it a little while ago. And—well, we know it couldn't have been Billi. I understand your concern. But—well, Carrie, I'll worry about you if you get involved. As usual."

A lot of noise sounded around us, and Arvie trooped into the hall with an Irish setter on a leash, followed by several twenty-something guys.

"Hi, Carrie," he called. "Can you help with a patient? Change first, of course, but I'd like you to join me."

And I needed a little space from Reed, though I'd want to talk with him later.

"Sure," I said. "Be there as soon as I can." After turning and waving toward Reed, I hurried to the locker room to put on my scrubs as fast as I could. I stuck the remaining treats in my locker.

Arvie must have been watching for me, since when I returned to the hall he immediately reappeared without the dog and led me into one of the treatment rooms. There, a familiar woman named Elva stood holding an even more familiar cat, Leo, against her as he stood on the metal examination table. Leo had been injured, scratched up in an actual cat fight, and not for the first time. Maybe for the sixth or seventh, or even more if he hadn't been brought to our clinic each time. Apparently the sleek and golden Leo, perhaps considering himself a lion, liked to fight. Since we were the only veterinary clinic in town, I suspected his adversary today might be here soon as well.

"You know what to do," Arvie whispered to me as he walked forward to talk to Elva, holding the clipboard with Leo's chart. I approached them as well and used a sterile towel to carefully pick Leo up. He glared at me but didn't attempt to scratch or get away. He knew what came next.

First, though, Arvie once more scolded Elva for allowing her cat, who should clearly be kept inside and away from the neighbors' pets, to go outside and pick a fight.

Of course, Elva protested—again—that poor Leo was the one who was always being picked on. I listened to Arvie's firm but kind protestations and warnings while I carried slumping Leo to our treatment room. Ron, another vet tech, was there and assisted me by holding the cat while I shaved the wounded areas and treated them with antiseptics, sticking bandages on the couple of worst ones.

"You'd think his owner would learn," Ron said, shaking his head.

"You'd think so," I agreed.

When I was finished, I carried towel-clad Leo back to the examination room. Arvie was no longer there, but Elva was.

I placed Leo gingerly on the table and took the towel away. "I suspect I don't have to tell you what to do for him now," I said.

"I already have the antibiotics from Dr. Kline, and I have the special soap and ointment at home still, and—okay. I heard him this time, honest. I'll take better care of my little Leo." The last was said in baby talk, right to her cat's face.

"I'm really glad to hear that." I said my goodbyes and left the room, recalling that promise from previous visits, too. And not believing that Elva would change what she was doing—or not doing—to protect her poor ornery pet.

When I got into the hall, I was surprised to see Arvie waiting there. "Let's talk, shall we, Carrie?" he asked.

"Sure."

I followed him down the hall, through the reception area, and onto the front porch of the blue chalet-like building that housed the animal hospital. It was nearly empty now, even though it was a place where people often waited till they could have their pets seen. No wonder; it was chilly out here and rain seemed even more threatening.

Arvie stopped at the wooden rail at the farthest end of the porch from the entry door. When he turned, the expression on his sweet face seemed concerned.

I had a feeling I knew what he wanted to discuss. Just like with Reed.

I decided to preempt it. "Yes, I've heard about Wanda. And since I heard about it from Jack, who's likely a suspect and also kind of a friend of mine, I realize you might think I'm going to jump right in and start my own investigation. Again. But—"

As I spoke, I continued to watch Arvie closely, and concluded that maybe I was wrong about what he'd wanted. He looked confused at first. Then amused. And now, brown eyes twinkling beneath white brows that matched the wispy hair on his head, he started to laugh, at least a little.

"Well, I did hear about that," he said. "Reed mentioned it in passing. He's worried about you. Again. But what I wanted to ask you was something different. Related, perhaps, since I know you've been negotiating with Jack to sell recipes to his company, and what I gathered was that Wanda also worked for VimPets and the two of them were competing over you."

I nodded, figuring that he and Reed must have shared several conversations about what was going on with this cast of characters.

"That's possibly why Jack will be considered a suspect," I said. "When he called me, it wasn't completely clear that Wanda was dead." Although his description of her hadn't allowed for much dispute. "And Wanda had threatened his job, too."

"Well, I'd really rather you stay out of it, for your sake and for Reed's."

I began to protest Reed's involvement, but Arvie just laughed again. "Oh, he's involved, all right, if you are. But in any event, what I wanted to ask you about is recipes and baking. We have a couple of new dog patients with irritable bowel disease. I've gotten them on the prescription food, but I wanted to suggest that you come up with some additional low-fat treats for them. And then maybe you can sell the new recipes to VimPets. Or not. Whichever you choose."

"Oh," I said. "I have some ideas for that but haven't implemented them yet."

"Anyway, just be careful, Carrie." Now Arvie's eyes were caring, his head cocked, and I wanted to give him a hug.

He initiated one instead. And as I stood there with my arms around him, holding his thin body close, he continued, "But I won't be at all surprised if this becomes your third murder investigation."

EIGHT

THE REST OF MY three-hour shift was busy. I assisted Arvie a couple more times, and then worked with Reed on taking case histories of two new dog patients and giving them shots.

We were all acting totally professional. No more talk about murders or even treats and their recipes.

I took time between patients to retrieve some remaining treats from my locker. I left them at the main reception desk in the waiting room with the person signing patients in that day—Yolanda, a highly skilled but often grumpy vet tech. She didn't seem exactly impressed about my creations, but that wasn't anything new with her.

While I worked, I was able to concentrate fully on my responsibilities, my love of our patients, and my desire to have them all leave here well and happy. That was the outcome with most of them that day, although we did have to hospitalize a young French bulldog who had eaten rat poison in a neighbor's yard. He was ill and weak but had been brought in soon enough to get the poison purged.

He stood a good chance of recovery, but we needed to keep watch over him.

On the whole, it was a good shift, but the moment it was over and I'd changed back to my regular clothes and grabbed what was left of the dog treats I'd brought, I needed to run. I'd already decided to visit Billi at Mountaintop Rescue but I wouldn't be able to stay long. I'd need to return to my shops as soon as possible.

Despite my concern about timing, though, I hoped to say goodbye to both Reed and Arvie. I hurried down the hall to Arvie when I saw him leave an examination room. "My next shift is on Saturday," I said. This was Thursday. "I can't say I'll keep my nose out of the Wanda situation. It really depends." Like, I was about to see Billi, and her possible involvement as a murder suspect would affect how much I tried to learn the truth—if at all. "We can talk then and I'll let you know. I'll also consider a new recipe or two, like we discussed. You can always call me."

"I know I can." He stepped forward and gave me a hug. "You can always call me, as well. I wish you would. I'll be concerned about you all over again."

"And call me, too." That was Reed, who had just exited from the next examination room and joined us. "In fact, how's dinner tonight? You can join us, Arvie, if you'd like."

"Can't," he said. "I've got a poker game. But let me know what she says." He directed that to Reed. Then to me, he said, "You *will* join him for dinner, won't you? The two of you need to do that more."

I laughed. "So where's your bow and arrow, Cupid?"

Both guys laughed but neither disputed the image.

I said to Reed, "Yes, that sounds good to me. But I'm off to Mountaintop Rescue now and might need to spend more time than usual at the shops, after being away so long this afternoon."

I didn't mention my visit to Cuppa-Joe's, though that had definitely added to my time away. Not that I didn't trust my assistants, but there were things I needed to do before the shops were closed each day.

"We'll talk later and figure out a time," Reed said. Arvie nodded and strode away. Reed, though, walked toward me. He reached out and grasped my arm gently. His expression suggested he'd like to kiss me, but a couple of the other techs passed us in the hall, leading a couple of medium-sized dogs and their owners to other rooms.

"Yes," I said. "We'll talk later." I turned and headed toward doggy daycare to pick up Biscuit.

Mountaintop Rescue was only a couple of blocks along Hill Street from the veterinary clinic. Biscuit and I walked there in just a few minutes, even as other people and their pets, many of whom were local residents, passed us and either said or sniffed their greetings.

As seen from the road, Mountaintop Rescue was an attractive, gold-colored stucco building, a couple of floors tall and well-decorated with windows surrounded in tile. Beyond the administration building was the heart of the place: other structures that housed the resident animals in nice enclosures that weren't difficult to keep clean.

When we arrived, Billi wasn't there. The receptionist, Mimi, greeted us with big smiles, especially when I handed her the bag of remaining treats. She was in college part-time, busty and pale and enthusiastic. She always wore shirts with dogs, or sometimes cats, on them—this time, a bright blue one that said *Every day's a dog day* and had a picture of a German shepherd on it.

"Our residents really love your stuff, Carrie," she said. "I love to give them biscuits. It helps them feel better about not having forever homes yet."

"I hope so," I said. "I'm sorry I missed Billi."

"She'll be sorry too. She said she had to give a class or something at her spa." That would be the Robust Retreat, which Billi owned. She loved it, and went there often to manage it and participate in or teach some of its exercise programs and massages.

"I'll drop in on her there," I told Mimi. "In case I miss her again, though, please let her know I was here."

"Definitely. And Biscuit too, of course."

"Of course," I said with a big grin, stooping to give the object of our current discussion a gentle pat.

Biscuit and I walked quickly from the shelter back to the shops, which were on the way. I left my dog for a minute in the Barkery while I checked to make sure all was okay—which it was. In fact, it was quite good, since both shops were busy. But my assistants didn't appear stressed. Janelle was in the Barkery, and Vicky and Dinah were in Icing.

"I'll be back in less than an hour," I told Dinah.

"No problem," she said.

Biscuit and I then headed down Peak Road several blocks till we reached Robust Retreat. Located in a nice retail area of Knobcone Heights, the spa had a large storefront with attractive marble-veneered exterior walls as well as wide windows that allowed passersby to peek into the front room, toward the main exercise area. The heated spa and massage sections sat behind the walls at the other end of the reception desk.

I pulled open the front door and let Biscuit walk in on her leash ahead of me. I was immediately struck by the loud voice from the filled workout area to the right. More than a dozen women were on wide woven mats on the floor, following the instructions of their leader—who was, in fact, Billi.

One of her assistants, standing near the entrance to the workout room, looked up and motioned toward me. She probably thought I had come to participate in the exercises but arrived late.

I enlightened her quickly. I directed Biscuit toward the wall to our left, hurrying toward the reception desk without interrupting the program.

I met Billi's eyes momentarily, though. She stood at the front in a form-fitting charcoal exercise outfit, her eyes huge, her expression more intense than I'd ever seen before … and I'd seen her pretty intense at times. As she punched the air, one fist at a time, rolling her entire body with the punches, she counted aloud, "Eighteen. Nineteen. Twenty." The students did the same, in varying degrees of strength and agility. But no one else's punches appeared as powerful as Billi's.

It looked like fun—hard work, but with the possibility of good strength and fitness resulting. I'd have to give it a try one of these days. But not now.

When we reached the reception desk I told the woman who sat there, who was middle-aged and definitely physically fit, that I was a friend of Billi's and wanted to say hi once her class was over.

"Fine." She looked me over as if she thought she might be able to sell me on a membership along with exercise. I believed myself to be in fairly good condition and walked quite a bit, especially with Biscuit, but I didn't belong to a gym or anything like Robust Retreat. I hadn't really considered joining before.

But my friendship with Billi had gotten deeper recently. Maybe I would think about joining … someday.

"They have another five minutes," the receptionist said. "Would you like a tour of the place?"

"Oh, I've been here before, but thanks." I'd met Billi here now and then and walked with her either to my shops or Mountaintop Rescue. She'd showed me the facility without pushing me to join or even suggesting it. She wasn't the kind of person to ram something unwanted down a friend's throat. When it came to an animal abuser or political foe, though? That would be a way different story.

As I stood there, I started participating in the exercises just a little, standing on Biscuit's leash so she wouldn't wander. I punched the air, did curls from my waist, and touched my toes a few times.

It wasn't lost on Billi, whose gaze often met mine.

Then she was done. She smiled at her students, who were similarly dressed in exercise clothing, and thanked them as they thanked her in return.

Eventually, she was alone in the exercise area. I stooped to pick up Biscuit's leash, and when I stood again Billi was right in front of me.

"I know why you're here," she said. "Let's go into my office."

She'd shown that to me before, too. It wasn't a huge room, and although it had a not-so-elite metal desk, the walls were decorated with photographs of some of the world's most famous places—places Billi had visited, like Paris, Venice, Sydney, and more. Bookshelves lined one wall, and on them, in addition to volumes on exercise and yoga and other aspects of physical fitness, were antique vases and dog statuettes.

I knew Billi left her dogs, Fanny and Flip, at home some of the time, and on those days a dog walker visited morning and afternoon. She also brought them to Mountaintop Rescue, to stay in the reception area, if she knew she would be at the shelter all day.

A door opened to another room in her office, which contained a conversation area. That was where she directed Biscuit and me now, and I sat down on one of the plush magenta armchairs, my pup settling on the hardwood floor beside me.

Billi took another chair, facing me. And stared.

"I take it you know about Wanda," I began.

"Yes," she said stonily. "And yes, I know where Jack lives, and that Wanda was staying with him, but he told me she moved into a nearby short-term rental after their fight. I also know she professed to have a relationship with him, and I thought he and I had a relationship, and I was beginning to care."

Her voice started to rise, and I had a suspicion as to why she was declaring these things, most of which I already knew. She'd been asked questions by one or more of the Knobcone police detectives.

"And I was angry with him. And her. And—"

"I know you didn't kill her, Billi," I interrupted softly.

"You and nobody else." Her brown eyes teared up and she dropped her now-pale face into her hands, causing her highlighted dark hair to fall forward.

She began to sob, this strong animal advocate, physical fitness guru, and avid City Councilwoman, and the idea that she was so upset brought tears to my eyes, too.

I stood and hurried over to her. I stooped to put my arms around her narrow, solid shoulders, even as Biscuit joined us and, sweet little dog that she is, stood on her hind legs with her front paws on Billi's legs, her head on her lap, as though also trying to comfort her.

We just stayed there, all of us, for some time. I felt Billi's shudders of emotion and put my own head against hers.

I wanted to tell her it would all be okay. But would it?

Could she have killed Wanda? That would explain all this emotionalism.

So would her actually having fallen in love with Jack.

Or both.

Eventually—twenty minutes later? Or was it only two?—Billi began to settle down. Soon, she pulled her hands away from her now-puffy face.

"You've gone through this, Carrie—being accused of a murder you didn't commit." Her voice was moist and throaty. "How did you live with that?"

"I just assumed that the truth would win out." I also jumped in to make sure it would, but I didn't suggest this to Billi. She was so prominent in Knobcone Heights, given her family background and her many roles. If she started snooping around and asking questions, it would be obvious. And it might even make her look guilty, as if she were trying to figure out who would be the best person to pin it on. As merely a vet tech and the owner of a couple of shops, I'd had no problem asking those questions when I was accused, or when Janelle was accused.

From my perspective, though, there appeared to be two major suspects in Wanda's murder: Billi and Jack. I was friends with both. I didn't want either to be guilty.

Yet I continued to suspect both, individually or even together.

Still…

Well, I needed a lot more information. "This isn't a good time," I told Billi. "I've been away from my shops too long and have to get back, and I know you have things to do, too." Like get herself back under control. "But let's have coffee together tomorrow or sometime soon so we can talk about this."

"You'll help to find the killer?" Billi's head was up, her eyes bright as she looked into mine.

Was that what this was all about—her way of recruiting me to help her?

No, I couldn't really think that of my strong, kind, smart friend. Yet I couldn't help wondering.

"I'm not making any promises," I told her. "And if I do look into it, I'll be seeking the truth, from you, from Jack, from everyone. But I've learned a lot about conducting an amateur investigation, so my answer is a definite maybe."

She smiled. I smiled back.

"Then yes, let's have coffee tomorrow morning," she responded. "At my office at Mountaintop Rescue so we can be alone. Okay?"

"Okay," I said.

NINE

When I returned to my shops, my mind was spinning and I needed to stabilize it.

Time for me to bake. And for an ideal distraction, I could come up with another treat we could sell in the shop.

And could I sell the recipe to VimPets? Would they be interested any longer? What if Jack was found guilty in Wanda's murder? Or even if he wasn't, what would the company executives think about Jack surviving and continuing his work, when Wanda didn't?

Especially that one exec she'd hinted was her lover?

Darn. I had to stop thinking about all that—my remote connection to it, everything—and start baking.

I walked into my shops via the Barkery door since I had Biscuit with me. Dinah was behind the counter waiting on some customers, so I just waved to her, closed Biscuit into her roomy crate, and headed straight for the kitchen. I immediately washed my hands and dug into some of the ingredients I had in mind.

I'd bought some pure, unsweetened applesauce a day or so before that I wanted to try out in a recipe, along with pumpkin. My mind had been baking the treats before my hands put them together, and I figured they might even be healthy and low-fat enough to try out on some dogs at the clinic who had tummy issues like irritable bowel, as Arvie had suggested. I'd learned that both of these main ingredients were beneficial to dogs with that kind of illness, so why not put them together—along with other ingredients that were considered healthful? I would double check with Reed or Arvie before promoting them as medically healthy treats, of course.

But first, I had to actually bake some—which I did after adding wheat flour and water and a few other ingredients to the applesauce, then rolling the dough into small balls that I squashed before placing in the oven … and after I ate a little bit just to make sure things tasted okay. Which they did. Much more than okay. I could hardly wait till the treats were ready and I could give a couple to Biscuit to try out. She was nice and healthy, and I always liked giving her treats that should help keep her that way.

"Hey, what are you making?" Vicky had just entered the kitchen from Icing. My expert scheduler had her nose in the air, as if sniffing the aroma of my new Barkery treats, and a large smile on her face beneath her glasses.

"A surprise," I told her.

I couldn't read the odd expression that suddenly covered her face. "Is that a good idea on a day like this?"

"What do you mean?"

She drew closer but stayed across from me, on the Icing side of the baking utility counter. "It sounds to me like this town has received all the surprises it can handle today."

"You mean something besides the murder?"

Her dark eyebrows shot upward. "Isn't that enough of a surprise?"

Vicky had been a new employee of mine when the last murder occurred. She and I hadn't discussed it much, so I didn't really know what she was thinking. In fact, I'd tried not to discuss the murder much with any of my assistants—except for Janelle, who of course was deeply involved, and Dinah, who'd wanted some details since she liked to write. But scheduler Vicky and chef Frida? Not so much. Sure, they all lived in the town and undoubtedly had opinions—and feelings—about the situation, and I knew no one wanted murders to occur here, but why did Vicky sound so emotional?

Easy enough to find out, I hoped. I asked.

"What have you heard?"

Her eyes teared up behind her glasses and her mouth molded into a frown. "That lady who came in here wanting some of our recipes for VimPets, right? She's the one who was killed?"

I nodded. I wasn't about to tell Vicky my opinion of that lady, which didn't really matter. I didn't have to like or respect Wanda to still feel awful that she was dead. Murdered. Here in my town—where some friends of mine were likely murder suspects.

"That's right," I said softly. "It's another terrible situation."

"You don't have to tell me," said a voice from behind me. Janelle had entered the kitchen. "I just don't get it. I like this town a lot, but I guess it can be dangerous to live here."

I turned and shot her a wry smile. "In more ways than one," I said—to the former murder suspect.

"I was waiting on a customer and couldn't answer the phone when Neal called me back," Janelle said. "I assume he's heard about the situation by now anyway."

"Probably." I knew for sure, then, where I would meet Reed for dinner that night—and not just because I wanted to make sure my brother knew about this latest sad incident in the town we'd both adopted not long ago. The resort would be an interesting place to learn how word had gotten out about Wanda's death, and maybe I could figure out some other potential suspects, too.

Which gave me another thought. "How did you hear what happened, Vicky?"

"Some of our regular customers came in talking about Wanda being found apparently murdered," she replied.

A buzzer sounded from the dog biscuit oven, signaling that time was up and my new dog treats should be done.

And a bell sounded from outside the kitchen, indicating that someone had entered one of the shops—most likely Icing, judging by the location of the sound.

Vicky and Janelle looked at one another, as if challenging each other about who should take care of the customer.

"Why don't both of you go find out who's come in and how much help they need?" I asked, grabbing oven mitts and turning toward the oven. "I'll let these cool, then bring some into the Barkery to be given out as samples. See you in a few."

I was glad when both complied with my wishes, even though I hadn't exactly phrased it as an order. Maybe they both wanted to go into the shops anyway to continue gossiping about the apparent murder.

But I doubted Janelle would find that a fun pastime—not after having been a suspect herself in a similar situation. I knew I wasn't thrilled about hearing of another murder, especially since I'd met the victim and seemed to know the most likely suspects, too.

As soon as I removed the tray of baked treats from the oven and put it on the counter to cool, I pulled my cell phone from my pocket.

Time to call Reed to firm up our evening plans.

Accompanied by Hugo, Reed picked Biscuit and me up at my stores at six thirty, after we closed. Tonight, he wore dressy jeans—an oxymoron, yes, but they looked crisp and new. He also had on a plaid button-down shirt.

I wore a cotton shirt, too, over my beige Barkery and Icing knit shirt, to look a little dressier. My slacks were deep green.

"I suspect I know what our main topic of discussion will be tonight," he said, getting into the driver's seat once the dogs and I were situated in his car. "Same as everyone's. Rumors are being shouted all over the place."

"About Wanda's murder?" I surmised.

"What else? And, Carrie, I've been thinking about it a lot. Too much." He hadn't started driving yet, and now, beneath the illumination of the streetlight above us, he looked at me, his deep brown eyes clearly worried but his expression firm. "I know I said before that you might not be able to solve this one—but my fear is that you *will* solve it—and get hurt, or worse. I'd really, really like for you to stay out of it this time."

I sighed. "I could promise you that, and I'd really like to stay out of it—but I've already got a good idea who the main suspects will be. They're both friends, so that's a promise I'd probably break. So—"

"So no promises. I get it. But I thought I'd try. I'm just worried about you. You keep putting yourself in danger."

We subsequently drove to the resort in silence. He stopped his car just before turning into the resort's parking lot and looked over at me, his expression so sad that I had an urge to kiss it away. Or even make that promise for him... but, yeah, even if I meant it right now, I couldn't guarantee I'd feel the same as the investigation went forward.

Especially if Billi became the police's main suspect. If Jack was considered more of a suspect, I wouldn't like it, but I might not fight for him. It was different with Billi, though. I considered her a really good friend. Yet … well, I couldn't completely dump the idea that she could have actually done it. Not that I believed Billi would harm me. But to protect herself … ?

Heck, she wasn't the killer. And I'd be careful. I'd learned to be careful.

For the moment, I chose to ignore the fact that I had indeed been in a bit of danger before.

I exited Reed's car the same time he did, and we both opened the back doors to extract our dogs. I held Biscuit's leash in one hand and my purse in the other as I walked toward the front of the car. As Reed and I met up, he looked down at me, then up again to scan the car-filled parking lot, and then he bent to kiss me.

What? If someone had been around to see us, would he have skipped the kiss? "Hey," I said. "Are you—"

He interrupted me by putting his arms around me, drawing me close, and giving me an even longer, sexier kiss—even as I heard people chattering behind us.

As the kiss ended and we pulled away from each other, I couldn't help laughing. "So much for hiding what you were doing."

We both started walking forward, our dogs sniffing the paving. "Who said I was hiding?" he asked. "Maybe I wanted an audience."

I laughed all the harder.

We were soon at the resort's entrance, and Reed held the door open for me. "Is a visit to the bar first okay with you?"

"Make it second," I said. "I want to see if Neal is on duty."

I quickly headed past all the offices along the nearest wall of the posh and crowded lobby, glancing at the people who stood in groups having conversations or seated in attractive chairs, either facing the multiple fireplaces or staring up at the television sets that hung at intervals from the slanted ceiling.

At the reception area, I caught Neal leaving his post, having just finished straightening up the main desk. "Hey, Neal," I said. "Are you—"

"Good timing, sis," he said, interrupting me. "I was just going to call to see if you could come here this evening. Hi, Reed," he added belatedly.

"Well, here I am," I responded. "But—"

"But come with me," he again interrupted. "Just you." He looked apologetically toward Reed, then back at me again. "We need to go into Elise's office."

"But—" I began again.

"I'll validate your parking ticket—Reed's?—if you do. I can't always, you know, but I can tonight, if… "

If I complied. And since parking at the resort wasn't cheap, whatever validation Neal could provide tonight was welcome.

Besides, I was curious. Why did Elise want to talk to me?

Elise Ethman Hainner, the resort manager and Neal's boss, was a member of the elite Ethman family that owned the Knobcone Heights Resort. Her husband, Walt Hainner, was a well-respected contractor in the area.

But why were we going into Elise's office?

"Okay." I knew my tone sounded a little hesitant, and I aimed my gaze at Reed. "I'll meet you in the bar in a little while."

"Want me to take Biscuit?"

"Sure," I said. Even though that would limit Neal's ability to play with his Bug for a short while, I figured that whatever was going on, I'd probably prefer not having the distraction of my dog with me.

My bro looked good, as always, as I strode beside his six-foot frame the short distance to the main resort office. Tonight he wore a deep blue shirt tucked into matching blue pants, professional without being all dressed up. He stopped in front of a door I knew was the resort's primary office, even though it had no sign on it.

Elise's office.

I heard voices from inside. Sure enough, when Neal knocked, then opened the door without waiting for a response, I immediately saw the crowd that was gathered inside, standing in the middle of the nicely furnished but compact room, talking. Well, not much of a crowd, I guessed—but it consisted of most of the Ethman family living in this area: Elise Ethman Hainner, her brother Harris Ethman—the pet store owner—and their parents, Trask and Susan Ethman, plus Les Ethman, a City Councilman who was also my friend.

I walked inside, with Neal behind me.

I didn't see Elise's husband, Walt Hainner, but of course he was only an Ethman by marriage.

What were they all doing here? And why did they want to talk to me?

Suddenly, I wished I was in the bar with Reed and the dogs, sipping on a glass of wine. Or maybe the feeling wasn't really so sudden.

Harris was the first to approach me, his hands out as if in sympathy. Why? "Hi, Carrie. How are you?"

Harris and I had only recently become friends of sorts. His wife, Myra, had been dead set against me opening my Barkery—"dead" being the operative word. I'd been the primary suspect in her murder for a while, so I hadn't really had the chance to express my sympathy to Harris then. But I had, subsequently, and we'd become cordial enough to send customers to each other's stores.

As was usually the case when I saw him, Harris wore a Knob Hill Pet Emporium shirt. He was of moderate height, with narrow shoulders, dark hair, and a hint of beard. He looked like a normal human being, not necessarily royalty, despite how his family was viewed here in Knobcone Heights. And as always, his eyes turned down at the corners, which was a common Ethman trait. He wasn't especially tall or especially thin, but now that I'd gotten to know him a little better, he seemed like a nice-enough guy.

It had been his wife who'd been most upset about my Barkery, or so I chose to believe now.

I put my hands out, too, and we engaged in a mutual shake.

"I guess you've heard the latest news," he began as his family members started drawing closer, tucking us in the middle. I supposed they all wanted to hear what I would say, although I didn't know why.

"You mean about Wanda Addler?"

"Yes. You know, don't you, that she came to the Emporium a few times recently? I gathered that she was taking over representing VimPets from Jack—but then he came in, too. Do you know what was going on there?"

"Not really," I said quickly. And I didn't.

"Do you think Mr. Loroco had something to do with Wanda's death?" That was Susan Ethman. Was Harris's mother concerned that her son was going to become a suspect in the murder?

Should he become a suspect in the murder? Is that why I was here—because his family wanted to know my take on what had happened, and because they wanted to make it clear what a wonderful and innocent person Harris was?

They hadn't confronted me when I'd considered him a potential suspect in his wife's murder. But if I'd zeroed in on him more then, maybe they would have.

I turned to face Susan. She was short and definitely looked like a senior—a well-to-do senior. There were lines and ridges in her face, but her light brown hair was immaculately styled. She wore a lavender dress that flattered her thin figure and matching, low-heeled shoes. I suspected both were from designers that charged as much for their names as for their stylishness.

"Honestly?" I began. "I don't have an opinion about what happened to Ms. Addler. I met her only recently, and, yes, she worked with Jack Loroco, so he knew her better, I suppose, than anyone else here in Knobcone Heights. But we're all aware that whoever knows someone the best isn't necessarily their killer." I looked over Susan's shoulder and grinned at Harris. His smile back at me was wry, but he appeared accepting of what I said.

"And despite her skills in having figured out what happened those two times before," my friend Les, the Councilman, said, moving to my side, "that doesn't mean she should or will get involved this time. Right, Carrie?"

"Right, Les," I agreed. But when I looked him straight in the eye I could see his amusement—and, possibly, his assumption that no matter what I said, I would somehow get involved.

Maybe I was already, not just because I happened to know Jack Loroco probably better than most other people in Knobcone Heights did. I didn't think he'd done it—even though I really had no knowledge yet about how Wanda had died, or what the murder weapon was or anything like that.

I suspected I'd find out, intentionally or not.

And, if necessary, I would use my knowledge—and the little bit of skill I'd developed the first two times—to make sure that Billi Matlock was treated fairly, even after her not-so-pleasant meeting in public with the murder victim.

I considered this meeting very interesting, though. Were the Ethmans sounding me out only for my interest in the case and what I suspected?

Or was this a backhanded warning that their entire privileged and connected family would be watching me?

Were they, like Reed, telling me to stay out of it?

Well, maybe I would. And maybe I wouldn't.

We'd all have to just wait and see.

TEN

"So what was that really about?" I asked Neal a minute later, after we'd walked out of the office and he'd closed the door behind us. I was a little peeved that my brother hadn't said anything. On the other hand, he had remained with me, like backup.

What would he have done if they'd gotten nasty?

"I think they wanted information more than anything." Neal began leading our way through the typical crowd toward the back of the lobby, where the bar was located on one side.

"Maybe. You don't think they were warning me to stay out of any investigation?"

"You'd have to ask them. All they seemed to do was ask what you knew, but I sensed … well, you might be right that it wasn't all they intended."

We reached the bar door, and before Neal pushed it open I said, "But you didn't ask them what they really intended. You didn't say anything while they were badgering—er, questioning—me."

He looked me straight in the eye with an expression I read as frustrated. With me?

But what he said clarified what he was feeling. "I like working here, Carrie. I brought you in there because they asked me to. I stayed because I wasn't sure what was going on and wanted to be there for you, although I had no reason to think they'd get nasty. But I've experienced times when the Ethmans gang up ... well, never mind. As long as they were relatively nice, I figured you, of all people, could handle what they might dish out. Right?"

I couldn't help it. I smiled at my little bro. Well, not so little if you counted his height. "Right," I said, then pushed past him into the lounge.

It was even busier than the lobby, with people occupying all the stools at the bar and most of the small, wood veneer tables. It wasn't hard to find Reed, though. He sat against the far wall and, instead of having people sitting with him, he'd offered one of the seats at his table to my small-sized Biscuit. Hugo's head rose above the table at Reed's other side.

Neal and I soon joined them, with Biscuit continuing to sit on one of the seats. A server came over and looked down at Biscuit first. "Have you decided yet what you want?" The twinkle remained in her eyes as she turned to look at me instead. "I don't suppose you have this youngster's ID with you, do you? I suspect she isn't old enough to order anything from the bar."

"Except water," I confirmed. I chose a glass of cabernet, and Neal ordered the same kind of imported beer that sat on the table in front of Reed.

"So, everything okay?" Reed asked when the server left.

I gave him a quick rundown of what had happened. "I think they were just sounding me out for my knowledge and opinion," I said.

We all changed the subject, then, and started chatting again about whether Neal would lead one or more hikes around Halloween and whether the weather would cooperate.

My drink soon appeared, as did Neal's. My brother took a large sip of his beer, and the expression on his face told me there was something on his mind.

"What's going on, Neal?" I traded quick looks with Reed, who clearly didn't know why I'd asked.

Neal took a deep breath. "I think my bosses asked the wrong person in that room what they knew."

Now, that certainly piqued my interest. "What do you mean?"

He looked around. The tables around us were fully occupied, and the people sitting at them seemed engaged in conversations. If Neal was concerned anyone would eavesdrop, the likelihood appeared small.

He still took his time answering, swigging his beer a couple of times first. "The thing is—" His voice was low, especially considering the loud voices chattering around us. I leaned toward him, and so did Reed. Biscuit and Hugo seemed really interested, too, but just watched us humans without getting closer.

"Yes?" I finally prompted.

"I think they asked the wrong person about who knows what. Not—" Neal held his hand up to silence what I intended to say. "Not that I am getting involved in any investigation or anything like that. But—well, I hope the cops don't decide to question me. I can't imagine they'd think they had any reason to, of course. But—"

"But tell us," I finally hissed quietly, staring into my brother's eyes.

"Well … I saw Harris Ethman having a drink with Wanda here in the bar a couple of nights ago. They knew each other. And—well, I had the impression that they were arguing."

That wasn't a good time for me to press my brother for additional details. But I gathered he really hadn't heard anything anyway. He'd just happened to notice them together, since he was aware of my prior dislike of Harris and my more current dislike of Wanda.

We all chose not to talk about it further, though. Instead, after Reed paid for all of us—nice guy—we picked up our drinks and the dogs' leashes and walked next door to the restaurant. It was fairly late, and I think all of us were getting hungry, including Hugo and Biscuit.

We were seated, as anticipated, outside on the balcony after walking through the restaurant with the dogs. Heaters were turned on above us, since the air was crisp.

Even so, there were people out here, too, sitting nearby, so talking much wasn't a good option.

Not that we'd stopped thinking about it. I already seemed unable to separate myself from this latest murder—now partly thanks to my brother. Even if we weren't discussing any aspect of it, the idea that a third murder had happened in this town blanketed us with a slew of questions that had no answers. Not yet, at least.

I'd asked Neal if Janelle was going to join us that night for dinner, but she wasn't. Neal was going to stop at her apartment later, though, at least so he could accompany Janelle and her dog, Go, on a walk.

Reed began a new conversation then. "I won't get into the gory details, but I'm happy to report that we saved the life of a pregnant

Weimaraner today. She'd been out for a walk and, thanks to her extra weight, apparently lost her balance on a hillside." He proceeded, as promised, not to get too gory about it, and it sounded as if both mama and her babies should be fine. The Weimaraner belonged to someone who'd recently moved to Knobcone Heights and had participated in dog shows with her mama dog, and had just bred her for the first time.

I clapped when Reed was done and even stood to give him a congratulatory kiss on the cheek, which stirred up Biscuit and Hugo. Of course I had to pet them, too.

Good. We'd gotten past our previous unwanted topic of conversation … not.

Apparently the owners of the Knobcone Heights Resort weren't the only ones around who were interested in rumors that were more than just rumors. Our server that night, once again, was Neal's prior romantic interest, Gwen. I wasn't very hungry, so I stuck to a salad with a burger on the side … which was more for Biscuit and Hugo than me. Reed ordered a steak, probably for the same reason, while Neal asked for a roast beef sandwich.

When she seemed ready to go place our orders, Gwen stopped. She looked at me, not Neal, which seemed a little odd. Until she asked, "Have you heard what happened to that Wanda Addler who ate here a few times?"

I closed my eyes briefly and nodded. "We've heard some rumors, at least."

People in this town certainly liked to gossip about murders—but I'd learned that before.

"Well, I haven't seen anything, of course," Gwen said, "but lots of people who come here talk, including some members of the police department. Did you hear anything about what happened to her?"

"No," I said warily, assuming we were about to be hit on the head by some of the rumors.

Probably not a good analogy, I thought immediately. Jack had said Wanda was stabbed, but what if she'd died of a head wound? I still didn't know.

I sat up straighter and looked with more interest at Gwen. What she knew, or thought she knew, might not be correct, but I wanted to hear it.

"What I heard," she began, "is that she was found early in the morning behind some apartment complex. She'd been stabbed—with part of a poop scooper, of all things. They're still trying to confirm where it came from—Mountaintop Rescue, maybe, since it looks like a kind they use there. Supposedly the shelter's owner—your friend, isn't she, Carrie? Our Councilwoman Matlock. She and Wanda had met and seemed to dislike each other, or at least Billie disliked Wanda. Maybe it was because of VimPets, or because of its representative here, Jack—I don't know. But at least some people now think Billi Matlock is involved. And I know—well, Carrie, you've solved some murders before. Are you going to try to figure this one out?"

I didn't need to let Gwen know one way or the other, even though she'd provided me with some interesting information—or rumors, at least. "I've gotten involved in enough murders," I told her. "We've got a good police department, and I've met some of the detectives." Unfortunately. And they certainly hadn't done the best job of figuring out the other murders. "I think I'll pass this time."

"I'm really glad to hear that," Gwen said. "When I heard about it, I couldn't help visualizing whoever did it having access to more poop scoopers—and maybe even using one on you. Please be careful in any case, Carrie."

I caught Neal's eye then. He looked concerned. And when I looked over toward Reed, his expression wasn't exactly readable, maybe because of the number of emotions in it. I thought I saw worry and anger and some commands like *Stay out of this* all written there somehow.

And I had to admit to myself that the rumored cause of death was really horrible—not that all murder weapons aren't horrible.

"I'll definitely be careful, Gwen," was all I said. I'd already said I wasn't planning to get involved.

But I doubted I'd told the truth.

My mind also started revolving around our earlier conversation. Neal had seen Harris Ethman talking to Wanda here.

Harris owned the Knob Hill Pet Emporium.

The Pet Emporium sold lots of pet supplies—including poop scoopers of many sizes, including large ones. Probably the same kind they used at Mountaintop Rescue.

But if it had been Harris, why would he have been anywhere near Jack's apartment building? Following Wanda there?

"Carrie? Are you okay?" Reed stared at me as if I'd just sprouted horns. Neal was looking at me, too.

"I'm fine," I said, then took a sip of my wine. "Hey, Reed. My next shift at the clinic isn't till Saturday. Do you have any interesting appointments scheduled then?"

I recognized that he was unlikely to know, and, besides, anticipated appointments generally consisted of checkups and shots, though people could schedule regular surgeries like spaying/neutering.

But we started talking about the clinic then, which was a great way to change the subject of our conversation.

Even though part of my mind was still picturing Wanda and a poop scooper …

ELEVEN

Our meals came at last. Gwen asked if we wanted anything else, then left.

I did want something else: peace of mind. And maybe to get out of the restaurant, since from the moment I'd gotten to the resort Wanda's murder had been forced back into my thoughts and mashed around there, along with different scenarios about who might have done it.

No matter what it looked like, I really preferred not to get involved.

I hadn't wanted to get involved with the other murders either, of course. But the situations had kind of forced me into it. This situation seemed as if it might do the same…

"Don't even think about it," Reed warned, as if reading my mind. I'd been staring at my salad, my wine glass in my hand, and supposed it hadn't actually been too hard for him to see into my thoughts.

"I'd really rather you stay out of it this time, too, sis," Neal said. What, he was also reading my mind? I was a lot more skilled at reading his, most of the time.

"You didn't mind my snooping around last time," I said, looking into my brother's blue eyes, which were so like my own. I figured I'd deal with Reed in a moment.

"Well, last time Janelle was a suspect. This time—"

"Okay, I really don't want to get into it, but you took me to see your bosses about Wanda."

"Yeah, and I told you I didn't have much choice."

"Hi, Carrie. Neal. Reed." A familiar voice drew my gaze up and away from my brother's face. Les Ethman stood behind Neal, smiling at us, but I couldn't help wondering why he'd come out here. I'd said hello to him earlier, at the meeting in Elise's office.

Les was a nice-looking senior, dressed this evening in a gray shirt and dark trousers instead of one of the suits he wore to City Council meetings—not surprising, considering the hour. I didn't know if the Council had met today anyway.

"Would you like to join us?" That was Reed talking, and I suspected he didn't know Les even as well as the rest of us. Of course, Les was owned by a sweet English bulldog named Sam who occasionally visited our veterinary clinic, so they'd most likely seen each other there.

Les's smile emphasized his Ethman turned-down eyes. "I'd love to, for a minute. I'll just have a beer, not dinner." He started toward the only empty chair at the table, which was no longer occupied by Biscuit.

Like the rest of the Ethmans, Les had apparently lived in Knobcone Heights for a long time. Unlike them, he actually did have a good reason to act as if he ruled the place, since he had been elected to City Council repeatedly.

He sat down, and immediately Gwen came over to ask for his order. The resort's employees were primed to take good care of the Ethmans.

My salad was good. The bite I'd taken of my hamburger was even better, but, as planned, I shared it with the dogs, giving Hugo the bigger piece.

Gwen brought Les's beer quickly, along with some taco chips and salsa, which we all sampled. Neal again brought up his proposed hikes around Halloween, to get Les's opinion.

The night air remained brisk but the lamps kept us warm. And Les kept looking from one to the other of us, as if waiting for us to start talking about the elephant on the patio—and probably everywhere in Knobcone Heights at the moment: Wanda's murder.

But what could we say to, and in front of, a City Councilman?

Neal bent over to hand his friend Bug and the other pup some roast beef from his sandwich. I'd have to give both dogs some healthy treats from my Barkery. Of course, meat was generally good for dogs, but my stuff was better.

That was when Les finally said, "Okay. Forget my family's pushiness, Carrie. Or that I told them you're fine with not getting involved this time. Who here has an idea what happened to Wanda Addler?"

He looked at me first, then at Reed and Neal, then aimed his gaze back at me.

I raised my eyebrows in a look I hoped appeared completely innocent. "Like you said, I'm fine with not getting involved this time. Isn't solving murders what the police are supposed to do?"

The lines beside Les's mouth grew deeper as he aimed a sardonic smile at me. "Yes, but that didn't stop you before, Carrie."

"Oh, but the other people at this table are stopping me." I aimed my own perky smile at Neal, then at Reed.

"You would look into it otherwise?"

My smile faded, and not just because I saw Reed and Neal both stare hard at me, as if daring me to say yes. "I never intended to get involved the other times, Les. I thought you knew that. But when I was a major suspect I really had no choice. And then a friend, who also has become an assistant at my shops, became a suspect."

"So, this time you don't consider Jack Loroco or any other potential suspect to be your friend?"

I really didn't want to get into this now, and with Les. Especially with the two men I was closest to listening. Besides, Les knew I was friends with his fellow City Councilperson Billi.

So I just aimed a puzzled look at Les. "I don't understand why you're pushing this now, Les, especially since you stood up for me making my own decisions in front of your family." I paused, but he said nothing, so I continued. "Jack and I are friends, sure, but not that close. And I gather your family may have ideas about other potential suspects, although they didn't mention who. Do you know who they are?"

Les glared at me this time, but only for an instant before taking a swig of his beer and ending the drink with a sigh. "I've got some ideas, but mostly I'm really unhappy that nice, quiet Knobcone Heights has become a murder location lately. You're right. You should stay out of it this time, Carrie. But I'm always happy to ask citizens for ideas, so if you can tell me how we can calm down our wonderful town again and make sure people are safe from any kind of issue, most especially murder, please let me know."

"Absolutely," I assured him—while wondering how to protect a whole town from that kind of thing, especially when the murders had happened weeks or months apart and were totally unrelated.

My dear brother took over the conversation once more at the table, so the rest of our meal was spent talking about how wonderful Knobcone Heights was for sightseeing, especially on hikes.

Les stayed even after he finished his beer. I wondered what was really on his mind. He, of all the Ethmans, had always been a very nice and rational person before. I supposed he was now, too.

But I wondered if all this was because he actually *did* want me to try to solve this murder, which was absurd.

Wasn't it?

Or was it the opposite?

This was becoming rather confusing…

Eventually we all finished eating and drinking, and I soon learned that, on top of all the tension and speculation, the evening wasn't ending as I'd hoped.

Les left before the rest of us. First, though, he took me aside briefly to look over the balcony down toward the lake. Its surface shimmered with lights reflected from the resort and other nearby buildings.

I was glad to accompany Les there to stare at the lovely view and speak privately with him. I expected some kind of explanation about what he really was thinking. Maybe even an apology for bringing the latest murder up more than once.

Instead, though, he said, "I want to chat with you about all this soon, Carrie. Now's not the time or place, but you probably figured that I have some concerns—about you, and about other related things. I'll give you a call tomorrow, if that's all right with you."

Of course it was. I was intrigued, for one thing. What was really on this City Councilman's mind? Just ways to protect Knobcone Heights from future murders?

If so, I wasn't the best citizen to talk to. A store owner and veterinary technician wasn't anything like a city administrator or cop—the kinds of people he had easy access too—even though this vet tech and entrepreneur had done some things beyond the scope of what was expected of her.

I'd have to wait to find out, though. "Sure, Les," I told him. "I'll look forward to talking with you tomorrow."

He preceded me back to our table, where he quickly patted both dogs in farewell and said goodbye to Neal, Reed, and me. Then he left.

"Is everything okay with Les?" Neal asked, as he and Reed stood.

"I'm not sure," I responded honestly.

Then came my big disappointment of the evening. Not that I dislike my brother, or the home where we live—not at all, I love them both—but instead of Biscuit and me getting invited to Reed and Hugo's for a nightcap, Neal drove me to my car, which was parked at the shops. That meant no fun activities with Reed before bedtime.

And Reed seemed fine with this idea. Maybe he was tired. Maybe he was upset about the possibility that, no matter what I said or did, I seemed to be getting sucked into this murder investigation despite his encouraging me strongly to stay away.

Which irritated me. Even if he was right and I should stay out of it, that was my decision to make. I didn't take orders well, except on the job when he or one of the other veterinarians instructed me about what to do to help one of our patients.

But this had nothing to do with saving an animal's life—although it could ultimately boil down to saving the future of a falsely accused suspect, as it had the previous times.

Well, I wasn't going to learn any more about it tonight.

Nor was I going to get anything more from Reed than a goodbye and quick good night kiss.

"You okay, Carrie?" Neal asked as Biscuit and I got into his car.

"I may need another drink," I told him, though just a nightcap was far from what I'd hoped for with Reed. "Care to join me with some beer at home while we watch tonight's news?"

He liked the idea, and so did I.

Biscuit stayed in Neal's car when he dropped me off behind the stores to grab my own, and I followed my brother through downtown and into the residential area where we lived.

It turned out to be a good thing that I did have a beer bottle in hand as we sat on the fluffy old beige couch in the living room and watched the local channel's news broadcast on the TV mounted on the wall. Unsurprisingly, Wanda Addler's death was mentioned, as Police Chief Loretta Jonas was interviewed on camera on the sidewalk in front of the police station.

As usual when confronted by a reporter and microphone, Chief Loretta was dressed in a formal police uniform, complete with dark jacket decorated with medals. She looked serious and concerned, although the frown on her dark-complected face was there nearly every time I saw her—except when she was with her dog Jellybean, a schnauzer mix adopted a while ago from Mountaintop Rescue. I'd guessed when I'd first met her that she was in her fifties and dyed her medium-brown hair, since it was all one shade.

Yes, she said into the microphone held by solemn Silas Perring, anchor of the local station's evening news, there had been an apparent homicide in Knobcone Heights. The victim was not a local resident, and an investigation was being conducted. Nothing outstanding or particularly informational there.

But who were her detectives, Bridget Morana and Wayne Crunoll, interrogating this time … anyone I thought of as a suspect?

Possibly, although the people they were most likely to zero in on might not be the ones I considered the most probable killers.

When the interview was over, I swigged the rest of my beer, then started to rise. "Bedtime," I told Neal—and Biscuit, too, since I'd be taking her out for her last walk of the night.

"What did you think?" My brother stood, too. "About that interview, I mean."

"Our illustrious police chief didn't really say anything, at least nothing new." I sighed. "And I wish I didn't care."

"I wish you didn't, too," Neal said, his voice firm and his light brows knitted in worry. "I don't suppose I could bribe you to stay out of it this time, could I, sis?"

"What would you bribe me with?"

"Oh, how about if all the hikes you take with me in the future are free?"

"They already are," I said dryly.

"Then I'll up the amount of rent I pay you."

"What, from nearly nothing to a few dollars more than nearly nothing?"

"I'll walk Biscuit for you more."

"You take her for lots of walks already. Hey, with all this I'm beginning to think you actually like it when I figure out who murderers are."

Neal smiled, his eyes drooping as if he were as tired as I felt. "I did appreciate it the last couple of times. This time, not so much, maybe. But I've got to admit that it's been fun telling my friends and people I work with that yes, I'm that Carrie Kennersly's brother."

I drew near to him, gently swatted him with the end of Biscuit's leash, and gave him a hug.

"Good night, bro," I said. "And if you happen to see the murder in your dreams, be sure to let me know whodunit."

"Count on it. And you do the same."

"Sure," I said, lying. If I dreamed about the killer, I'd still want to do some digging to make sure my mind wasn't just telling me who I wanted to have done it.

And assuming I ignored Reed and Neal and possibly Les, and stayed involved in solving this murder—due to knowing and liking both Billi and Jack—then I wanted to make sure that I did it the right way, once more.

TWELVE

My bedtime walk with Biscuit along the sidewalk of our quiet residential street under the sparse streetlights was short and to the point. She apparently was tired, too.

Just as we returned to the house, my phone rang. I opened the door quickly, then pulled the phone from my pocket.

It was Reed. "I hope I didn't wake you," he said.

"No, I'm about to go to bed." I knew my voice sounded cool, but I felt a little irritated toward him. Not that I minded spending time with Neal, but still…

I bent down, phone to my ear, to let Biscuit off her leash and give her a big hug.

"I want to apologize, Carrie." Reed's words and tone made all that iciness inside me start melting.

Hey, I told myself. He might want to apologize for something totally illogical.

But no. He continued by saying, "I miss you tonight, and I kind of pulled away because you're clearly getting involved with this latest murder situation. But it's not up to me to tell you what you can and can't do. Except at the clinic." Okay, he was trying to lighten this up a bit.

"True," I told him, but without removing the bite from my tone. He could grovel some more.

Meanwhile, I checked that the doors were locked, then followed Biscuit down the hall to our bedroom. I heard the shower as we passed Neal's room so I figured he hadn't gone to bed yet.

"Although I can at least make suggestions if I'm worried about you, like now," Reed said. "And I want you to promise me something."

"What's that?" I walked into my bedroom, Biscuit in front of me, and closed the door behind us.

I anticipated Reed saying something like he wanted me to drop all interest in murders, or only to snoop into them from some faraway location, or let him do it all for me. And I was sure his form of investigating would be, if anything, to check long-distance into what was going on, maybe just researching online.

I was therefore surprised when, as I sat down on the edge of my bed on top of the lavender coverlet, he said, "Several things. Promise to be careful—I've told you this before, but I'm repeating it, especially since things got pretty nasty those other times. And I know you're smart, much smarter than you should be about things like murder investigations, but I'm asking you not to talk one-on-one with anyone you think could be the real killer, not unless you're in public and safe—although I know you can't always choose time and place and who you're with. Just take good care of yourself."

"And bad care of the person I think is guilty, if I figure that out." I watched Biscuit turn in circles on top of her fluffy bed on the floor beside mine.

"Exactly. Like, put 'em in the hands of the cops fast."

I laughed. "I got it, Reed. And I appreciate your concern."

"Oh, yeah, I'm concerned about you, Carrie Kennersly. And I'd like for us to have dinner here at my place tomorrow night, just ourselves. Is that okay?"

"That's very okay." We soon hung up—and I knew at last that I'd be able to sleep that night.

Well, I slept some that night, although I did have dreams wake me. In one, I saw Billi killing Wanda, hitting her with a poop scooper till she bled. In another, it was Jack. In another, interestingly, it was Harris Ethman. And, yes, in yet another, I couldn't see who it was, but it was none of the above.

Too many dreams. Too little time. Four o'clock in the morning came much too quickly.

But I rose on schedule and also arrived at my stores on schedule a while later, Biscuit accompanying me. I gave her a big hug as I left her in the Barkery, making sure, since she was loose for now, that the shop door couldn't be opened by anyone else. Then I returned to the kitchen to scrub my hands and don my apron.

First thing, I started on some of the Icing baked goods, including the excellent red velvet cupcakes whose recipe I'd bought from Brenda. As I stood by the Icing part of the counter, I kept seeing those dreams again in my mind. Maybe everyone was right. I had to stop getting involved with murders. They took up too much of my consciousness and unconsciousness.

Enough, I told myself. *Listen to Reed. Listen to Neal. And even listen to Les.*

But would I listen even to myself? That remained to be seen.

Soon Janelle came in via the back door. "Good morning, Carrie."

"Good morning." I saw her glance toward where I stood.

"Looks like I'm baking dog treats this morning," she said. "Love it!"

She quickly got started on the gingerbread dog treats that had been created by Chef Manfred Indor for me. Manfred was a really great chef for human food who'd been fired from the Knobcone Heights Resort a while ago. I liked the guy, especially since he'd promised to come up with some new dog treat recipes for me and then delivered on his promise—the gingerbread recipe was from him. He'd fortunately found a couple of other jobs in the San Bernardino Mountains, so I still saw him now and then.

The recipe was quick, easy, and tasty not only for dogs but also for the people who tried them. I always tried to have some of those treats around.

"I really like this recipe," Janelle said. "But I like everything you bake here. We need something new, though, since I want to take some more photographs to post on our website and social media."

Janelle was, first and foremost, a photographer. Which also turned her into the absolute best person to provide promotion for both of my shops. She could arrange baked goods into all kinds of formations to attract potential customers' attention and had been doing so for several months now. And the only compensation she ever let me give her was to employ her at my shops.

That was probably because she was Neal's girlfriend. And also because I'd ensured she was cleared of the murder allegation against her.

Could I wind up doing that for Billi, and Jack, too?

"Great idea," I said. "I've been working on some low-fat applesauce-and-pumpkin treats but have only made them look like little squashed balls. I'll have to come up with some other shapes—maybe our traditional bones, or some appropriate cookie-cutter form."

I'd already put a couple of batches of red velvet cupcakes into the Icing oven and now got started on cranberry scones.

I saw the irony, of course. I was working on a baked good that had red coloration ... was that a result of my dreams, in which I'd imagined blood? Ridiculous! I had to move my mind far away from the whole scenario of murder.

Just when I thought I'd convinced myself, though, Janelle stopped her work on the gingerbread treats and looked at me in a way I realized right away had nothing to do with baked goods. I tried not to look back, but she said, "Neal called me late last night."

"He shouldn't wake you," I said, ignoring what this was probably about. "He knows your schedule. He must have known you'd be here early this morning."

"He's worried about you, Carrie."

"And I'm worried about him." Was this never going to end—everyone reminding me to be careful, which was a way of pounding on me to not get involved in the latest murder? Even someone like Janelle, who should like it if I jumped in to try to clear someone innocent?

"You know what I'm talking about. And I told him I'd mention it to you. And now I have. You won't hear any more from me about it, Carrie. I promise."

At those words I did look up at her and smile. "Thanks," I said.

I knew the next person I'd talk to that day on the subject of murder would have an entirely different agenda than everyone else. Billi Matlock would definitely continue to encourage me to try to figure out who killed Wanda Addler.

In the meantime, my shops opened at seven o'clock sharp, and I was delighted at the immediate influx of customers into Icing—people on their way to work who wanted to start their day on a sweet note. We sold lots of scones and people biscuits and even red velvet cupcakes at that early hour.

I loved it!

I loved it even more when I left Janelle in Icing and headed into the Barkery, where Dinah was busy waiting on customers, too—most of them with their dogs along indulging in samples and helping their human companions choose what to buy.

This was me. My life. These shops, and my work as a part-time vet tech. I wasn't a police investigator. Maybe my friends and family were right. After all, I'd barely known Wanda Addler, and there was no reason to really believe that the people I was a bit worried about, Billi and Jack, would be the sole subjects of the police investigation, the ones they'd focus on—right?

Only … I received a call from Billi at around ten that morning, confirming that she wanted me to come talk with her at Mountaintop Rescue around eleven. By then, Frida had arrived.

Billi sounded a bit frantic. That caused me to feel—well, concerned. And more.

As a result, Biscuit and I arrived at Cuppa-Joe's at ten fifteen, a bag of leftover Barkery treats in my hand to bring to the residents of Mountaintop Rescue. Maybe it was silly, but I wanted just a few minutes to visit with my close buddies, the Joes, before getting into an emotional discussion with Billi. Once again, Biscuit and I headed to a table along the fence on the outside patio, beneath one of the heaters. I didn't have to peek inside since server Kit, today wearing a dark blue shirt with the traditional coffee cup logo, saw me as she came out the door and turned back.

In moments, Joe and Irma were outside with us.

"Hi, Carrie." Joe bent down to hug me and pat Biscuit. He felt warm and supportive and solid.

"What's wrong, honey?" Irma asked, hands on her hips as she regarded me, worry wrinkling her very attractive face. "As if I can't guess."

They both sat down and in a minute Kit reappeared with cups of coffee for all of us, mine in a to-go cup.

Rather than jumping on me about what might be bothering me, my dear pseudo parents started talking about the weather and how they hoped their patio heaters would continue to keep patrons warm. They asked how business was at my shops, then about my latest work at the veterinary clinic.

I relaxed, drank my coffee, and smiled as both gave Biscuit attention, too.

But then I glanced at the time on my phone. "I've got to leave." I knew I didn't sound happy about it. "I'm heading to Mountaintop Rescue to talk with Billi."

"I wondered." Irma reached her hands across the table, and I placed mine into them. "I know they're looking at her as a person of interest in that killing, aren't they?" She paused. "No, never mind. Don't talk about it unless you want to. And don't talk to Billi or anyone else unless you want to—and I hope you know you can talk with us anytime about anything, right?"

I felt tears in my eyes as I smiled at these two wonderful people. "I do know that, and that's why I'm here. I love you both." I forced myself to rise and pick up my coffee cup from the table. Biscuit got to her feet, too, and I made sure the loop of her leash was securely around my wrist. "I'll be back soon."

My goal in coming here had been fulfilled, I thought, as Biscuit and I hurried out onto the relatively empty sidewalk. I'd talked with people who cared about me yet didn't tell me what to do, who trusted me to get involved, or not, based on my own good judgment.

So what would I do now when I talked with Billi?

I found that out about fifteen minutes later.

She'd said yesterday at the spa that she wanted me to help find Wanda's killer.

I'd said I'd think about it. My thoughts since then had been gravitating toward yes, but that was before everyone but the Joes had come down on me to keep out of it.

So why was I here at Mountaintop Rescue—to reassure my friend that I was going to dig in nevertheless and try to figure out what happened? Or to let her know that, on further consideration, I would be staying out of it this time?

After all, I hadn't made any promises, except that if I did get involved, I'd look for the truth and wouldn't try to shield anyone, friend or not.

Having Biscuit with me, I wasn't going to visit any of the residents today. Instead, I stopped at the reception desk.

"Hi, Carrie." Today, Mimi's shirt said *Dogs Rule—Unless You're A Cat* and had a feline with a Cheshire Cat smile on it. "And hi, Biscuit. Billi's expecting you. Go on up to her office."

I handed Mimi the bag of leftover treats to distribute to the shelter's residents. Then Biscuit and I walked up the clean wooden stairs to the upper hallway and passed a few doors till we reached

Billi's hangout. The sign on the door now identified her as *Councilwoman Wilhelmina Matlock, Boss of the City, Canines, and Cats*.

I smiled at that, knocked on the door, and didn't wait for a response before I opened it.

Billi had decorated her office here, more than at the spa, in a way that conveyed she was a Matlock, one of Knobcone Heights' ruling families. The desk didn't look like the run-down piece of pre-used furniture that animal shelters usually used so that all their funds could go toward the animals. Billi had paid for the furniture herself, and had an attractive, professional-looking wooden desk. It sat on an antique area rug with faded gold trim.

My friend appeared professional-looking, too, whenever she sat behind it, even while wearing the standard *Mountaintop Rescue* T-shirt and jeans—most of the time, that is. This morning, she looked exhausted.

"Hi, Carrie." She sounded exhausted, too. She had a cup of coffee in front of her, which was a good thing. I should have called to offer to bring one for her from Cuppa's, like the one I carried.

"Hi, Billi." I moved one of the wooden chairs facing her desk so I could get closer to her than the people who sat here usually did—often potential adopters. "How are you getting along?" I thought I knew what her answer would be, but she surprised me.

"Okay, I guess. Look, Carrie, I really appreciate you saying you might be willing to help figure out who really killed Wanda for me, but after thinking about it, I don't want to make you do that again. I know how stressful it can be to investigate something, and like last time, you'd just be doing it to be a good friend."

"You are a good friend," I responded. "Tell me what's been going on."

Softly, she described being confronted a couple of times since the murder by the Knobcone Heights PD, including both detectives—who'd been the banes of my existence when I was a suspect, and who'd even interrogated me briefly this time, when I had nothing to do with the situation. Well, not much, anyway.

"At least Wanda's body wasn't found near here, but they know I know where Jack's apartment is and that Wanda was still bothering him. Since they're at least considering me a possible suspect, I did the right thing and hired an attorney. I considered getting a high-powered criminal lawyer from LA, but I figured someone who knew this town and its quirks would be better, so I've hired your former lawyer, Ted Culbert. Just in time, by the way. He indicated he'd been approached by someone else regarding the same situation—Jack, probably—but hadn't taken the case yet."

"But he took on your defense?"

"Yes, and I'm glad. Since he's from the area, he knows me as a City Councilwoman and local businesswoman."

And probably as a Matlock, too, I thought—and Matlocks were big wheels in town even though, except for Billi, they weren't always around.

So now my mind was twirling once more. I could stay out of this.

Did I want to stay out of this?

Billi was acting responsibly under the circumstances. Maybe Jack was, too. And the fact I thought neither of them had killed Wanda … I could be wrong.

"So this time, please stay out of it, Carrie." Billi's look toward me was sad but resigned.

"Why, because you're guilty?" That just blurted from my mouth. I clearly wasn't thinking straight.

"No!" Billi's shout reverberated through the room. "No," she repeated more quietly. "Of course not."

"Then are you trying to protect Jack because you think he's guilty—and you know that if I do investigate, I'll figure out the truth?"

What was I doing? Trying to convince myself I was a detective, despite all the concerns and warnings voiced to me in the past day or so?

Being the person the Joes thought I was and making the best decision possible?

Heck if I knew.

"No, I don't believe he's guilty, and I think he and I will try to help each other, but—Carrie, I think we've talked this over enough. I appreciate your interest and experience and all, but I don't want to do this to you again. I don't want to do it to *me* at all, but I'm stuck with it till the truth comes out. But thanks anyway."

Her attitude stoked my curiosity. Even if I told her I wouldn't try to help her, that didn't mean I'd have no interest in figuring out what really happened. After all, someone had killed Wanda. I didn't truly think it was Billi, although now that she'd invited me to keep my nose out of it, I kind of wondered...

And if it wasn't her, it might be Jack, who remained my friend, at least for now—and possibly Billi's friend, too.

Besides, maybe the killer was someone else altogether, I thought, recalling Neal's report of Harris Ethman arguing with Wanda at the resort.

Or—

"There is one thing, though," Billi said. "I know we were talking about having an adoption event in a week or two at the Barkery, but I'm just not going to be able to handle that and everything else, too.

If we do one of these again, it'll have to be in the future … and that could wind up being a big *if*, depending on how things go."

When I first opened my shops, Billi and I had talked for quite a while about possibly doing an adoption event with dogs from Mountaintop Rescue at Barkery and Biscuits. We'd finally done one a few weeks ago. It had gone great! Not only had some wonderful dogs who needed a forever home found them with people who'd come to check them out at my store, but we'd sold—and given away—a lot of treats.

And lots of people had begged us to do it again.

Okay. Maybe this was a dumb reason to postpone it, but it made sense to me. And if we couldn't count on doing another adoption event at my Barkery as long as Wanda's murder remained unsolved and Billi was a suspect, I had to help figure things out as fast as possible.

Don't try to change my mind, I called out silently to Reed and Neal and the whole world.

Or maybe my mind had already been made up …

"We'll throw another adoption event soon," I told Billi, looking straight into her sad brown eyes. "I've decided that I *am* getting involved, no matter what, and I'll try to find out what happened to Wanda as fast as I can."

THIRTEEN

A CRISP BREEZE WAS blowing as Biscuit and I left the shelter to head back to our stores. Good. The chill boosted my circulation, especially since I'd worn only a light jacket over my knit shirt.

Or maybe my inner warmth was due to thoughts of facing down those who cared about me but who'd tried, with the best of intentions, to tell me what to do. Reed and Neal, Les, and now even Billi had expressed concern about me. Reed had acknowledged that it was my decision, but he clearly wished he could order me to back off, sweet and caring guy that he was.

Of course, he couldn't.

And now, after talking to Billi, I was very concerned that the adoption events we'd started might evaporate. Not to mention that her life was in danger of doing the same.

People who cared about me giving orders or not, I had reasons to get involved this time. Multiple reasons.

As we reached the sidewalk, I decided to take a brief detour, one I'd purposely avoided even thinking about on our walk here.

Exactly where had Wanda been killed?

I didn't know which apartment Jack was living in, or which one Wanda had apparently moved into. I googled the news report on my phone, to see if the media had pinpointed the location of the murder scene. I found only general speculation, but it did appear to have occurred east of here, in the area I'd have guessed—not the most elite residential area, but a place where several apartment complexes blended with supermarkets, liquor stores, and general retail outlets where locals often bought supplies.

That area wasn't on our way back to my shops, unfortunately, but I led Biscuit along Hill Street in that direction—passing the police station and City Hall across the street from us. My dog seemed fine about heading in a direction we rarely took on foot, sniffing lots of new spots and earning smiles from the few people who were walking around us. Traffic was fairly sparse this way, too.

The location wasn't hard to spot. Police tape still blocked off the rear part of a parking lot near the closest apartment building. The rest of the parking lot held a lot of cars—and people seemed to get in and out of them slowly, observing that far side where someone had been killed.

I wondered what kinds of crime scene investigators were still around. And what they'd found—in addition to the poop scooper that the media claimed was the murder weapon.

The scoopers I'd seen being used at Mountaintop Rescue didn't have points on them, so how was she stabbed? Had someone used the scooper like a bat, as in my dream? Had the killer modified the scooper to put a point on one or both of its crossed handles—the upper ends of them, farthest from the metal parts that actually did the scooping—specifically to use it as a murder weapon?

I hoped no one was watching me as I pulled gently on Biscuit's leash, urging her to join me as I turned and walked away. I was smiling, but grimly—and not because I was happy to have observed a murder scene, even at this distance.

But I was happy that I was listening to my own mind and heart again—still—and considering how to satisfy my curiosity and hopefully help my friends in the process.

I stopped smiling when Biscuit and I passed Mountaintop Rescue again and reached the corner of Pacific Street. If we continued straight ahead, we would arrive at the veterinary clinic. My clinic, where Reed currently was at work—and he and I were to meet for dinner tonight.

I considered calling him right away as Biscuit and I turned down Pacific. If he was going to return to giving me a hard time about the choices I was making, even in a nice and caring way, I could call off our dinner date.

But that wasn't the kind of conversation that should interrupt any veterinary exams, and I certainly didn't want to leave a message.

No, I'd tell him first thing about my decision to investigate, and dare him to kick me out of his house.

I gave a quick nod, as if in commitment to that thought, as I waited for the traffic to pass, at the edge of the town square across the street from my shops. I was ready.

I was very busy for the rest of the day, since the shops were crowded. Locals seemed to love both stores. Plus, although Knobcone Heights wasn't a huge tourist spot, it did attract a lot of visitors. Today, a tour bus had stopped on its way to nearby Big Bear, and the occupants had gotten out to stretch their legs—and visit the town's upscale retail area.

Apparently a lot of the tourists had dogs at home, and apparently they felt guilty about leaving their canine kids behind, since they bought a lot of treats at the Barkery. They also must have thought they deserved some treats of their own, since they swept into Icing and left with nearly everything there. I sent Dinah and Frida scrambling into the kitchen to bake a few more things so we'd be able to end the day with enough if any other customers dropped in.

By our closing time of six o'clock, I was exhausted. And I was smiling.

I loved being an entrepreneur, especially since I was successful.

Plus, it was Friday, and I'd have a shift at the clinic as a vet tech tomorrow.

Life was good—as long as I didn't think too much about the latest murder and how, after all, it was going to affect me.

I said goodbye and gave heartfelt thanks to my assistants, who'd worked till the day's bitter end. No, *sweet* end, thanks to the Icing half of the stores. Leaving Biscuit in the Barkery for a few minutes, I slipped into my office in the back part of the kitchen to do a final quick tally for the day and close down my computer.

My phone rang and I pulled it from my pocket. It was Neal.

"Hi, Carrie," he said. "I need to ask you a favor."

Uh-oh. And this was before I'd had a chance to tell *him* my decision about snooping around Wanda's murder. "What's that?"

"Can you come to the resort for dinner? Les Ethman wants to talk to you again—although he asked me not to tell you that, but to tell you I really wanted you to come visit tonight. He'll even pay for our dinner."

"But he doesn't want you to tell me that? Why not?"

"You'll have to chat with him to find out."

Hmmm. My curiosity wasn't just humming now; it was on overdrive. Les had already given me his two cents worth about my looking into Wanda's murder—more than once. What did he want now?

"The thing is," I said, still sitting at my desk, staring at the dog biscuit that was the wallpaper for my computer, "I'm supposed to have dinner with Reed tonight to talk about—well, you can guess."

"Yes, I can guess, and I can also guess that you're—never mind. Tell you what. I'll let Les know and tell him you're only coming if I can arrange dinner for Reed, too. You're supposed to think I'm paying, so the deal, before you get here, will be that we'll all have to order frugally."

"But as soon as I 'realize' that it's Les who's treating, I can eat anything I want." It wasn't a question, and I felt the smile that erupted on my face.

"You got it."

"Then so do you. I'll let Reed know what's going on, although we'll both be discreet for you."

"I knew there was a reason I love you, sis." Neal said that a lot, especially when the topic of how much rent he was—or wasn't—paying came up.

"See you soon," I said. After I hung up with him, I pressed the button on my phone to call Reed.

He answered right away, so I figured his shift had ended for the evening—as it should, since we were supposed to get together in half an hour.

"Hi, Carrie. Are you still coming to my place for dinner tonight?" he asked. "If so, I'm stopping someplace special to bring home our meal."

"No," I told him. "I've got to go to Knobcone Resort. Neal needs me there because Les Ethman wants to talk to me. But you're invited for dinner, too. I assume you'll come pick Biscuit and me up? And—well, we have other things to discuss, too."

Something in my voice at that last comment might have suggested what it was I wanted to talk to him about. I figured we would have some kind of potentially heated discussion, whether in the car or at the resort or afterward, about my decision to snoop more into the murder—and despite Reed's acknowledgment that I could do what I wanted.

"I have a feeling I need to stop in the bar to get fortified before we eat," he said.

"Me, too," I agreed.

I'd visited the Knobcone Heights Resort a lot since moving to town, especially after Neal joined me and landed a job there.

I wondered, as Biscuit and I waited on the sidewalk in front of my shops for Reed to pick us up, if I should start staying far away from the place. The times I seemed to visit most were when murders were committed.

"Hi, Carrie," said a familiar voice. I turned and saw one of our most loyal customers, Cecelia—Cece—Young approaching from down the street. She was an older lady, a sixth grade teacher at our local elementary school, and a great fan of Icing on the Cake. "Is Icing still open?"

"Sorry," I said. "Both shops are closed. I'm just waiting here for a ride."

She looked disappointed. "Oh, I was hoping to bring home some scones."

"Tell you what," I said. "Come in to buy some when we open at seven tomorrow and I'll give you a half dozen extra."

"Really? That'll be great! I wanted to bring some in to school for an early teachers' meeting. Everyone will be thrilled."

Me, too, I thought—as long as she told the group where the scones had come from.

As soon as she said goodbye I spotted Reed's car slowing down in front of the shops. "Here we go," I told Biscuit, and we piled into the passenger seat of his black luxury sedan.

Reed had on a gray shirt that complemented both the color of the car and his dark, wavy hair. He looked over at us, his smile not really looking happy. What was he thinking? Was he disappointed I wasn't coming to his place?

But dinner at the resort didn't mean I wouldn't end up at his home for a nightcap later—assuming we were still speaking to one another at that point.

"Hope you don't mind that I didn't open your door like a gentleman, Carrie," he said, "but I didn't want it to look like I was parking here at this hour. I saw a couple of cop cars prowling around, maybe staking out your shops. Do they know they have to compete with you in solving that murder?"

"No," I said, startled. "And how do you know that?"

He started the car again, his smile looking more real. "I've come to know you, Carrie. I also figured, since you wanted to talk tonight even before we'd decided to go to the resort, that you're going to lay the reality in front of me that you're going to do whatever you damn well please, even though I've kind of already agreed. Right?"

My laugh was more of a snort. "You could phrase it differently. And maybe I won't tell you anything. The Joes told me not to talk to anyone unless I want to. Maybe I'll just clam up altogether rather than talk to you about the murder, or whether I give a damn about it, or whether I intend to try to figure it out."

"Which you are, aren't you?" His tone was neutral, but I knew that this man—who in some situations was my boss, in other situations my friend, and more—still had his own opinion about what I should or shouldn't do, and believed his way was in my best interests.

"If I tell you no, you won't believe me. And if I tell you yes, you'll be unhappy that I'm not obeying your orders."

"Phrasing it that way tells me a lot, too. I never gave you orders, just requests. And expressions of concern."

We had just pulled up to the gate to the resort's parking lot. I hadn't asked Neal if he was validating our parking ticket again—or if Les was paying for that, too. I vowed to try to ensure that we paid little, if anything.

First, though, as Reed pulled in and found an empty spot, I tried to finalize that conversation, for now, at least. "I've heard what you said, Reed, and I always appreciate your concern for me. A lot. And it's not like I'm going out and seeking out murders because of the fun I have trying to solve the crimes. But as odd as it is—"

"Murders are seeking you out. And yes, it is odd. But just remember I'm here for you and have your back—as long as I know what you're doing and where you're doing it. Just be careful, Carrie." With that, he turned off the engine and looked at me for a long moment before he leaned toward me.

Our kiss lasted a nice, hot, sexy while before I reluctantly backed away.

"I've got to find Neal and have him make sure Les 'accidentally' runs into us," I said.

FOURTEEN

UNSURPRISINGLY, NEAL WAS AT the reception desk. "Oh, good, you're here," he said. He turned the desk over to one of his colleagues, who was as professionally dressed as he was, and walked to where I stood at the edge of the lobby with Reed and Biscuit. "So, Reed," he began, "I really want us to get a drink at the bar, but Carrie's going to order her dinner in the restaurant. And I need a little dog time with my Bug. Got it?"

He looked at me, and I interpreted what he was doing: keeping Reed—and Biscuit—occupied while Les got an opportunity to talk to me alone. And not just at the edge of the patio for a few minutes this time. Les had said he would call me, and he hadn't. Why was he doing all this so sneakily?

Well, hopefully he would explain. And for now, at least for my brother's sake and the sake of his relationship with the family that owned this place, I'd play along.

I felt lonesome heading through the arched doorway into the restaurant alone, though. I looked around the semi-crowded place and decided on a table in the rear corner, one without too many people around so Les and I could talk—assuming he did as Neal indicated and joined me.

My server wasn't Gwen today, although I saw her waiting on some customers near the door to the patio. I was unfamiliar with the guy who appeared and just asked for a glass of wine to start with—a zinfandel this time. "I'll probably go out on the patio when the rest of my party comes, since one of them's a dog," I told him. "But till they join me, I'll enjoy a drink."

I hadn't yet gotten my wine, though, when I saw Les, dressed in athletic pants and a hoodie, nearly walk past me. He stopped a few steps away and turned back, as if it was a big surprise to see me there. "Hi, Carrie. Are you alone? May I join you?"

"Of course, Les." I really wished I understood what this was about. Why was he putting on this act, assuming either that I didn't know about his plan for the evening or that I was willing to play along?

He sat down in a chair beside me, and I figured we'd be able to hear one another better that way than if he faced me. The room wasn't extremely crowded or noisy, but he probably didn't want us to have to shout about whatever he wanted to talk about.

The server brought my wine then, placing it on the white tablecloth before me, and Les ordered a gin and tonic. "I assume you've got people joining you for dinner, so I won't order a meal," he said.

"That's right." And then I grew completely silent, waiting for him to begin.

When I'd seen Les the night before, he'd looked like the elder of his family that he was. Now, he appeared even older, with more lines in his aging face and an added sag to his Ethman eyes.

"All right, Carrie," he said softly. "I'm not sure what Neal told you, but I appreciate your cooperation."

"You know we're friends, Les," I told him. "I don't know why we're playing games, though. I'll do what I can do to help you—if I can?" I was making no promises, especially since I didn't know what he wanted. Whatever it was had probably been on his mind at least since we'd chatted so briefly on the patio, probably longer.

"Thank you. I appreciate it," he said.

His gin and tonic was placed before him then, and he became all gracious to our server—one of the royal Ethmans thanking a subject. But Les was usually more down-to-earth than the rest of his family. He took a long, drawn-out gulp and I wondered if he thought he'd feel more comfortable talking to me if he had a buzz on. Or maybe this was just another way to delay it.

"Okay, Carrie," he said softly. "Let me just lay this out—although if you tell anyone what I say, I'll deny it." He narrowed his eyes, then used them to scan me up and down. "You're not recording anything, are you?"

I laughed in disbelief. "Of course not. What, are you going to tell me you're the murderer? Or that you want me to go kill someone?"

"Not exactly."

That answer both intrigued and worried me. I leaned even closer to him. "Then tell me exactly what's going on, Les. Please."

"Okay. Now's the time." He was the one to lean closer, then. "Carrie, my family asked me to talk with you again, since you and I are friends. The thing is—well, my brother and sister-in-law in particular are concerned that … " He hesitated, as if it was painful to continue. "That this time, Harris really is the killer." He winced, again indicating pain.

"Why is that?" I asked gently. "What motive would he have for killing Wanda Addler?"

"I can't tell you that. No, I *won't* tell you that. But the thing you need to know is, he didn't do it—even though he doesn't have a good alibi for that night. He was alone, so no one can vouch that he didn't go after her."

"The family didn't seem to worry so much about Harris when Myra was killed," I said. And I had been all but accused of that murder, despite the fact that Harris, as Myra's husband, was surely more of a viable suspect than I was.

"No, but not only did Harris not kill his wife, he had good reason not to. He was the Ethman, with the money and all, even though Myra had the smarts and ambition. She used his money to buy him the Pet Emporium, and she helped ensure he knew how to run it. He felt, for the first time I gather, that he was successful at business and fit well into our family."

I took a sip of my wine as I pondered this. I'd also kind of gotten that impression at the time, even though Harris had been on my list when I tried to find out what really happened in Myra's death.

"But Harris *had* a motive to kill Wanda," I said, again hoping Les would change his mind and tell me what it was.

"Yes. But he didn't do it, no matter what you may find during your investigation. And—well, that was one reason I hoped initially that you'd stay out of it this time, even though I figured you wouldn't. And if I thought it would do any good, I'd pay you to plant evidence against Jack Loroco. I think he did it anyway. I really don't think it was Billi, even though I know she had reason to be angry with Wanda."

"Wait a minute, Les. Let's go back to you paying me to plant evidence. Surely you know I'd never—"

"Yes, I know. It was just a thought . . . "

"A bad one." I realized that I'd already finished my wine. I waved our server back over and gestured to let him know I wanted another one.

I *needed* another one. This conversation should not have been happening, yet there we were in public, being seen together.

What if the cops had some idea what it was about? What if, after this meeting with Les, they found evidence against Jack that Jack said must have been planted?

What if—?

It couldn't have been Les, could it? Was this all a ploy to make me dig deeper into Harris and the possibility of him killing Wanda, so that Les wouldn't get caught?

Les bent over then, placing his head in his hands. I could barely hear him when he began talking. "Oh, lord, Carrie. This is all so wrong. I love my family and its status in this town. I love my position on City Council. I didn't want any of this to happen, especially the deaths that have occurred recently. All three of them. What are we going to do?"

He was on the City Council, and I was just a concerned citizen. But I did think it was time for me to give him the best advice I could. "I'm not sure, Les," I told him. "But you're in charge, or at least our mayor and City Council are in charge. My suggestion is that you have a discussion with Chief Loretta about what the police think, how they believe any future situations like these can be avoided. Plus, I think we'll all be happier if the detectives on the case actually determine what happened this time—and who did it." *Even if the murderer was Harris—or you.* But I didn't say that.

Les straightened and looked me in the eye. "You're right, Carrie. We need the truth here—and I genuinely don't think Harris is to blame. We also need better ways of preventing murders in the future, and that might mean creation of a special task force to figure out why these killings happened and how others can be avoided. You're one smart shopkeeper." His smile this time almost appeared genuine, despite the ongoing sadness in his eyes. "Anyway, thank you for putting up with me—and Neal may have told you that your dinner tonight is on me, as is his and Reed's, since I saw the two of them heading for the bar together. Biscuit, too."

He rose, and so did I. I wasn't surprised when he stepped nearer and gave me a hug.

We'd hugged before, now and then. He felt frail this time.

I only hoped, no matter who solved this crime and who the killer was, that Les would be okay.

Of course, that still assumed that he wasn't the most recent murderer…

After Les left the restaurant, I approached our server, who assured me our drinks had been taken care of. "I'm going to get my friends together, and we'll eat on the patio since my dog is with them," I said.

"Great. I'm serving an area out there tonight as well, so maybe I'll be able to wait on you again."

"Sounds good. What's your name?" I glanced down at the name-tag pinned to the pocket of his white shirt. "Stu," I said at the same time he did. "Good to meet you, and thanks."

With that, I started toward the arched doorway so I could head into the bar and get the rest of my gang together for the evening. As I neared it, though, I was startled to see Jack Loroco in a dark corner of the restaurant. What really startled me, though, was the person he was with: Dinah Greeley. My assistant Dinah.

They looked deeply engaged in a conversation, heads bent toward one another.

I knew Dinah had met Jack at the shops, probably last spring, since he'd started coming to town to attempt to woo recipes from me at that point.

But how well did they know one another? And what were they talking about here?

Dinah loved to write, so my initial speculation was that she was talking to Jack, maybe interviewing him, so she could get his side of the story and incorporate it, perhaps fictionalized, into a book.

Was that too obvious an explanation, though?

Did Dinah know Wanda and have reason to rid the world of her?

Oh, heavens, this was getting out of hand—as did all my murder investigations.

The others had borne fruit, though. I'd figured out who the killer was. It didn't hurt—did it?—to suspect everyone till I'd narrowed things down.

But even Dinah?

I left the restaurant then and slipped into the crowded lobby, aiming for the bar.

I still carried my glass of wine, and I wondered how many more I'd drink that evening before I felt able to face all the stuff going on around me and to me—like another murder investigation.

Entering the lounge, I ignored the loud hum of many conversations and the blare of the sports announcer from the television on the wall. I looked around, finally spotting Reed and Neal at a table near the bank of windows at the back. They weren't alone.

Not only was Biscuit with them, but I saw Janelle, too, sitting beside my brother.

That wasn't really a surprise, since they were an item. And I figured that having Janelle here might actually work to my advantage. We could talk shop, not murder … I hoped.

Since it was getting late, all they could probably see of the lake now were the reflections off it, which might have been romantic for Neal and Janelle if Reed wasn't there. Maybe I'd be enough of a distraction, joining them, to make their evening more fun. I doubted Biscuit's presence had been enough.

As soon as I maneuvered my way through the dense crowd and reached the table, Biscuit stood on her hind legs and pawed at me—for attention, or because my darling pup sensed my disquiet? It didn't matter. I bent to hug her as Reed pulled the chair beside him out for me.

I obediently rose from my knees and sat down on the chair, putting my glass on the table only after I took the last sip from it. "I didn't realize you were coming, Janelle," I said. She had a bottle of beer in front of her, like both of the guys did.

"I didn't either, but Neal and I had talked about getting together this evening and he called to tell me he was still here, and why. I hope you don't mind, but it seemed like a good idea for me to come." My part-time assistant had changed out of the casual, promotion-oriented wear I insisted on at the stores and into a red and orange print dress with buttons down the front. Since I now sat beside her, I could see that she wore dressy, low-heeled pumps instead of her usual purple athletic shoes. She looked lovely—and I thought she should take a selfie, especially because she was a photographer.

"Well, glad you're here. Are you all ready for dinner?"

That was one of many words that Biscuit recognized, and she rose on her hind legs again to paw me. I laughed.

"Looks like we'd better get a table for five, Bug," Neal said.

They'd already taken care of payment for their drinks—it appeared that Les would take care of Janelle's meal, too, whether or not he knew it. We all headed outside to the patio, where we went through the gate in the low, ornate fence to the restaurant area.

Stu was, in fact, our server at our table for four. It had plenty of floor-space beneath and around it for Biscuit, had an overhead heater nearby, and was positioned near the fence overlooking the lake. Our orders here were somewhat standard: again, a salad for me, and Janelle asked for one as well. A burger for Biscuit, and sandwiches for the men.

And yes, another glass of zinfandel for me, beer for the guys. Janelle was still nursing her last one.

"So how was your discussion with Les?" Neal finally asked. I was wondering who'd bring it up. "We kept speculating about what you and Les were discussing—well, what aspect of it, anyway. Now that you've made up your mind to investigate, did he try to talk you out of it like the rest of us?"

"No, he just wanted to make sure I didn't zero in on one particular suspect. And that's all I'm going to say. I don't want to get into which suspect or why." Or anything else that had been said, like Les's claim he might have wanted to try to bribe me ... "In fact," I finished, "this whole subject is now off limits for the night, and preferably forever."

"For now," Reed amended.

Even so, it was in fact the last time Les or murder or Wanda was brought up that night.

Which suited me just fine.

———

This time, Biscuit and I rode with Reed when we finally left.

We didn't go back to the stores to get my car. Not right away.

And it wasn't because I'd drunk too much to drive.

I hadn't ordered any more wine, though, and eating had helped to rid me of the slight buzz I'd achieved before. Not that the buzz had emptied my mind of the things I didn't want to think of.

Even so, Reed made his point clear when he drove from the resort parking lot toward his home in a nice, hilly residential area south of town. "The nightcap I'll give you tonight will be water, tea, or coffee. Okay?"

I laughed. "What, you don't want to get me drunk so you can have your way with me?"

"I'm hoping I can have my way with you while you're still at least somewhat sober."

I laughed—and he did. I had my way with him, as well.

Later, as we lay snuggled together in Reed's bed, Biscuit snoring softly on the floor beside me, the things we hadn't yet discussed imposed themselves back into my mind.

I must have stiffened, since Reed's arms pulled me even closer. "I won't tell you not to think about—whatever—but just remember I'm here for you." I felt him kiss the top of my head.

"Thank you." I couldn't help it, though. I wasn't able to control my thoughts—or my fears, not at that moment. Maybe that was the result of having drunk too much earlier. I pulled the covers to me tightly and moved a bit away from Reed.

There wasn't much light in his room, but enough entered through the windows for me to see how messy his wavy black hair was, how his short shadow of beard darkened his cheeks and chin.

He was a good-looking guy. A nice guy. A wonderful guy who saved animals' lives on a daily basis.

"I want you to promise me something, Reed," I said suddenly, surprised at the fierceness in my own tone.

"What's that?" He cocked his head a little in obvious puzzlement.

"Promise you will never get involved in a murder—either as a suspect or a victim."

There was no humor in his laugh, only a touch of surprise. "I definitely promise you that. Or at least I want to."

"Good." I snuggled back up against him, but only for a minute. "It's getting late," I said regretfully.

"And even though tomorrow's Saturday, you still have to get up at an ungodly hour to get to your shops," he added.

"Right."

We both rose to get ready, since Reed had to drive Biscuit and me to our car at the shops. He came over to me and pulled me back into his arms. "I really care about you, Carrie. I wish you'd promise me the same thing you asked me to promise you. I know you can't, and won't. But like I said, please remember that no matter what, I'll be here for you. And—"

"And?" I prompted as he didn't continue.

"I really, really hope this is the last time you get involved with a murder."

FIFTEEN

I HAD A HARD time dragging myself out of bed the next morning. Good thing that Biscuit woke up with the clock radio as usual and was raring to go—outside, that is. I could hardly refuse.

Which got me up and going, too.

Also as usual, I reached the shops before any of my assistants, even though I was running a couple of minutes late. I took Biscuit into the Barkery, hugged her for her alertness and for getting me going, and rewarded her with an apple treat left over from yesterday. Then I dashed into the kitchen and began preparing products for Icing.

Janelle joined me about twenty minutes later. She looked as exhausted as I felt—and I figured she'd spent at least as much time as I had after dinner last night having fun with the guy in her life, who just happened to be my brother. She'd brought Go with her today, so Biscuit had a playmate.

"Do you want to talk this morning about what you didn't want to talk about last night in front of the whole gang?" Janelle asked from across the counter as she started getting ingredients together for carob-and-peanut-butter biscuits. She was dressed for work, in a beige T-shirt with the Barkery and Biscuits logo on it.

"Nope." I glanced up for a moment from where I was rolling dough for chocolate chip cookies before I looked back down and smiled. But her question caused my mind to start rehashing my discussion with Les last night.

Well—not really. It wasn't as if my mind had ever left that subject since I'd gotten up and into the shower that morning.

"Neal told me to push you to talk about it." Janelle's tone sounded amused. "I'd have done so even if he hadn't pushed me to push you."

I laughed. Then I grew sober. "I'm still mulling it over," I said honestly. "I don't want to talk about speculations and all."

"But we're all speculating about what you said last night. Who is it that Les doesn't want you to zero in on? I think it must be Billi since she's on City Council with him. But Neal—well, he knows Les's family a lot better than I do and he's trying to figure out which one of the Ethmans Les wants to protect. Himself?"

Maybe, I thought again. As well as Harris. But I didn't want to mention either of them now.

"Sorry," I said. "You can tell my brother you tried to get me to talk. Right now, though, I need to take some scones out of the oven and start stocking the shelves in the Icing display case."

"That's just an excuse," she said, sticking her bottom lip out as if in a pout.

"You got it," I agreed, but I did as I'd said and began taking baked goods into Icing.

It took me about fifteen minutes to put things on display and make sure they looked good enough to eat—and buy. It was nearly seven o'clock by then. When I popped into the Barkery, I wasn't surprised to see Dinah there, also waiting for the day to begin.

I looked at the display case in that shop first, glad to see that lots of fresh dog treats had magically—not!—appeared on the shelves behind the glass, although not all the shelves were full yet. I then went over to the area where Biscuit and Go had been confined, presumably by Dinah, and gave them pats on the head, although they seemed to believe they were getting treats.

"Later," I told them.

Then I did what I'd been wanting to do all along while trying to appear nonchalant. I headed behind the counter, where Dinah was still arranging treats, and asked, "Did you have a good dinner at the resort last night?"

"I wondered if you'd noticed me," she said, her brows raised in an expression of innocence—which increased my curiosity about why she'd been with Jack. "I hoped you hadn't."

Well, maybe not so innocent.

"Yep," I said. "I did. What did Jack and you talk about?" As if I couldn't guess.

"The poor guy is so upset," Dinah said, finishing her ministrations with one of the trays and placing it inside the display case. "He's been interrogated by the police, which didn't surprise him, but he hates that they're still after him as a major suspect in Wanda's death. He was angry with her, so he understands why he's under suspicion, but he swears he would never have hurt her—except to get her fired, if that had been possible."

"From what I gathered, she was more likely to get him fired," I countered. "So what did you think? Would you cross him off your suspect list now? And—well, why were you even talking with him?"

Turns out my guess had been correct. "Research," Dinah said. Her grin lit up her round face, and I couldn't help smiling back. "With all the murders around here—well, you know I like to write. I've been working on a fictionalized version of the earlier killings and now I can add this one, too."

A horrible thought passed through my mind. I had no idea how Dinah plotted her stories—but what if, in the interest of getting her book published in the future, she'd decided to expand this terrible situation in Knobcone Heights? I knew who'd committed the two earlier murders—thanks to my own snooping—but what if Dinah had decided three murders were better to write about than two? Could she have chosen Wanda because she was aware of the dissension between the VimPets employee and her colleague? Or maybe the fact that someone else who was at odds with Wanda was also a big wheel in the local government—Billi.

How fun for her, maybe, that there were two such credible suspects.

And if my musings turned out to be correct, then what about four murders? Five? More?

I worked with the electronic cash register as I stood there by the counter, not really making any entries but telling myself that I was making sure it was ready for that day's business.

But Dinah had worked for me for months now. She knew me. And I thought I knew her.

"Uh-oh," she said softly.

Concerned she had found something wrong with some of our biscuits, I hurriedly looked over toward her.

She was staring at me, not any of our products.

"I'm in trouble, aren't I?" she asked.

"What do you mean?" I tried to sound confused. I actually was confused. Surely she couldn't read my thoughts—could she?

Yes, she could and did. "I can see the wheels turning in your head," she said. "You're trying to figure out if you should add me to your list of possible murder suspects, aren't you? I figure you're going to look into this case, too, right?"

I let out a deep sigh even as I smiled at her. "You're right on both counts. I don't want to consider you a suspect, but I'm keeping my mind open right now. You can help me close it. Did you kill Wanda?"

"Of course not!"

Not that I'd have expected her to say otherwise. I didn't want to suspect Dinah, although my mind kept circling around that very difficult possibility.

But what I said was, "Great. That's what I figured." I quickly pulled my phone out of my pocket. "It's almost seven. Time to open the shops."

"And time," Dinah said, "for me to convince you that I didn't hurt anyone except on the computer screen. Do I think Jack did it? I'd say you can remove me from your suspect list, but I wouldn't eliminate him, at least not yet."

I pondered that conversation along with everything else regarding the murder—but was careful to keep those thoughts at the back of my mind, not allowing them to distract me from what was important to me as the day progressed: making sure each customer in both shops got what they were looking for and enjoyed their visit. Having three assistants working made that part easy, at least during the morning. But I had a shift at the veterinary clinic scheduled for the afternoon, so part of what I had to do was make sure Dinah, Frida, and Janelle all felt comfortable taking over when I was gone. Which they did. My vet tech shifts were part of the reality of my shops and their responsibilities. They were used to them.

And even though murder investigations had a tendency to slip in, too, I was through talking about this one, at least here and now. Instead, red velvet cupcakes, chocolate chip cookies, and blueberry and cranberry scones for humans were my main topic of conversation, along with pumpkin-and-yam biscuits and carob-and-oatmeal cookies for dogs.

Cece came in early, as discussed the previous day, and I gave her the extra scones I'd promised.

Both shops stayed busy. Biscuit and Go had a lot of canine visitors in the Barkery while owners chose treats for their cute pets, most of whom had accompanied them, and Icing was always filled with both locals and visitors. Everyone seemed to enjoy having a sweet tooth.

Noon seemed to arrive very quickly. My assistants got lunch breaks one at a time, starting then, and when I left at one o'clock, it meant there was one person to staff each store for an hour till all three assistants were back. I wouldn't return till four o'clock or after.

No one complained. Everyone encouraged me to do what I needed to.

I really liked my assistants.

I tried to keep my mind on them as Biscuit and I walked to the clinic, although my success rate was minimal. Murder suspects seemed to intervene, maneuvering through my thoughts like wraiths while I attempted to think of only good things.

At least the walk wasn't very long, even with my customary bagful of leftover dog treats for our patients in my hand. It was about as far to the clinic as it was to Mountaintop Rescue, although we turned left, rather than right, after crossing Hill Street. We immediately headed to the back of the structure that invariably reminded me of a blue Swiss chalet, and I opened the door to the doggy daycare facility for Biscuit.

"Hi, Carrie," called Faye from the check-in counter. The head daycare person's voice grew softer and warmer as she added, "Hi, Biscuit."

I talked to the staff for a few minutes—Faye, Al, and Charlie. The more I got to know them, the more certain I was that their decisions whether to attend veterinary school were almost made. Positive decisions. I knew they'd talked to my fellow vet tech Kayle a lot, though. Kayle had already started applying to veterinary schools.

Better that our topic of conversation remained on veterinary schools and doggy daycare than the other things on my mind that day.

I left after watching Biscuit join a few other dogs that were playing with stuffed animals at the far side of the room—supervised closely by Al, fortunately. The other dogs, from a small shih tzu mix to a large, furry collie, were frequent visitors here, too, and they all seemed to get along well.

I walked out the door into the hallway, where I headed for the locker room so I could change into my vet tech scrubs. When I exited, a couple other techs walked by, accompanying patients and their owners to some of the examination rooms, so I just stood against the wall, out of their way.

When the hallway emptied and I started toward the reception area to check in, one of the exam room doors opened and Arvie came out. As soon as he saw me, he frowned.

"Uh-oh," I said, approaching him. "What has Reed been saying to you?"

Like the Joes, Arvie always gave me advice in the most caring of ways. Only something bad would have made him look at me with that concerned expression. And where might he have heard something he didn't like about me?

"Reed didn't say anything till I pressed him," Arvie said in a low voice as Yolanda, the least friendly of my fellow vet techs, strode down the hall behind us carrying an armload of clean towels. "But it's about Wanda's murder. The more I hear about it, the more I realize you're friends with some of the people the media says are being considered 'persons of interest.' And Reed confirmed you're still looking into this one, even though I hoped you wouldn't."

"Did he also tell you that he and I have discussed the situation *ad nauseam* and I've promised him I'll be careful and all that?"

"Yes, I told him."

I jumped a little as Reed's voice, behind me, startled me. The fact that someone could sneak up on me that way, even as I was talking about being careful, was disconcerting. But I wouldn't let these two know that. Besides, other people—vets, technicians, patients, and pet owners—also strode up and down this hallway, so it wasn't surprising that I didn't notice someone walking up to me.

I laughed nervously. "Well, it's good to know that people care enough to talk about me behind my back." Literally, now, in the case of Reed.

"Of course we care about you," Arvie said. "And we admire your track record, too. You snooped into two murders before and figured them out better than the authorities did. What are the odds you'll do that now, or that the killer won't attack you like the other killers did?"

I started to shrug as Reed walked around me to stand by Arvie. He looked good in his white veterinary scrubs, which contrasted so well with his dark hair.

Of course, he looked good no matter what—although I wondered why the expression he aimed at me now looked more amused than irritated that I still dared to do my own investigation of who killed Wanda.

"I have a patient waiting," he said, "so I've got to go. One thing first, though. How many new suspects have you come up with since yesterday?"

If I thought I was startled before, what I felt now was multiplied.

Only one, I thought, recalling my discussion with Dinah that morning, but I certainly wasn't going to tell Reed that. And I also knew how I was going to use part of the rest of the afternoon to hopefully determine the viability of another potential suspect.

"What, do you have some ideas you haven't shared with me?" I asked. "Or how about you, Arvie?"

"Keep me out of this," our boss said. "But like Reed said, Carrie, be careful. Be very careful." He took a step forward and gave me a quick hug. "Hey, I'm about to work with a couple of patients who need some flea treatments fast. Want to help?"

Did I want to? No. But would I, for Arvie?

"What a wonderful way to start off my time here today," I said. "Lead me to them."

SIXTEEN

My shift was over at four. Reed knew that. He made sure my last assignment of the day was with him, assisting with general exams of a family's three dogs, then inoculating all of them with standard shots: rabies, distemper and parvo, and bordetella. The mother, father, and teenage son each took charge of one of the Great Dane mixes as they left. Fortunately, all three large dogs were well behaved even though they didn't seem thrilled to get their shots.

"Are you and Biscuit headed back to your shops now?" Reed asked when we were alone once more in the examination room.

"Yes." I half expected him to invite me to his place for dinner, and was considering inviting him to mine. But I had a stop planned on my way back to the shops, and I didn't want that to come up in any conversations, so the less I talked to Reed the rest of the day, the better.

But since Saturday is often considered date night, why didn't he ask me to dinner? Even though I was considering saying no.

My hurt feelings must have shown on my face. Either that, or Reed had already been planning on inviting me. "Care to join me at my place tonight?"

I considered saying no, but, heck, I really wanted to say yes. "Sure," I told him. "Should we aim for around seven o'clock?"

"Yep. That'll give me time to pick up our food, since we didn't end up doing that last night. I look forward to it."

"Me, too." I stepped forward and tilted my head upward, intending just a quick kiss. But it went on long enough that I wondered whether a vet tech or someone else would pull open the door to prepare the room for the next patient.

Fortunately, that didn't happen, and I soon changed into street clothes once more and went to get Biscuit. She was happy to see me, and the report I got on her from Faye was all good—good games with the other dogs, good behavior, and a good nap.

I got her leash from where I'd stuck it on one of the shelves behind the counter and we went on our way.

Would I end up telling Reed about the detour I had planned for Biscuit and me? That depended on how it went.

My excuse was that I needed to pick up a small bag of healthy kibble for my dog. This explanation would have been more realistic if I'd driven, since now I'd have to carry the bag, but I hardly ever drove to the vet clinic and hadn't wanted anyone to ask me questions today.

Our stop, which was just a bit out of the way on our walk back to the shops, was the Knob Hill Pet Emporium.

I hoped Harris would be there. Like me, he had a staff of employees who helped customers, but he hung around the place a lot, also like me—at least as far as I knew.

If he wasn't there, I could still pick up some food and, hopefully, ask some discreet questions.

As earlier in the day, the fall air was crisp and dry. Instead of walking along Pacific Street at the eastern edge of the town square, we stayed on the other side of the road and turned left on Peak Road. Harris Ethman's store wasn't far from there.

I'd adopted Biscuit after she was abandoned at the vet clinic, soon after I'd moved to Knobcone Heights and started working there. At first, I'd considered the Emporium too expensive and hadn't shopped there, but then I learned it was not only the most convenient but often the best place to buy food and supplies for my dog. Of course, when I opened my shops and Myra Ethman railed against me for it, viewing the Barkery as competition, I stopped going to the Emporium and drove far out of town to pick up healthy food for Biscuit. After Myra died—and I'd become a suspect—I remained far away from the Emporium whenever possible, since even after the killer was caught, I hadn't felt welcome. But I was pleased that over time—somewhat thanks to Jack, who'd convinced Harris to sell VimPets products—Harris and I had first become cordial, and by now somewhat friendly.

And I'd begun shopping there again.

I decided to rely on that friendliness for the upcoming conversation I planned—although I had no real sense of how to start it, or how to direct it. I'd have to improvise.

But Harris had mentioned, at the resort, that he'd met Wanda before, and that she'd visited his store. Les had expressed concern that the police could view Harris as a murder suspect, and I'd gotten this sense of concern from Harris's mother, too, when they'd summoned me to Elise's office.

Finally, there we were, right in front of the Emporium. Since it was still daytime, the neon sign with its elegant scripted font wasn't turned on. I looked in the window of the shop, where some of its most high-end goods were displayed: things like dog bowls that appeared plated in gold; diamond-studded, or more likely rhinestone studded, collars and leashes; and even stylish dog clothing. I saw people inside. One of them was Harris.

I had a feeling my visit was going to be quite interesting.

Or not. As Biscuit and I entered the upscale and attractive shop, I noticed Harris glance in our direction, then turn back to the customers he'd been talking to, in the area filled with dog toys. I could understand that. He was busy.

But I certainly hadn't gotten the impression that he was glad to see me. Not that it mattered. I'd still wrest a few minutes of conversation from him as soon as I could.

For now, I led Biscuit past groups of customers and employees toward the rear of the store, where the gleaming wooden shelves of food were. One area was filled with VimPets products—canned food and kibble in different flavors—for dogs of different sizes, ages, and dietary needs. Things had definitely changed from the time when Harris had refused to carry VimPets products.

There were several different size bags of each kind of kibble, and I picked out a five-pound sack, easy enough to carry, of the dry food Biscuit now enjoyed along with her canned food—all high-protein and organic.

When I turned back toward the front of the store, one of the employees, an attractive and thin young lady, approached me. "Can I help you with that?" She looked down at the bag I was carrying.

"Oh, no thanks, I'm fine," I said, and Biscuit and I kept walking.

But when I reached the place where I'd seen Harris before, he wasn't there. Nor did I see him anywhere else. Where had he gone?

Was he avoiding me, or was I just being paranoid?

Or was it a touch of both?

No matter.

I then did something that generally displeases owners or managers of retail stores: after glancing around to make sure the employee who'd offered to help me had her attention on another customer, I put the bag of food I was carrying on the nearest shelf—one not for food, but for dog collars. I'd return and get it soon; carrying Biscuit and five pounds of food, not to mention the purse over my shoulder, could get unwieldy. I stooped down and picked my dog up, holding her close as I began wandering again, this time toward the cash register counter.

As I recalled, there was a door behind that counter, and since it was the only closed door I saw other than the entrance onto the street and the exit to the rear parking lot, I assumed this one led to the Emporium's office.

Though Harris and I had become more cordial and even visited each other's shops now and then, we hadn't become friendly enough to be invited into each other's offices. As a result, all I could do was guess as to its location.

Was Harris there? I'd need to check.

I had to wait a couple of minutes, though, while the employee standing at the electronic register in front of the office door finished with a customer and bagged a huge order of food and toys and treats.

Treats? Bagged and pre-packaged ones. That customer needed to go to my Barkery… but I wasn't about to suggest that now.

Instead, I waited until the employee finally moved away from the cash register—fortunately, he wasn't simply working as a cashier. I then edged in that direction, only to see Harris exit through the door I'd been aiming for.

I'd presumably been right about the office, but at the moment it didn't matter. What did matter was that Harris was now visible. I continued edging toward him.

He noticed me, which wasn't surprising. I saw him freeze for a moment, then aim a very quick look behind him, as if he contemplated fleeing back into his office.

I'd seen him looking gaunt and frail after losing Myra, and somewhat healthier recently. Right now, he appeared pale and edgy, or maybe he was simply not thrilled to see me here. Why? I was a customer, after all.

I half expected him to stride off to find some customers to wait on. Instead, he actually approached Biscuit and me. As usual, he wore what I'd come to understand was the tradition in this shop: a black knit shirt with a golden Emporium crown logo sparkling on the pocket.

"Hi, Carrie," he said. "What brings you here?"

"I need some food for Biscuit," I replied. "And—well, I thought, with your background, that you'd be the right person to talk to about a concern I have." I watched his face as I spoke. He seemed to wince slightly but didn't tell me to get lost. "Could we go to your office or someplace quiet to talk?" I added.

"Yeah. Sure. This way." He turned his back on me and headed for the door he had just exited.

For a moment, I hesitated about following him. Heck, I'd been noticed at least somewhat by this crowd. And I didn't really think Harris was the killer—did I? Plus, even if he wanted to get rid of me somehow, he surely wouldn't harm me right here, where it would be obvious.

I realized I was overreacting as I reached the office door. But looking into a murder tended to stretch my emotions thin.

I'd learned this before—including when I'd investigated the murder of this man's wife.

He opened the door and waved me in. Still holding Biscuit, I walked inside.

The place looked every bit as posh as Elise's office at the Knobcone Heights Resort, which wasn't any big surprise since it had always been occupied by an Ethman, either by blood or by marriage. That had been Myra's view before she was killed, and she'd been the one to start the Emporium for her husband, to give him something worthwhile to do even as an Ethman.

The furniture looked more refined than standard retail office stuff. The desk and chairs were either actual mahogany antiques or excellent replicas. Artwork on the walls depicted cats and dogs, and although I couldn't name the artists, these modern renditions of animals, mostly in multiple colors with big eyes and sweet expressions, drew me to them. I wondered if the paintings were on sale, like the merchandise in the store—but decided I wouldn't ask. I doubted I could afford even the cheapest of them.

"Have a seat, Carrie." Harris sat down in the chair behind his desk. After kneeling to place Biscuit on the area rug that appeared Asian and, yes, expensive, I followed his instruction and planted myself in one of the two chairs that matched the desk. "So what's up?" he finally asked.

I'd been pondering how to start this conversation and hadn't come up with a good way. I just decided to jump in. "Well, the last time we spoke, the rest of your family was there—and the topic was what had happened to Wanda Addler. It's been on my mind a lot this week, as it probably is with everyone around here who met her."

“So you’re sticking your nose into that situation, like you did before.” His frown seemed to squeeze his entire face into a caricature that wasn’t nearly as attractive as the pet paintings around him.

“It sounded, when we got together, like you and your family anticipated that, and you wanted to make sure to look at Jack Loroco as a possibility.”

“That’s right. So have you found the evidence that’ll convict him?”

“Still working on it, but maybe you can help.” *Or, at least, help me learn more about your involvement.* “I gather you met Wanda, from what you said. I also gather that she wasn’t the nicest person, especially not when someone like Jack stood in the way of her getting what she wanted.” I paused, fascinated by how Harris’s face had reddened, as if he was holding inside his head something that threatened to make it explode. But I wasn’t sure how to continue. I finally came up with, “What did she tell you about Jack?”

Harris stood abruptly and turned his back on me. What was he thinking? I was dying to know…

No, poor choice of words. But what had really happened between him and Wanda?

I remained quiet, hoping that whatever was going on in Harris’s head would come pouring out.

And I wasn’t disappointed.

At least not completely.

He finally turned back to face me, but he didn’t sit down. “If anyone deserved to be murdered, it was that woman,” he said.

SEVENTEEN

I WAITED FOR HARRIS to explain his outburst, but he just stood there, no longer looking at me but somewhere over my shoulder.

Once again, I wished I could read what he was thinking.

Finally, I had to interrupt the silence—with more than the muffled hum of conversations out in the store. "What did she do that was so disturbing?" I asked softly.

He took a deep breath, then looked down at me. He smiled then, but it appeared more furious than happy. "She tried to get me involved in her war against Jack, and the weapon she used against me was my own store and its success."

He moved slightly, then crumpled back down into his chair. The movement apparently startled Biscuit, who'd been lying beside me. She was on her feet all of a sudden, appearing to guard me.

I bent over and patted her head, hoping she would remain quiet. I didn't want anything, even a beloved dog's bark, to interrupt this moment.

"How, Harris?" I finally prompted.

For the few next minutes, I forced my eyes to remain compassionate and not widen with surprise. At first I thought he might actually wind up confessing to killing her.

Not exactly.

His story came flooding out, as if it had been on the tip of his tongue for a long time but had been swallowed, maybe thanks to orders from members of his family.

The beginning was nothing new—how his wonderful Myra had wanted him to do something he loved, even if it wasn't a standard Ethman activity. She'd bought this shop for him, made it first rate and excellent and started ramping up its reputation.

"Even though I thought she worried too much when you opened your Barkery," he said, "I can't tell you how much I appreciated her drive to help me be successful. And I was, thanks to her. And then… And then…"

He paused without finishing that thought, but I knew what it was. "I'm so sorry, Harris," I said, half driven to walk over and give him a hug. But that wouldn't really be appropriate, and it might make him stop talking.

He resettled himself in his chair, straightening his back as if gathering his courage to go on. Finally, he did. "The Emporium was successful before I lost her, and we got even more customers for a while after she was gone. Maybe some were curious… I don't know. But then things started quieting down a bit, and Jack happened to come by again on a day I was particularly worried about my store's future. That's why I started carrying VimPets products, even though Myra had been against it before. But Jack promised that VimPets would promote the Emporium and they did, and business actually started picking up again."

Still not wanting to interrupt, but hoping to encourage Harris to continue, I made a small, happy noise at the back of my throat. It was enough to stimulate Biscuit to stand up on her hind legs and put her front paws on my thigh. I petted her but kept looking at Harris.

He smiled slightly toward my dog and then, fortunately, began speaking again. "I don't want to get into a lot of detail now, but I hated what happened. Things were going okay, and then Wanda arrived a week or so ago. She came to see me, congratulated me on my success—and told me she needed my help, which kind of puzzled me at first, until I realized the help she wanted was to ruin Jack."

I nodded, again saying nothing.

Harris ran one hand through his hair as if in utter exasperation. "She threatened me. Threatened my shop. She said she would go public with a lie—that I was taking the high quality dry pet foods we sell here and adulterating them with fillers, like the cheap, crappy food from some really inferior mass marketers, and then resealing each of the bags. Plus, she threatened to say that I took empty bags of the good stuff and poured equal amounts of good and bad food into them, and sealed them as well. But she'd never make any of these claims if I went along with her to hurt Jack."

I felt my eyes widen in sympathy. "What—"

But he was on a sad, angry roll and didn't stop this time. "She said that the more I protested that she was wrong about me adulterating the food, the more publicity the whole scandal would get. And if I wanted to keep it all from happening, I had to lie the way she told me. She wanted me to tell the VimPets people that Jack had proposed tainting some of *their* food that way. He supposedly told me that I could then sell their products for the same amount of money and make a higher profit, and he'd want a percentage of the increase."

"What did you do?" I exclaimed. Surely this was a no-win situation.

Or had it become a motive for murder … ?

"I told her no. I let a few of my family members know what she'd threatened—well, maybe I ranted about it to them while I tried to figure out what to do—and they agreed I'd better not do what she said. I tried to warn Jack, tell him what she was up to since she might have been doing it with other retailers who sold VimPets products, but Jack started off on his own rant about Wanda, so I just shut up. I was about to call the VimPets execs—but that was when Wanda died."

So he'd really had a motive—and that was why Les, and the other Ethmans, had wanted me to look elsewhere if I decided to try to solve Wanda's murder. They were worried about Harris, because of his anger against the woman who had died, but they believed in him, knew he wouldn't do it—maybe. Yet they, too, or at least Les, were willing to commit bribery or extortion to get me to zero in on someone else as the killer. Someone like Jack.

"That's all horrible," I commiserated with Harris.

His return smile this time was heartrending. "I knew you'd probably be looking into what happened to her, especially since you did such a good job before. And I know my family's concerned about me. I told myself to keep quiet, not let you in on any of this, since the only two people who knew all the details were Wanda and me. But I'd talked to my family, hinted about it to Jack—and, anyway, I knew you'd decide somehow that I was a suspect. Better to let you know the truth. And now, here's the last thing I want to say about it."

He paused, obviously wanting me to ask.

"What's that?"

"I hated that woman, mistrusted her, had a motive, and all that. But Carrie, you can be certain of one thing."

I knew what was coming but had to repeat, "And what's that?"

"I did not kill Wanda Addler."

So did I believe him?

My mind churned round and round about the discussion with Harris as Biscuit and I walked slowly back to the shops. At least I walked slowly. Biscuit did her usual thing of sniffing a lot, especially along the grassy edge of the town square, but she still seemed in more of a hurry than I did. The air was a touch chilly now, but I nevertheless felt too warm.

I wanted to get my mind around all Harris had said.

I found myself smiling distractedly at people walking by, especially those holding dog leashes with canines of all sizes attached. Some locals I knew even said hi, and I greeted them, too, but without stopping to talk.

Had Harris and I actually had a discussion? No. Harris had ejected some pretty emotional thoughts from his mind, and all I'd done was encourage him to continue.

But had it all been the truth? Particularly the last thing he'd said? Was he innocent of Wanda's murder despite his admission of a darned good reason to get rid of her—like potential ruination of his own reputation and his store?

He certainly remained among the people I would consider suspects. What should I do now?

I'd already talked with Billi enough to figure that the likelihood of her having killed Wanda was slim. But I hadn't yet spent much time quizzing—or listening to—Jack.

Dinah had, of course, but I doubted her conversation with him had convinced her one way or the other about his innocence—although I would ask her about it further.

I really needed to talk to Jack myself. Soon. Maybe even get his ideas, now that a few days had passed, about other possible suspects in his coworker's murder. He surely wouldn't admit to doing it, and I hoped he wouldn't try to pin it all on Billi, whom he'd been dating.

Anyone else—besides Harris? Not that I was eliminating him. But I really hoped there were other possibilities, assuming I wasn't totally wrong, and that I should zero in on someone in my core group of suspects.

Maybe I could even get Jack's thoughts on it tonight, before Reed and I had dinner.

Biscuit and I had reached the sidewalk in front of my shops. I peeked in the windows and was glad to see that both were filled with customers, and my assistants appeared to have everything under control.

That gave me the leeway to duck to the side of the first of the stores we'd come to, the Barkery. I stopped near the wall, even as Biscuit again started pulling on her leash. This was a sort of emergency, so I dug into my purse and pulled out two tiny treats. "Sit, Biscuit," I told her, and she obeyed immediately, which she undoubtedly would have even without the bribe. "Stay," I added, then gave her the treats.

Even though she gobbled them fast, the distraction had slowed her down and she started to sniff the dirty pavement beneath us.

The next thing I pulled from my purse was my phone.

How should I handle this? I didn't want to call Reed and tell him I might be late to dinner, or a no-show, if I happened to reach Jack and he agreed to meet with me.

I turned to face the street and watched the traffic roll by as I considered what to do. Who to call. What to say to whom.

Although … Well, Reed and I had reached an understanding of sorts. And the likelihood of reaching him was slight anyway, since he was still on duty at the clinic.

Even after all my pondering, I called Reed first—and was relieved when I was right and he didn't immediately answer. So I left a message. "I learned some interesting things today," I said, "and yes, I was careful." I wasn't going to tell him I'd planned the stop at the Emporium before leaving my shift, since I hadn't mentioned it at the time, although I'd admit to it later if he asked. "I might need to do something before we get together for dinner tonight," I went on. "I'll let you know." And then I hung up.

Next, I called Jack, whose number was also programmed into my phone. He answered right away.

Now, what would work best for chatting with him?

A drink was always a good idea.

"Hi, Jack," I said. "I've been thinking about you."

"I figured. Your buddies the detectives have been thinking about me, too. Hounding me—and as an animal lover and employee of a pet food company, I use that word in both its contexts."

I laughed, then said, "I've been wanting to talk to you. And, yes, some of it's about the murder. I'm being a bad girl and looking into it despite the controversy about that."

"Oh, it's fine with me, as long as you don't get hurt," he said, somewhat latching on to the position Reed had convinced himself to take.

"Then you're willing to talk to me about it? Be my sounding board?"

"Sure. What do you have in mind?"

For Reed not to explode about the idea—and, actually, for my own peace of mind and potential safety—I knew what the best idea was: to meet in public, and probably not alone with Jack despite my need to talk with him. The best place would be the one that was becoming my daily habit recently: the resort where my brother worked.

But it was also where the Ethmans, or at least some of them, hung out.

Well, at least Les and I were still speaking to one another, and I could tell him my side of it later—or at least what I wanted him and the rest of his family to know about my skepticism.

"Let's grab a drink this evening at the Knobcone Heights Resort bar," I said. "About six thirty, after I've closed my shops?" The bar was usually busy enough then that, though we'd find a table, the undercurrent of conversation would keep what we said to one another fairly private.

"Sounds good. See you then."

I confined Biscuit in the Barkery as usual when I entered, and she seemed happy since several customers had their friendly pups along to trade nose sniffs with her. I waved hi to Janelle, who was waiting on some customers, and scooted through the door into the kitchen, heading for my office.

After leaving my purse in a drawer, I'd barely put my phone in my pocket when it vibrated. I didn't really need to look to see who it was—although I looked anyway.

“Hi, Reed.” I kept my tone light despite feeling my shoulders cringe as I awaited a scolding.

“You’re at it again. Still.” But he didn’t sound angry or unhappy, just maybe a bit resigned, which was a good thing.

“That’s right. And—well, I need to grab a drink with Jack before I head to your place tonight. We’re meeting at the resort. Care to join us?” Again, I cringed as I waited for his reply.

“Of course,” he said, as if I needn’t have asked. I gave him the particulars, checked the time on my phone—which indicated the meeting was only a couple hours away—and we worked out the details of getting together there.

I realized that shouldn’t be the end of who I notified, either—but I didn’t call Neal. Instead, after washing my hands, I returned to the Barkery and watched Janelle end a transaction by handing a full bag of treats, plus change, to her customer and cordially inviting the twenty-something mom of both a human child and a pug to come back soon.

Then, before Janelle headed for one of the other two customers currently examining the contents of our display case, I motioned for her to join me near where Biscuit was waiting.

“Are you getting together with Neal tonight?” I asked.

“Don’t know yet.” Her brow lowered in a frown, as if she expected me to tell her to back off, and I laughed.

“I don’t want to bother him at the reception desk right now, but if you talk to him, let him know that Jack and Reed are meeting me for drinks in the bar around six thirty tonight.” Did I want more company?

The whole thing might appear more innocent that way.

“You two are welcome to join us,” I added, “assuming Neal’s off duty. And even if he’s not, you can come.”

"Sounds good." But Janelle's forehead puckered once more as her big blue eyes studied my face. "This isn't just a meeting among friends for a drink, is it? I mean, I gather that the resort has turned into the place to nose around and talk to people about murder, right? It seemed that way before, and it does again now."

I lifted my brows and shoulders in an attempt to appear the picture of complete innocence. "What do you mean? Of course this is just a fun get-together among friends—and family, too, if Neal joins us. And if we happen to talk a bit about things going on around town, like a murder investigation … Well, let's just see if we hear anything interesting, shall we?"

Janelle laughed. "Yes," she responded, "we shall."

EIGHTEEN

THERE WAS STILL MORE than an hour left before I was to close the shops, and a while beyond that before I went to the resort.

Heading into Icing, I considered throwing my latest bits of information—or at least claims of info—to Dinah, for the story she was writing.

Which I did in generalities, between customers. I wanted to see her reaction, just in case she gave something away—like hints that I should keep her among my most-likely suspects.

Not that I wanted to. And all she did when we spoke was to act excited about this other possible angle to insert into her plot.

"This might be the most exciting of all the murders that happened around here," she said happily as we later stood behind the refrigerated counter pulling out the few human baked goods that were getting too old to maintain overnight.

I looked into her bright blue eyes, which were glowing now with excitement. "You mean you'll use the real low-down, rather than make more stuff up for your fiction?"

"Reality is always more fun to use in a story," she said. "Or at least pretend reality."

I just laughed at that. And hoped that her attitude was a good reason not to consider her a viable murder suspect.

Once we'd completed our assessment and I'd placed the gently aging treats into a box, to be refrigerated and saved till someone from one of the charities down the mountain came to pick them up, I thanked Dinah for her excellent help. Since she had the next two days off from work, I wouldn't be able to easily quiz her as a potential murder suspect, or find out what she'd learned from Jack as a potential suspect, for a while. But nothing urgent came to me.

I'd just have to see how I felt after talking with Jack that evening. Hopefully, any questions that formed for Dinah could wait till I saw her again on Tuesday.

I said goodbye to Dinah, then went into the Barkery to say bye to Janelle, until later. Both Frida and Vicky were scheduled to come in the next day, which was Sunday. I was too, of course.

"Did you talk with Neal?" I asked Janelle as we began clearing out some of the older dog treats from the refrigerated display case.

"I did. He's off at around—" She used a paper towel to pull her phone from her pocket to check the time. "Right now, I think." As far as I knew, it was approximately ten after six. "He said he'd hang around and grab a drink with us."

"Great." But I did wonder how things would go with a big crowd having drinks while I tried nonchalantly—this time—to quiz Jack on what he knew and who he still suspected.

As we closed the display case, I looked over to where Biscuit and Go still hung out—and then to the chairs on the blue tile floor with the beige representation of a bone in the center. This area had proven perfect for the adoption event we'd recently held in conjunction with Mountaintop Rescue.

The kind of event I'd been really looking forward to hosting again. Soon.

But I hadn't figured on this latest murder. Even if I had, Billi Matlock was one of the last people in the world I'd have thought might become a murder suspect.

I absolutely had to figure Wanda's murder out fast, if for no other reason than to permit us to hold that wonderful adoption event here soon.

And it couldn't happen until Billi was cleared.

Maybe the detectives would figure it all out even faster than me. I certainly hoped so. But they had protocol and rules to follow.

I didn't—except for having promised so many people, so often, to be careful, which I intended to do anyway.

Would this evening's discussion help me solve this murder, and fast?

Or would it just be an enjoyable—I hoped—meeting among friends?

I would do all I could to ensure it accomplished both.

Reed picked Biscuit and me up a short while later. He'd called back to suggest it to save a little parking money—and to have some good company coming and going. That was fine with me.

"I hope we're not planning to spend a lot of time there tonight," he said once I was ensconced in his passenger seat and Biscuit was in the back. "I promised Hugo a nice dinner, too, but he's at home."

I grinned at Reed as he looked out the windshield. "I wouldn't want to disappoint Hugo. Right, Biscuit?" I looked at the rear seat, and she cocked her head as she looked at me. "She says 'right.'"

"Are you going to tell me why this drink with Jack became so urgent tonight?"

"Sure." I gave him an abbreviated version of my discussion with Harris.

"And that's supposed to make you feel that Harris Ethman is innocent." Reed's words were far from a question, yet I knew what he was asking.

"It makes me feel like I need even more information," I said. I was glad that Reed pulled into the parking lot right then.

As I'd recognized before, I was spending a lot of time these days at the resort. Was the Knobcone Heights Resort somehow a magnet for people who got involved in murders, or in solving them, or…

Well, no matter. Here I was, and I would soon see Neal—and, hopefully, have an opportunity to casually ask Jack some more questions relating to Wanda's murder.

Despite the large number of cars in the lot, Reed found a great spot not far from the resort's door, and I exited the car before he could do his gentlemanly thing and come around for me. I opened the rear door and scooped my little Biscuit into my arms. Reed closed that door for us and, taking my arm, led us to the front of the large, sprawling white building.

The lobby was busy, but when wasn't it? The large televisions hung from the ceiling had a couple of different football games on. I suspected they were recordings of earlier games, since it was past seven thirty in California, but I wasn't interested enough in them to try to find out.

Neal's workday had already ended, so I didn't try to walk by the registration desk as I usually did. Instead, I accompanied Reed into the traditionally dark and noisy bar.

Sure enough, in an area against the far wall, some tables had been pushed together and Neal sat there with Janelle, apparently waiting for the gang. But the gang wasn't all I'd hoped for at this moment, since Jack wasn't there yet.

What would I do if he didn't show?

Well, I'd enjoy a drink or two at least. And storm—internally only—about not being able to accomplish what I'd hoped to do that night.

Reed and I joined the others, and although I considered ordering a stronger-than-usual drink, I instead just stuck with wine, a rosé this time.

Then, so I could get my head together and decide how I'd handle things next if Jack didn't appear, I handed Neal his Bug and headed to the restroom.

On the way there, I wasn't surprised to see Elise Ethman Hainner, chin up, strutting in the same direction. This resort was her realm, after all.

She surely wasn't aware that I'd been talking with her brother—was she?

Judging by the determined expression on her face as she got closer, I wouldn't have been surprised if she did. But if so, why would Harris have said anything to her?

"Carrie, I'm glad I caught you," she said as we both reached the restroom door at the same time. Her outfit today appeared designer chic, as I had come to expect. Her gray suit jacket, its sleeves three-quarter-length, was trimmed in black, matching her mid-thigh skirt. She had a colorful, leaf-like necklace over her white shirt, and her black shoes had high heels that were far shorter than stilettos but still looked uncomfortable.

And here I was, still in my knit shirt with a store logo on the pocket and dark slacks. But our careers were quite different, and I refused to feel out-fashioned.

Elise's face was attractive, her makeup impeccable, and I wondered why she had wanted to catch me. I really didn't want to talk to her about Harris or Wanda—unless she was about to confess to the murder to save her brother from suspicion.

Fat chance. Although if Harris had told her what Wanda was up to, maybe she would have felt compelled, on behalf of her family's reputation, to do something to prevent her brother's downfall.

"How are you, Elise?" I asked politely, turning to open the restroom door. I would at least pretend to assume that she simply had the standard reason to go inside, as I did.

"I'm fine," she said, then barely paused before she continued. "We need to talk. Come to my office when you're through in here."

No invitation, just a command. I wanted to tell her no, but what if she told me something useful—about Harris or otherwise?

Before I answered, though, I noticed that the door was already open, and Gwen had exited, but we blocked her ability to get back to the restaurant. The expression the server leveled on me appeared quizzical, as if she could see how conflicted I was feeling. I just rolled my eyes.

"Hi, Gwen," I said, moving out of her way. "And okay, Elise. I'll see you in your office in a few minutes. I'll have to tell the people I'm having drinks with where I'm going, though."

"Fine."

She pushed past me into the restroom, and Gwen was already on her way toward the restaurant. I had a slight respite from talking to anyone, thank heavens, as I strode inside and found an empty stall. I felt pleased to lock it, as if I was locking everything else in the world out, but that lasted only for a minute. I fortunately didn't see Elise as I exited after washing my hands, but I'd already decided to conform to her edict.

I headed into the bar, where I told everyone, my eyes on Neal, that Elise and I were getting together briefly. My brother's expression went grim. "Just be careful with her, Carrie."

"I won't say anything to jeopardize your job," I assured him, although I knew that wasn't what he'd meant.

"And don't say anything to jeopardize *you*," Reed added. He was the only one with whom I'd shared any details of my conversation with Harris. Plus, he was the most inclined to try to warn me away from nosing around about the murder.

I just said, "There are a lot of people around here, so I should be safe. I don't know what she wants to talk about, but my preference will be just to listen. I'll be back soon, I promise."

I looked at Janelle, who appeared skeptical, then bent to pat Biscuit. "You stay here," I told my dog. "Take care of these people. They need it as much as I do."

I slipped out of the bar and into the lobby crowd. As I headed to the far side I saw Gwen coming toward me, a tray in her hands. We met up right outside the office door, which surprised me. Her skirt today was beige, her blouse white, and she wore a traditional coppery pinecone necklace to call to mind Knobcone Heights, which was named after knobcone pine trees.

The tray she held was moderate-sized, metallic, and round. "I hope you don't mind," she said, "but I eavesdropped a little and I know Elise wants to talk to you. I just figured I'd bring some refreshments—not as good as what you'll get in the bar, but maybe it'll make this meeting more fun. I saw your face—"

"And I know I didn't look thrilled. Thanks," I told her.

I looked at the tray and saw two large orange mugs of coffee, some taco chips, and salsa.

"No problem. But—" She hesitated.

"But what?"

"I gather you're looking into that latest murder, right? I overheard your friends and family telling you not to the other day. Does your meeting with Elise have anything to do with that?"

"I don't know," I lied. "I'm not sure what she wants to talk about. Maybe she wants to have some of my dog treats available for guests, for all I know."

Gwen appeared relieved. "Oh, that would be a good thing, wouldn't it? It's none of my business but I could see how much everyone was concerned about you the other day, worried that you could get hurt—Neal included. We're still friends, even though we're not dating now, you know."

"That's great. Anyway … " I turned, knocked on Elise's door, and then pushed it open. "You go ahead in and put all that down. It looks heavy. And thanks again."

I heard a voice say, "Come in," which was a good thing since we were already inside.

Elise's office looked just as it had the other day, when I'd been granted a reception with the queen of the Knobcone Heights Resort and her royal family, only today it was empty of everyone but her—and now Gwen and me. It was small but nicely furnished, and Elise stood behind her desk frowning at Gwen.

"What's this about?" she asked the server.

“I thought you might want refreshments.” Gwen bent her head and smiled a little as if hoping for forgiveness—or maybe recognition that she was one really good server.

“Good idea. Thanks.” Thus, Gwen was dismissed and all but backed out of the room. Then it was my turn. “Have a seat, Carrie,” Elise commanded.

So who was I but another subject of this queen—not. Nevertheless, I wanted to get as much out of this meeting as I could, so I obeyed.

I immediately bent forward, though, and took a coffee mug off the tray, as well as a couple of chips, which I dipped into the salsa.

Then I looked up at Elise, raised my eyebrows, and smiled a bit grimly, inviting her silently to explain why she wanted to talk to me.

She immediately complied. “Why did you do it, Carrie? Are you protecting the people you’re friendliest with now that you think you’re some kind of detective?”

I assumed my confusion showed on my face. “What do you think I did, Elise?”

“You were at the Emporium, weren’t you?”

“Yes.” I had already figured that this meeting had something to do with my speaking with Harris, but what was she driving at?

Elise rose, all but hovering over me despite remaining across the desk. “Harris called and told me what you did. You went to his store and confronted him and called him a murderer. You can’t do things like that in Knobcone Heights. Not if you want to stay here and have your brother work at this resort and make sure your own businesses are successful. Got it? You can never, ever attack an Ethman that way.”

NINETEEN

My mind swirled. How *could* I attack an Ethman—like this one, who was all but attacking me?

More importantly, how could I get her to stand down and tell me what, if anything, she knew about the situation, such as whether she or her brother actually was the murderer?

I attempted to sound calm. "You got part of that right. I did visit the Emporium. I also had a conversation with Harris. But—"

"He says you barged into his office and began accusing him. You claimed he argued with that Wanda woman, then killed her."

"It wasn't like that." I finally rose to my feet, crossed my arms, and grew confrontational, too. "Now, if you want to discuss what really happened, sit down and let's talk."

To my surprise, she listened to me even though she didn't appear at all happy about it. "Okay," she grumbled. "Tell me your version."

I started doing so slowly, from the time I entered the Emporium till I suggested I wanted to talk to Harris and he invited me into his office. How he'd told me that, if anyone deserved to be murdered, it had been Wanda. But I didn't want to feed Elise any information that might be important, so instead of continuing, such as disclosing his possible motive, I asked, "Do you know why he thought that? Why he might have argued with Wanda in the first place? I didn't accuse him of anything." Not directly, at least. "But did he tell you anything about knowing Wanda, or what she might have said to him?"

Elise seemed to calm, if only a little. Her expression, from enraged, turned sad. "Yes, my brother talks with me a lot, especially now that he's lost his poor wife."

It didn't matter that I hadn't been especially fond of Myra. Elise was right. Harris deserved to be treated sympathetically because of his loss.

Even so—"I'm sure your closeness means a lot to him. But I'd still like to know what he told you about Wanda, and why he'd been upset about her." And why one of them had made up this story about me supposedly accusing Harris directly of the murder.

"I don't know who Wanda thought she was. Harris told me she was trying to coerce him—an Ethman—into carrying out something he definitely had no intention of doing. Something illegal, something that could not only ruin his reputation but destroy his whole wonderful store if he ever got caught." She glared at me. "Did he tell you the details?"

"I'm not sure I got it all," I told her, settling back onto the chair. "Something about changing the quality of some products?" I purposely kept it vague, hoping she would reveal what she actually knew.

"Exactly. She wanted him to taint some of the healthy products he sold, supposedly under Jack's orders. And if he didn't do it, she would tell the world he was doing it anyway, on his own. To make money at the pets' expense, and to harm her poor VimPets company's reputation.

It's no wonder he considered her scum. Maybe she even deserved to be killed."

So said another Ethman. Well, Wanda might have deserved some kind of comeuppance, though I didn't think getting killed was the right thing. But that was just me.

I wondered about Harris and Elise's latest conversation, and any others they had shared. When had Harris told her about Wanda's threats? After he'd killed Wanda? Or at a time that allowed Elise to get so furious that she killed the woman?

Or did they simply both have motives for murder yet remain innocent?

And want to dump some level of guilt on me, at least for making possibly false accusations.

Elise knew what I was thinking, of course. "Don't even bother asking. Yes, she deserved it. And no, neither my brother nor I is mourning that bitch's death. But did either of us kill her? Nope. No way. N-O. You got that, Ms. snoopy, inexpert, incompetent, unprofessional amateur detective?"

"Yes," I said. "I've got that." I didn't bother correcting her largely inappropriate adjectives about me. Nor did I remind her she'd claimed just a minute ago that I had been brazen enough to falsely accuse Harris.

Even more important, I didn't necessarily believe the rest of what she'd said either.

But at least she'd said it. That gave me more to mull over about Harris's involvement—and Elise's.

I took a sip of coffee from the mug that I now held on my lap. It was time to go. I doubted I'd get anything else out of Elise, particularly anything useful.

And I'd achieved, more or less, what I'd hoped to—learning from Elise what she apparently knew, which did provide a possible motive for her, as well as her brother, to have murdered Wanda.

I wasn't certain how I'd ensure that my detective friends learned about this, if they didn't already know, but I'd do something. The knowledge should hopefully remove at least some of their attention from Billi, and even Jack, as the top suspects.

"I'm glad we had this conversation," I told Elise. "Of course I don't condone murder, but no matter who got to Wanda, I'm glad she didn't have the opportunity to harm any animals with poor quality foods—or to blame an innocent person for it."

"Amen." Elise stood. I was obviously being dismissed, which was fine with me. She shook her head, slightly messing up her deep blonde hair. "I don't know how you can handle nosing into all these terrible situations, Carrie. Just be careful."

How many times had I heard that lately? I was close to most of the other people I'd heard it from and appreciated their concern, even if I didn't just back off and stick my head in a hole. But I didn't know the Ethmans very well, nor what they were capable of doing to protect themselves and each other.

Those words could definitely have been a warning, coming from Elise.

I was glad to rejoin Reed, Neal, and Janelle, particularly since they were still sitting in the bar. Biscuit, too.

But Jack apparently remained a no-show, darn him. He wasn't with them.

Without saying anything, I slid into my empty chair at the table. "I need a drink," I announced as they all looked toward me, Biscuit standing on her hind legs with her front paws on my thighs. I resisted getting on the floor with her, although a big doggy hug sounded good to me.

Maybe from one of the people, instead. Later. Any of them, but preferably Reed.

"The fee for your drink," Neal said from across the table, "will be your description of what that was all about." His voice was so soft in the noisy environment that I could hardly hear him, and he spoke only after looking around, presumably to make sure that neither his boss nor any member of her family were close by.

"Wine first," I insisted. "Whining later."

That brought a grin from Reed—a sexy one that appeared fond, and I found myself smiling back, kind of. Smiling took energy, and often was meant to express happiness. If anything, my grin was small and wry.

Neal gestured toward a nearby server, and despite what I'd said, I ordered a piña colada, a sweet drink, sure, but with rum—a harder alcohol than either wine or beer. I needed that.

"Are you okay, Carrie?" That was Janelle, and her expression was full of concern and compassion. "You look—well, exhausted."

"Arguing with an Ethman has always taken a lot out of me," I half joked, though it was definitely true the couple of times it had happened—with Myra, and now with Elise.

"What did you argue about?" Reed asked. He was sitting right beside me, and his gin and tonic looked great and I was suddenly very thirsty, maybe from drinking the coffee before. I reached for his glass and took a sip without responding. Just a sip. I wasn't driving for a while, and I needed some alcoholic sustenance—quickly.

"It wasn't exactly an argument," I began, returning his glass to where it had been. "We discussed—okay, all of you can guess the underlying topic, right?"

"Wanda," Janelle said, and at the same time both of the guys proclaimed, "Murder."

"You're all spot-on." I opened my mouth to start explaining the Harris-Wanda connection to Neal and Janelle, who hadn't heard it before, but before I spoke I was surprised to see Jack edge up through the crowd behind Janelle. "Oh, hi, Jack," I said. I didn't want to get into a discussion of any other potential suspects with him there—not yet, at least.

He held a half-empty beer glass, which he raised slightly as if to toast me. "Hi, Carrie. I'll go get another chair." He bent to put his glass on the table, then walked off again.

"Was he here before?" I asked the others. Maybe I'd stolen his chair, which was fine with me. I didn't mind a minute of respite before I got into whatever discussion we would have.

"Yes, but he excused himself a few minutes ago," Janelle said. "He said he had to go say hi to someone."

"Oh, really? Who?" I was curious who Jack would be talking to around here, but he'd come to the resort often enough before the current difficult situation to know quite a few people in town. Not that it really mattered, since I doubted he'd admitted—or denied—anything about the murder in conversations he held here. Even so, it wouldn't hurt for me to follow up with anyone he'd spoken with, just to learn what they'd talked about and if it had anything to do with Wanda, or VimPets, or anything else of interest.

Although if he'd popped in to say hi to Elise, I wouldn't follow up directly with her.

I didn't get a response to my question, so I assumed he hadn't mentioned anyone, and he returned just then with the extra chair.

"So how are you doing, Carrie?" Jack inquired before I could ask him the same thing. He looked a bit pale, and not just because he was wearing a beige long-sleeved T-shirt, which was a lot more casual than I was used to seeing on him. His straight nose, as always, was prominent over a wide mouth that was generally smiling, but not now. His light brown hair was cut even shorter than usual, adding to an impression I got that this good-looking guy was falling apart.

Because he was a killer, or only because some people thought he was?

"I'm okay," I replied to him. "I suspect you can't say the same."

"I could say it," he said, "but it wouldn't be entirely true." He took a swig of his beer, looked around at the others at our table as if to acknowledge their presence, and then centered his attention back on me. "How did you do it, Carrie?" he asked in a tired voice that he raised loudly enough to be heard over the crowd. "I mean, survived day to day with the fear you might be arrested for something you never did."

"You just do it," I said, then looked toward my other side. "Right, Janelle?"

"Hey." Jack looked from me to Janelle, then back again. "How about if we start some kind of support group. Call it something like Murder Suspects Not-So-Anonymous."

I smiled, and so did Janelle, though neither Reed nor Neal did.

"Well, at least the truth won out with Janelle and me," I said. "And neither of us was guilty. Can you honestly say the same?" I leaned toward him with my elbows on the table, batting my eyelashes as if eager for his answer.

"Honestly and truthfully and accurately and absolutely." The words came out in a rush. Then he lifted his beer glass, as if in a toast, and chugged the rest of his drink.

But as much as I wanted to believe it, that didn't convince me so absolutely that Jack was telling the truth.

My piña colada arrived, then, along with another beer for Jack. I knew that his apartment wasn't very close and I wondered if he was drinking too much.

I, on the other hand, didn't finish my drink, as much as I'd have liked to. As was often the case, Reed was going to drive Biscuit and me back to my stores to get my car. Then each of us would drive to his place, where he would feed Hugo and I'd make sure Biscuit wasn't starving, either. Reed was going to pick up a pizza dinner on the way home so that neither he nor I would go hungry as well.

After that, we might satisfy another kind of appetite, depending on our mood.

As a result of those plans, Reed and I didn't stay much longer. Neal and Janelle said they were leaving, too, and I wondered if they had a similar arrangement in mind.

That would leave poor Jack alone for the evening—maybe. I wasn't going to ask.

He might just stay at the resort and soothe himself with more to drink, or maybe he could join up with whomever he had spoken with before.

But as the rest of us stood, including Biscuit, so did Jack. Our tabs were paid, so we just headed into the lobby, which seemed a little less crowded than usual. This was somewhat surprising for a Saturday evening, but it was getting late.

As we walked through the lobby, Gwen caught up with us. Apparently her work for this day was done. She wore a denim jacket that hid what was underneath, which was probably her serving uniform.

"Did—was your meeting okay, Carrie?" she asked.

"Okay's a good word for it," I assured her. "And thanks again for the refreshments."

"Oh, you're very welcome. Besides, Mrs. Hainner paid for them."

"I thought she might have."

"Anyway, good night to all of you." Her gaze took in Reed first, then Janelle and Neal and Jack. She seemed to look hardest at Neal, and I wondered if there was any regret on her part that they really hadn't entered into a relationship.

"Good night to you, too, Gwen. I'm sure at least some of us will be back soon to see you at the restaurant."

"I hope so," she said. Then, waving, she hurried ahead of us to the door.

As we got into the parking lot, I didn't ask Neal when he was likely to get home that night, and he didn't ask me, either.

But each set of couples headed off to wherever our plans took us that evening.

I looked forward to it, despite anticipating I'd have to give Reed more information about what I'd learned, or hadn't, from Harris and Elise. We revised our earlier plan and decided to go to his house first, picking up a pizza on the way, and he'd take me to my car later.

And as expected, Reed was definitely interested and concerned about any information I had—although he promised he'd stop asking questions on the subject once we were at his house and finished walking the dogs.

I held him to that.

TWENTY

I WAS TIRED THE next morning, but in a good way. Biscuit and I had stayed longer at Reed and Hugo's than we should have, and even though this was a Sunday my hours didn't change.

That meant needing to hurry to my shops and start baking, when I felt like I could have remained in bed—alone, at my house—for a long time.

I started out by making some fresh scones and muffins and biscuits for Icing, since customers had proven they were more likely to want people treats for breakfast early than to get out of bed and dash here for good stuff for their dogs. Besides, I had some leftover dog treats from yesterday still in the refrigerated display case that were far from going stale.

Frida and Vicky were coming in to work that day, thanks to Vicky's highly competent scheduling, and she had even determined that she would arrive first. But since it was Sunday and I'd still open at seven, I'd told her she didn't need to arrive before eight.

That meant I had to start on dog treats as soon as I got the first trays of human goods into the oven. Biscuit remained quiet in the Barkery, so I figured at least one of us was enjoying catching up on her sleep.

To keep myself awake, I rehashed things in my mind from yesterday—primarily the good things, like being at the bar with friends, and afterward with Reed.

I inhaled deeply and often, appreciating, as always, the sweet, alluring aromas caused by my baking while I blended new doughs and formed them into dog biscuit shapes and round cookies.

And, yes, I couldn't help it. I soon started to rehash the things I knew about Wanda and her life and what could have led to her murder, as well as to think through who would have been the most upset about which of her actions and perhaps even angry enough to kill her.

That last thought still puzzled me. A lot. Yes, Wanda wasn't a nice person; in fact, from the little I knew about her, she'd spent her entire life trying to figure out how to put herself in the best of positions, all at the expense of other people. But still, someone must have been pretty angry.

One person I knew very little about was the VimPets executive she'd apparently been dating, the guy who'd been helping her rise through the corporate ranks no matter who got hurt—like Jack.

Did that executive have a motive to kill her? Maybe, since nearly everyone Wanda knew did.

But to murder her, wouldn't he have had to be in Knobcone Heights? And wouldn't Jack, at least, have recognized him?

That was something I should ask Jack. He'd probably thought of it himself, though.

If the executive had come to town with the idea of killing Wanda, he could have worn a disguise—although some kinds of big-wheel executives would have the funds to hire a hit man. Were the cops looking into that possibility, too?

And did Jack know of a reason why one of his bosses, even one with some kind of romantic interest in Wanda, would want to get rid of her? I'd seen a few statements to the media online, from executives at VimPets, expressing sorrow and sympathy about losing this excellent employee, but nothing had stood out as coming from someone who cared for Wanda as anything more than a peon.

A buzzer sounded in front of me, signaling that the people goods I'd been baking were ready to be removed from the oven. The timing worked well, since I was nearly ready to stick a couple of trays of dog treats in the other oven, behind me. I'd soon be prepared for customers to start coming in—a good thing, since it was approaching seven o'clock.

I left the trays of scones and more out to cool, put the dog treats into their oven, then went into my office to check on some scheduling and financial stuff. I didn't really have time, but, seated at my desk, I booted up my laptop and quickly googled "Wanda Addler" yet again, to learn what was being said about her murder. There were still a lot of articles about her death here in Knobcone Heights, and the fact she was from LA and worked for VimPets, but nothing I found was helpful other than that the authorities were following up on some leads.

But were there actual leads, or was that only to ward off the pushy media? I wasn't about to contact anyone who might know, or I might be the one who got pushed, and not by any reporters.

Sighing, I put my computer into sleep mode, half wishing I could do the same for myself. I'd check on Biscuit, give her a quick walk, then open the Barkery, followed by Icing.

Biscuit seemed to like my plan, especially when we went outside onto the sidewalk and I gave her a minute to sniff the ground and a couple of other dogs walking by. "Come on into the Barkery in about half an hour," I told the owners at the other ends of the leashes. "I'll give your baby a sample treat." *And hope you buy more of them*, I thought.

Biscuit was well-versed in this kind of short morning outing and seemed happy enough to come back inside. I kept the Barkery's outer door open and checked to make sure the bell was working so I'd hear when someone came in.

Next, I enclosed Biscuit in her confined area and went through the door from the Barkery into Icing, to open it for the day, too.

Only then did I hop back into the kitchen to remove the day's newly baked Barkery treats from the oven and let them start cooling. I took the Icing items that were already cool into the shop to place into the display case.

While I was doing that, the bell on the Barkery's door chimed. Customers! I glanced at the time on my phone, made sure the trays of product were secure on the counter behind the display case, and hurried back to the Barkery.

Only it wasn't customers who'd triggered the bell. Or maybe it was. But the person who stood there surveying the contents of the glass-fronted case was Detective Wayne Crunoll.

I'd already primed myself for some fun taking care of someone who wanted to buy dog treats. The detective had brought both of his wife's dachshund mixes that morning—Blade and Magnum.

Did he actually want to buy something, or had he brought the dogs along in a feeble attempt to try to fool me into talking with him?

He appeared to be casual, wearing a gray hoodie with the large letters *KHPD* on the back. When he turned to look at me, his dark brows were raised and he appeared all friendly.

I didn't trust that.

Meanwhile, his two dogs were pulling on their leashes to go see Biscuit, who stood on her hind legs in her enclosure as if she wanted to greet them, too.

"Hello, Detective." I attempted to sound pleased to see him. "And Blade and Magnum, too. I assume it's okay for me to give them a treat?"

"Absolutely."

I went behind the case and pulled out three pumpkin biscuits. I didn't want Biscuit to feel slighted. After passing them out, I turned back to the cop. "What treats would you like to take home with you today?"

I'd thought about asking what I could help him with, which was often what I asked customers, but that was too broad. I didn't want to help him with anything related to Wanda Addler's murder—even if I could. Which I really couldn't.

"Oh, the biggest treat of all would be for me to haul you into the station for assaulting Harris Ethman." His round face turned up into a grin that looked entirely evil to me.

"What! I didn't assault anyone."

"Well, you barged into his office and threatened him, I understand. Claimed he murdered Wanda Addler. Are you sticking your pretty little nose into this homicide, too, Carrie?"

My nose wasn't pretty and little. It was the longish Kennersly nose. And though I supposed I was snooping into that homicide, I wasn't about to admit it to this difficult detective.

"Who told you that?" I countered. "I have to assume it was either Harris or his sister, Elise, but I thought I convinced her of the truth of what happened. So what is Harris trying to prove?"

Wayne's grin melted into a frown. "When did you supposedly convince Elise of that?"

I was glad there weren't any real customers in the store from whom I'd have to hide this conversation. I motioned for Wayne to join me at one of the nearby tables, where I melted onto a chair. I felt as if I were the one being assaulted. But I had to turn this around somehow. If I acted cooperative with the detective, maybe I could learn something helpful.

"I did have a conversation with Harris at his store yesterday, Wayne," I said, attempting to sound rational and friendly. "He in fact told me some pretty good reasons he should be considered a murder suspect. Have you talked with him?"

That frown grew even deeper. "Yes, briefly on the phone, but I didn't hear anything like that from him."

"Really? Well, maybe there's a reason for that—like his guilt. Unlike with our City Councilwoman Billi Matlock, or Wanda's coworker Jack Loroco. I gather your department has been investigating them in particular."

"Who told you that?" Wayne demanded, one of his hands, the one not holding the dog leashes, fisting on the table between us.

"They both hinted at it, not that either wants to talk to me about what's going on. But they're both friends of mine, and I hate to see them go through the same kind of circus I had to put up with a few months ago."

"I can't talk about a pending investigation. I'm sure you learned that from your two prior interferences with official cases."

"You've already approached me about this one," I said, looking him straight in the eye. "It would be a lot easier for me not to pay any attention to this case if you could convince me that you're looking into other potential suspects, too. Is anyone else on the table?"

Wayne looked as if he wanted to get up and throttle me. His two dogs, sensing his distress, dashed over to us, and even Biscuit gave a couple of sharp woofs.

"What. Did. I. Just. Remind. You?"

"You don't have to tell me details," I said innocently. "Although you might like to know the details of why Harris Ethman and maybe Elise, too, should be on your suspect list, if they aren't already. I'd be glad to tell you more, if you'll tell me more so I don't need to worry so much." I'd wondered previously how I would let my detective non-friends know about my Ethman conversations, and surprisingly I now had the opportunity. I hoped.

"Okay," he said through gritted teeth. "I can't give you any specific details, although I expect some from you. But, yes, there are other suspects. Ms. Addler had expressed some romantic interest in Mr. Loroco, although the two of them stopped getting along together, I gather. But she did have another boyfriend in Los Angeles, whose location at the time of her death is still being investigated."

The VimPets exec, I figured. Once again, I was reminded that I needed to quiz Jack about him.

"I see," I said. "Anyone else?"

For some reason, Wayne seemed to relax a little. "Do you want the whole list? Yeah, I bet you do. Suffice it to say that our victim did not always act like the nicest person, and that caused her to have enemies. We haven't discovered many who were treated badly enough to be likely to consider murdering her—but we're still looking into it. And now you're potentially adding another to our list."

"Two," I said, realizing he hadn't really given me much additional information that I could jump on to clear Billi—and hopefully Jack, too. But I decided to provide my little bit of info to confuse the cops even further. Or it might lead to their actually solving the case faster and accurately. Maybe.

"I assume from what you said that it was either Harris or Elise who got you sent here to interrogate me." I stared at Wayne's face to try to discern his internal response, but though he was fairly young, he'd apparently been a cop long enough to hide what he was thinking, at least sometimes. "Maybe it's because they're both concerned about my discussions with them yesterday—and the fact that if you now look into it further, you'd see that both of them could be viable murder suspects."

"Yeah? Convince me."

I tried to do just that, giving a brief rundown of my confrontation of sorts with Harris Ethman, his anger with Wanda for her threats to his store, and to him, if he didn't cooperate in ruining Jack. Then I explained my other confrontation with Elise Hainner, after her phone call with her brother and his supposed claim that I'd attacked him, at least verbally. "I guess that's what you heard about, maybe from Elise. I didn't attack anyone, and I don't want to point fingers without evidence, but I can assure you that Harris was very angry with Wanda, even after her death. Did he kill her? You'll need to look into that. And what he told his sister about what Wanda was doing could have made her angry enough to do something to protect him and the Ethman family name."

"Very interesting," Wayne said. I'd been glad to see that he'd removed a notepad from a pocket and had taken notes as I talked.

Maybe he actually would look into them as possible suspects. Even though he'd come here apparently ready to run me in for some kind of interference in his case—or maybe just because his superiors wanted to appease the angry Ethmans.

But not go after them as possible murder suspects?

Would they, or wouldn't they, now that I'd told Wayne some of the details about my conversations yesterday?

I considered mentioning Les Ethman, too, since he also had confronted me about this latest murder. I didn't really consider Les a suspect—well, I hoped not, anyway—but would the cops?

"You know," I began, "the Ethmans are very protective of one another. If you look at one or two, you might consider looking at others as well."

Fortunately, I heard the bell chime in Icing so I had an excuse not to answer any questions Wayne might have.

"Excuse me," I said, standing quickly.

"Sure. Thanks. And I will want some treats to take home for the dogs. Maybe some from next door for my wife and me, too."

Boy, had his attitude changed. That was a good thing.

Fortunately, my wonderful helper Vicky arrived just then. I figured she'd get the gist of what was going on when I greeted her warmly and asked her to take care of Detective Crunoll and his dogs.

Then I sped into Icing to help the several groups of customers who'd arrived there.

When I had a chance to go back into the Barkery a short while later, Wayne and his dogs were gone.

My concerns weren't, though. A few of the people and their dogs who'd been out walking before were there, and I passed out sample treats as I'd promised. They, in turn, oohed and aahed over

Biscuit as well as some of our products. And they bought treats, including some of the items their dogs had sampled.

I was glad I couldn't concentrate on my earlier visit from the detective, but it remained on my mind.

And when Billi Matlock called later in the morning, after Frida had come in, I decided that my lunch break would be spent meeting with my friend.

We met at Cuppa-Joe's. It was kind of in between our respective locations, and the Joes were also friends of Billi's.

I got there first and found a table in a corner, inside, which was, as always, crowded. I'd left Biscuit at the Barkery, so I didn't have to sit on the patio. Billi arrived only a few minutes after I did, joining Joe and Irma at the table with me.

And under the table—though she probably shouldn't have been inside the coffee shop—was Sweetie, the adorable golden toy poodle-terrier mix who resembled Biscuit, whom the Joes had adopted from Mountaintop Rescue a few months ago. When they'd heard Billi was coming, they brought her in from her fenced area near the door for just a few minutes, they told me, so she could meet with a couple of her favorite people in the world—Billi and me.

As always, it was delightful to spend time with my pseudo parents, but both of these wonderful seniors rose as soon as Billi got there. "You two have things to talk about," Irma said.

"But come back soon, when you have time to talk to us," said Joe.

"Did you tell them what was going on?" Billi asked in a hushed voice when they, and Sweetie, were gone. She looked pale and as exhausted as I felt. No, more so, and with good reason. Her outfit was casual, a loose T-shirt and fraying jeans, and I assumed she'd come straight from Mountaintop Rescue.

"I didn't have to," I told her. "Rumors about the latest murder are flying around town, I assume." I glanced at the nearest occupied tables, but no one paid us any attention—even when I used the word "murder."

"And around City Council." A look of utter sorrow passed over Billi's face. "Even Les Ethman suggested I might want to take a leave of absence while all this is going on."

"Really? Les? Although ... well, he may be trying to protect an Ethman, or the family's reputation." And himself? Could be, although I hated to think of Les as a murder suspect. He was so much nicer than most of the Ethmans that I hardly thought of him as one of the family. But of course he was.

"What do you mean?" Billi asked. I waited to answer for a few minutes as we both placed our orders with server Kit.

I requested—what else at Cuppa's?—coffee, as well as some cheese and crackers for us to share. Billi ordered a cafe mocha, as if hoping the rich chocolate taste would help reflavor her sadness.

As I had for the detective, I described for Billi my meetings with the Ethmans the day before. I also let her know that I'd passed the information along to the cops.

"Oh, my," Billi said. "Then they have someone else to look at, maybe more than one. But do you honestly think they'll zero in on an Ethman?"

"That family is no more elite than the Matlocks," I told her. "And you should remind them of that."

"Maybe so." Her lips pursed. "But the detectives who keep interrogating me don't seem to care that I'm a Matlock anyway, although Chief Loretta tries to assure me that all will be well."

"As long as they don't zero in on you as their main suspect," I concluded. "At least—well, are Jack and you still an item at all? Do you at least cry on each other's shoulders about being murder suspects?"

"A little. In fact, we've begun seeing each other briefly, nearly every day. He comes into the shelter for a short while to help socialize the animals and talk to me. Although—Carrie, I'm not sure Jack didn't do it. I know he was upset with Wanda. And—well, you of all people know that Jack isn't exactly the most loyal of guy friends."

"Very true." I recalled again that he'd once acted interested in me as a potential girlfriend, but I'd realized over time that he liked me more as a potential way to improve his position in his job.

I'd thought his interest in Billi was different, though.

"Anyway, at one point I thought he was actually falling for Wanda," Billi continued, "since she was going after him kind of the way he went after some other women. Although—well, for a while, I thought it was different between Jack and me, that he was genuinely smitten with me even though he might continue to use the others."

"But he wasn't actually interested in you?" I looked at her with sympathy.

"I don't know. We don't talk about it much, even when we get together now. But, yes, we do commiserate. And he does talk to me, as if it helps him to lay things out on the table."

"I assume that doesn't include a murder confession."

Kit arrived with our order so we quieted down and thanked her, then started indulging. Billi dug into the cheese and crackers along with me, and I was glad. She'd always been slim, but I wondered if she was eating much at all now. Or if she was spending a lot of time exercising at the spa to help get her mind off things, and losing weight that way. Or maybe I was just imagining her gauntness.

Soon, though, I directed our discussion back to where it had been. "You know I'm trying to figure out what really happened to Wanda, right, Billi?"

"Yes, and I appreciate it. As to whether Jack confessed to me, he is kind of opening up, but not about killing Wanda. He says he has regret about using people, mostly women—like you. And he says there've been others, like someone he promised a job to, who works here in Knobcone Heights and wanted to leave. And women in other cities he visited for VimPets sales purposes. But—well, Carrie, he still tells me he cares about me. A lot. And he says that when this is all over with, he'll show me." She shook her head and took a long swig of mocha. "But I'm not sure now that I want him to. I don't know what I want."

We didn't stay much longer. I gave Billi a hug on the street in front of Cuppa's since we were going in different directions.

She'd said she didn't know what she wanted. Of course, she was talking about Jack, and I wasn't sure whether it was good for her to remain in contact with him or not.

But one thing I was sure of. I did know what I wanted.

I wanted to find out who really killed Wanda, so Billi could finally return to her life.

TWENTY-ONE

THE LAST THING I talked about with Billi, as we were about to part ways on the sidewalk outside Cuppa's, was the adoption event we had intended to hold at Barkery. It was now iffy, or at least its timing was.

She'd made it clear, when we'd talked before, that she wanted to do it as much as I did. Maybe even more. So, I kept reminding myself, I didn't only have to help figure out who'd killed Wanda—I had to do it fast, so we could turn our attention to planning and carrying out the event.

Assuming, as I definitely did, that it wasn't Billi.

After my conversations that day, I couldn't help wondering how to find out whether the cops were talking to any VimPets people besides Jack, and wishing I'd asked this before. I had to assume they were, anyway, although since the company was in LA, it was likely that they'd sought cooperation from the LAPD, at least for any initial interrogations.

I really, really wanted the killer to be someone from VimPets. The most likely candidate, of course, was the executive Wanda seemed to be having an affair with—whom she used in her attempt to derail Jack's career in favor of her own.

Which meant there was another good reason to talk to Jack. Alone this time. Not with a group of friends and relatives, and not at the bar.

As a result, I called him as I walked back to my shops. Passing by on the town square side of the street, I watched several people playing with their dogs on the grass, all on leashes since it wasn't a dog park. But it was a place people frequently brought their dogs. I'd have to send one of my assistants there with treat samples, rather than having them pass the samples out on the sidewalk in front of the stores.

Jack answered immediately.

"I've got some other ideas to run by you," I told him. "Any chance we can get together to talk, just ourselves?"

"I'd love to hear them. Anything. In fact, I'll come by your stores at closing tonight—six o'clock, right? I'll bring Rigsley. I've been leaving my poor dog alone too much lately. It may get dark, but we can walk Rigsley and Biscuit in the town square since there are lots of lights there. And if we decide to, later, we can go grab a drink somewhere. Okay?"

Privacy with Jack, in public. I liked the idea.

On the other hand, there was one person I wouldn't mind joining us. I'd let Reed know, in case he could come. He might be able to "accidentally" show up at my stores around the same time.

I wanted to talk to Jack, but I didn't want to be foolish about it. He could, after all, be a murderer, even though I doubted it.

"Sounds good," I said. "See you later."

Reed, unfortunately, wasn't available then. An emergency cancer surgery had been scheduled for a dog that evening, and I certainly didn't want to interrupt that. I even offered to come in if he needed a technician, but he'd already lined up Yolanda, so that was fine.

My evening wasn't fine, though. I considered whether to ask Jack to join me at the resort instead, but we'd been there before—with others along, of course—and I hadn't heard as much as I wanted about what he was thinking.

So, okay, not Reed—but maybe one other person. I decided to call Neal, and as soon as I explained what was going on, my brother made it clear he'd be the one who would just happen to show up at my shops when they were closing.

I wanted to hug my little brother and probably would, later.

I ended my conversation with Neal right outside the Barkery, and then Biscuit and I hurried inside. There were a few customers, and Frida was helping a young couple with a terrier mix choose some treats. I quickly put Biscuit into her crate and hurried to help another group who stood pointing at treats in our refrigerated display case.

As soon as I could, I popped into Icing and found that Vicky also had her hands full providing service there, where one group was attempting to buy enough baked goods for a school party that night and was taking up a lot of my assistant's time.

And so things went for the rest of the afternoon.

I wasn't surprised when six o'clock rolled around, but I was sorry I hadn't had any free time to mush around in my head all the things I wanted to ask Jack.

Oh, well. I felt certain they'd come to me.

I'd said goodbye to my assistants and was still tidying the Barkery when I heard a woof outside. I looked out to see Rigsley near the door with Jack behind him.

I opened the door quickly and gave Rigsley a hug as he hurried in and ran right to the glassed-in display case. He knew where the treats were kept.

Because we were closed, I locked the door behind Jack, then let Biscuit out of her enclosure. Both dogs stayed around the display case, and I couldn't resist. I went behind it and got out a couple of apple treats, giving one to each of them.

"So, hi, Carrie," Jack said, smiling at me. He wore a black hoodie and appeared more relaxed than the last couple of times I'd seen him. Did that mean he was off the top of the cops' suspect list? As much as I hoped the answer was yes, I was afraid that it wouldn't bode well for Billi.

"Oops, was I ignoring you?"

"I know who's important around here." Which was generally true, but I had lots of questions for Jack, which put him at the top of the list of things I was thinking about at the moment.

A knock sounded on the window and I looked in that direction, figuring I'd see Neal. I was correct, and I let him in.

"Looks like my brother wants to go on the walk with us," I told Jack.

"Yeah, I'm rehearsing for the next hike I'm putting together," Neal explained. His blond hair was long enough to be mussed up already, so I figured we would run into a breeze on our walk. Neal had donned a sweatshirt that read *Hiking Builds Character*, highly appropriate for my character-filled brother.

"Fine with me," Jack said. "In fact, that hike sounds inviting, too. You'll have to tell us what you have in mind for it."

"Sure."

I went into the kitchen, then, to check that the back door and the door into my office were locked, then headed back into the Barkery with Biscuit's leash. I made sure the lights were out in both stores and those doors were locked, too, once we were all on the sidewalk.

There wasn't much traffic, either of the pedestrian type on the sidewalk or the vehicle type on the road in front of us. When we crossed Summit Avenue to reach the town square, we found the lighted area populated by some teens playing soccer on the grass beyond the benches, as well as a couple of other dog walkers.

Just another evening here in Knobcone Heights. And I certainly didn't feel uncomfortable being there with Jack—especially with Neal and the dogs along.

But did he happen to be a murderer?

I didn't plan to ask him outright this time. I wanted to make sure he answered my other questions.

I led Biscuit down a path beside the soccer area, and the others joined us. I held back a little, to start walking right beside Jack, holding Biscuit's leash as he held Rigsley's.

"You know what subject is foremost in my mind," I said as we walked, and then related to him my conversation with Detective Wayne Crunoll. "He seemed interested in my version of my confrontation with both Harris and Elise, but I gathered that one of them, probably Elise, had contacted the cops about my supposed attack on Harris at his shop. I don't feel like stepping away from trying to figure out who killed Wanda after that, not when I've been put even more into the police's crosshairs, so to speak."

"I feel for you, Carrie," Jack said with a sigh. "Do I ever. But at least you're not considered a suspect this time." He stopped briefly. "Are you?"

"No, of course not." But then, as we started walking again, I added, "I shouldn't phrase it that way. I know better. But I don't believe they're thinking of me as a murder suspect, just someone who might be interfering with their investigation. Which might be true, at least till they figure out who really did it."

I stopped speaking then, as Biscuit found a tree trunk—of course, a knobcone pine—particularly interesting and started sniffing it.

"It wasn't me," Jack said, as if I'd just accused him.

"Of course not," I said again, although this time I remained even less sure. "But I do have some questions for you, and you might not have the answers."

"Hey, how about if I grab those leashes and take the dogs for a run?" asked Neal, who'd come up beside me. I wasn't thrilled about the interruption, but I did like the idea.

"Sure," I said, pulling the loop of Biscuit's leash off my wrist and handing it to Neal.

"Sounds good to me, too." Jack did the same with Rigsley, and he and I stood there for a minute, both grinning, as Neal and the dogs loped off in front of us. Then Jack looked back at me. "So what are those questions?"

"Well, I couldn't get away with asking Detective Crunoll who all they were considering to be suspects, but I have to assume that at least one of your VimPets executives may be on their list, possibly their short list."

We started down the path Neal had taken into the more shadowy areas of the park, without the dogs this time, but there were still a few pets and their people nearby.

"You mean the man she was interested in, or at least pretending to be interested in. That would be our Products VP, Marv Langwell. Well, you may get an opportunity to interrogate him yourself, Carrie, if you're so inclined. He's let me know that he and our company president, Fitzgerald Jagit, will be here in Knobcone Heights in a couple of days to talk directly to the cops about Wanda's death and to show their caring and mourning and all that."

This time I grabbed Jack's arm as I stopped walking. "Really? That's great! And yes, I'd like to at least meet them. Any chance of your setting up some kind of get-together with them that I could attend?"

"I'll see what I can do. Oh, and Carrie, if you're keeping your nose in this situation to try to clear me—even if I'm not the only one you want to clear—thanks. I feel so bad about Billi. I really do care for her, you know."

The light around us was nearly nonexistent, but I nevertheless believed I saw sincerity in Jack's hazel eyes as he looked down at me, his other hand over my hand, which remained on his arm.

Did I believe him?

Let's just say that at that point I really hoped to find a way to zero in on Marv, or Fitzgerald, as the killer and thereby finally let Jack off the hook—including in my own mind. Of course, it seemed like the cops probably didn't view these executives as suspects. Then again, since when had I followed the cops' lead?

For now, I began talking about another thing I'd been wondering about. "I know Wanda was staying with you, and—"

"Not after that scene she made. And even when she was, nothing happened," Jack practically spat out. "She made up the supposed attraction between us, but it wasn't there."

"That's not what I was going to ask," I said. "I just wanted to know if you were aware of any other places she hung out, where she might have met other people whose toes she could have stepped on."

"I certainly wasn't with her 24/7," Jack said. "The only place I know she spent a lot of time when she wasn't hounding me was the resort. You've already talked to a lot of people there, haven't you?"

Neal must have heard the reference. He'd slowed down, so that he and the dogs were only a few feet ahead of us then. He stopped, then, until we caught up.

"Yes, she has," he said, responding to Jack's question. "Carrie already put my boss, Elise, on her suspect list. I'm not sure who else she's talked to, though. I'm pretty much tied to the reception desk when I'm on duty. But she's welcome to come back and ask around—as long as she doesn't say anything nasty that could affect my job."

Neal had been looking at Jack, talking to him as if I wasn't even there.

"Yes, I think she'll do just that," I told my brother. "It's too late tonight, but how about if I bring Janelle tomorrow—I think she's working at my shops—and you take lunchtime off to join us?"

"I think I'll pass on that," Jack inserted, as if I'd invited him, too. He apparently assumed it would have been okay to accept my non-invitation.

So it was only Neal who said, "Sounds good to me. I'll talk to Janelle. Just make sure you've got enough people scheduled at your shops tomorrow that you can both come."

I spent a little while on the phone that evening after Biscuit, Neal, and I got home. That was after a quick stop at a fast food place, where I indulged in a taco salad and Neal ordered a couple of hamburgers—one of which belonged to Biscuit.

My first call was to check to see if Frida was available to help out at the shops for a couple of hours around lunchtime tomorrow. It would be Monday, one of Dinah's traditional days off, and Janelle and Vicky were scheduled to come in. But if Janelle joined Neal and me for lunch, another assistant would be needed for a while.

Fortunately, although Frida's other sort-of job was creating new recipes for people—she'd indicated recently that she was considering writing a cookbook—she was kind and flexible enough to commit to coming in.

My second call was to Reed, just to say good night. I waited till I was in bed, ready to go to sleep, before calling him. Biscuit lay snoring a little on the floor beside me, and I smiled down at her as I pressed Reed's number into my phone.

He answered immediately, then asked, "So what mischief were you in today, and what do you plan for tomorrow?"

I laughed, but only a little. These days, he knew me too well. "Discussions with Billi and Jack today. Lunch with Neal and Janelle scheduled for tomorrow at the resort. I doubt it's possible, but I'd love to have you join us."

"You got it right the first time." His tone sounded rueful. "But it's been a day or two. How about dinner together tomorrow night?"

"I'll definitely look forward to it," I told him.

TWENTY-TWO

Monday morning at both my shops was productive. Quite a few locals as well as some out-of-town visitors stopped in to buy lots of tasty treats for themselves and their dogs. We—initially Janelle, Vicky, and I—were quite busy.

It didn't really slow down as lunchtime approached, and I was a bit concerned about leaving only two of my assistants there, but Frida arrived early and both she and Vicky encouraged me to go. In fact, they seemed to insist on it.

"It's not like you don't spend enough time here," Vicky said, her black eyebrows raised beneath her glasses. We'd all gone into the kitchen for a minute to talk, leaving a few customers in both stores who were still checking out our merchandise and making up their minds. "Maybe I should start including you in my scheduling so you'd take a full day or two off now and then."

"Forget that," I told her.

"Well, you can forget about acting like Vicky and I can't handle things here ourselves for a couple of hours," Frida said, hands on her ample hips. "We'll do so well that you'll even consider giving both of us raises."

"You wish," was my retort to her, given with a smile. I felt a lot better after talking with both of them. Plus, I'd keep the timing of the lunch at a minimum—or at least try to.

And one of these days, if business continued as it had been, I would in fact give my assistants raises.

Part of rationing my timing today involved driving to the resort, since it was a pleasant but not extremely short walk. Janelle and I took Biscuit and Go, who was also at the Barkery today, out for a walk before we left, and then, after hugging the dogs goodbye, I drove the two of us.

Neal turned his part of the registration desk over to another guy as soon as we reached his area. He motioned for us to join him in a corner of the busy lobby before we headed into the restaurant.

"Just wanted to let you know, Carrie, that I made a special point of asking a few of my closest friends and coworkers who they'd seen Wanda with." My tall brother slumped a little, as if trying to hide a bit from any prying eyes—his boss's, I presumed. He was dressed in a nice shirt and trousers, as he usually was at work, a contrast to his casual home wear and hiking things. "I made it clear I didn't want them to let Elise know I was asking, and I hinted that she seems to think her brother could be involved. I didn't hint that you considered her a suspect, too."

"Good," I said. "Did anyone mention someone who'd talked with Wanda, someone I should follow up on?"

"Not really. A couple mentioned Jack, since he's here enough for people to recognize. One remembered that dinner here on the patio where Jack first introduced Wanda, but he couldn't recall who was with them—besides you and Billi Matlock and Reed. Oh, and Janelle and me, too, but I don't think you need to follow up with us, either. Another one wondered if Wanda had introduced herself to any of the Ethmans, but that was just conjecture on his part. And a couple mentioned that the cops had been here once or twice asking questions but didn't know if they learned anything. Anyway, I thought you should know I tried."

"Thanks," I said. "We know Wanda ate here a few times. Did you question any of the servers at the restaurant or bar?"

"No," he said. "I thought that was part of the reason for our lunch today, at least in the restaurant."

"True," I said. "I just wondered."

Since I'd left Biscuit with my assistants at the Barkery—yes, another service they rendered for me today and at other times, too—we chose a table inside the restaurant. Gwen waited on us often, and if I remembered correctly, she was the server on the patio the night so many of us had gotten together for dinner. If in fact she was, would she remember what happened?

And might she have been Wanda's server on other occasions, with or without Jack? Had she paid any attention to who else Wanda had eaten with?

I figured it wouldn't hurt to ask, so I whispered to Neal where I thought we should sit, and he agreed.

He spoke briefly with the hostess and we soon were seated at a table in the middle of an area where I'd seen Gwen working. As always, the resort's restaurant had lots of patrons, the room resounding with the loud hum of many conversations, the air filled with tempting aromas. The hostess handed us menus, although we all probably had them memorized. I, at least, knew I'd order a Cobb salad.

In a minute a familiar female voice said, "Hi." Gwen had appeared, table setups in her hands and a smile on her face. "Good to see all of you." She placed the flatware she carried on the linen tablecloth. "What would you like to drink?"

I would have been happy with just water but ordered iced tea so our tab would increase, and so would Gwen's tip. I observed her interaction with Neal and Janelle, and all seemed cordial as usual.

I wasn't sure what the best time would be to ask Gwen my questions, but I figured this wasn't it. I doubted that we could catch her during a break, either.

She probably would spend a little more time at this table when she took our lunch orders, so I decided that would be the time to broach the subject.

"What are you two getting today?" Janelle asked after Gwen had left. She and Neal had also ordered iced tea to drink. "I'm considering just a cup of Manhattan style clam chowder."

"Barbecue sandwich for me," Neal said. My brother seemed to eat hearty but didn't gain weight—probably at least partly because of the hikes he led and those he took on his own.

We chatted for a couple of minutes about nothing important, and then Gwen returned. "What would you like today?" she asked when she'd put our drinks in front of us. Her expression appeared as interested and expectant as always.

How would she look in a minute, when I got off that topic completely?

I'd picked up the menu and tried to appear as if I were still deciding so she would ask Neal and Janelle first. When it was my turn, I didn't immediately tell her what I wanted.

"I've got a question for you first," I told her.

"Of course." She must have assumed I was going to ask about food since her expression didn't change—initially.

"I know this is a little—well, weird, but I'm trying to help some friends."

That brought a look of concern to her face, but she didn't say anything.

I smiled at her. "I know you're an excellent server and you don't interfere with anyone's conversations or anything. And I know you're aware of who Wanda Addler was."

Her eyebrows knitted in a frown. "The lady who was killed? I didn't know her, but I know her name."

"Were you ever her server? I know she ate here now and then after she arrived in town."

"Didn't she join your table once or twice? I thought about that after… after I heard she died. But if she spent much time here otherwise, I really didn't pay attention." Gwen was beginning to look antsy, glancing down at the notepad in her hand where she wrote orders.

"Then you can't tell us if she ever dined here with someone other than Jack?"

Surprisingly, Gwen gave me a small smile. "You're at it again, aren't you, Carrie? I know you were involved before, looking into those other killings." She glanced away from me and toward Janelle, but not for long. "I admire you for that—I guess. But if you're asking if I know anything about Wanda's death, sorry, I don't. I can ask around the kitchen if anyone else around here does, but you're not the first, you know. The police came here a few days ago and asked if any of us knew who she was or saw anything… well, unusual about her. Or anyone with her. No one said anything useful, I gather. I certainly didn't. But—well, good luck. Although from the news I think the police believe they have a couple of good persons of interest, right?"

"Maybe," I said. "Anyway, I just thought I'd ask. Thanks. And please bring me a Cobb salad."

Once she'd left, I looked from Neal to Janelle and back again. "That was useful," I said sarcastically.

"At least you tried," Neal said. "And I wasn't aware that the police asked around the restaurant. I know they snooped here a little bit after Wanda was killed because they were looking into Jack, who comes here often, as a potential suspect. They asked a few questions even of us at the registration desk, but I don't think anyone there had any answers. Maybe they even talked to Elise. Anyway, this turned out to be a dead end for you."

"But as you said, at least I tried. And if Gwen knew anything, or knew of a server or anyone else who knew anything, I have the sense she would have told us—as gossip or whatever."

"She's obviously aware of how good you are at solving murders," Janelle said, her smile on the wry side.

"I gather it wasn't a surprise that you were a suspect last time," I said to her. Then I turned slightly. "Now that we're done with that, tell me your latest ideas for the next hike, Neal—it'll be around Halloween, won't it?"

"I might do one or two before, like my regular ones, since that would be easier," Neal said. "For the Halloween one, I've changed my mind. I might try to set things up so the people on the hike can conduct a little trick-or-treat after all, at a few places. But I'll need to make sure the home and business owners know in advance and are okay with it."

We talked about his ideas, the timing, and how grueling he intended his Halloween hike to be. We were still discussing it when Gwen brought our meals.

"Enjoy," she said with her server-smile back in place. "Oh, and I did ask a couple of people in the kitchen what they knew about the murdered lady and only got a lot of demands from them to explain why I'd asked and what I knew—nothing that'll help you or the cops."

"I figured that would be the case," I said, "but it never hurts to inquire. Thanks for checking. And thanks for this, too." I gestured around the table toward our food. "It all looks and smells good—and reminds me of one of the reasons I like to eat here."

"One of the reasons?" Neal asked.

"Well, it never hurts that I get to say hi to my little brother when I'm here." I looked up toward Gwen and winked.

We enjoyed the rest of our lunch. At least I did—since I didn't ask more questions about the murder investigation.

I did still quiz Neal more about his upcoming hikes, though. I looked forward to participating in at least one of them—because it would be a diversion from the rest of my life, which I spent mostly baking and vet-teching. And, oh yes, solving murders.

That made me realize the extent of my frustration.

I tried to thrust it out of my mind as we talked and, afterward, when I paid for our lunches. After all, eating here—and being nosy—was something I'd wanted to do, and I did get a bit of a discount on the bill thanks to Neal being employed by the resort.

"Are you okay?" Janelle asked as I drove us back to the shops.

"Sure," I said, then changed the subject to one I knew she'd believe was actually on my mind: how the Barkery and Icing were doing. Fortunately, the results remained positive.

More than positive. The two stores were a subject I never got tired of talking about—and hearing suggestions for. Janelle told me she'd search again for some websites where she could send some of the photos she'd taken to promote the stores.

I thanked her. A lot. And felt even more glad about our discussion.

I soon parked behind the shops, and we entered through the kitchen to wash our hands. Then I disappeared into my office to call Reed while she hurried into the Barkery to help out.

I sat at my desk, phone to my ear, and stared at my blank computer screen as if it contained all the answers to my strange and difficult mood.

"Are we still on for tonight?" I asked when he answered.

"Of course." No hesitation.

Good.

But I wondered, through the rest of the afternoon, how I'd feel after I revealed to Reed more about the direction my mind was going.

I waited on customers in Icing first, then in the Barkery. And as I sold lots of dog treats I focused even more on the way my mind was heading.

When I solved the first murder, it was because I'd been the main suspect.

When I solved the second murder, it wasn't only because Neal's girlfriend Janelle was the main suspect. I had dogs in distress to rescue.

And now, with this latest murder, a couple of my friends appeared to be the primary suspects. But was that enough to keep me on this difficult path? Did I actually like solving murders, or was I just allowing myself to be drawn into the investigation because I considered helping my friends important?

Was I spending too much time on that, when I should be concentrating on my shops—and my part-time vet tech career?

Maybe I should stop. Now.

But I knew very soon, late that afternoon, why I wouldn't.

Billi appeared in the Barkery around five o'clock. She had her dogs with her—Flip, her black Lab, and Fanny, her beagle mix.

I was behind the register counter, having just finished with a customer, and Janelle was helping a couple of teens who'd come in with a Bichon. Seeing Billi and her babies, I smiled—but that smile drooped immediately when I saw her tearful expression.

I slipped away immediately and rushed to greet her. "Hi," I said, then whispered, "Are you all right?"

"Can you take Biscuit for a walk with us?" she asked, and I knew the answer.

She was definitely not all right. And I needed to know more.

TWENTY-THREE

Unlike my walk with Jack, which had been a bit after sundown, we didn't stay on the grass-lined sidewalks near the benches around the town square on this late, still sunny afternoon. Instead, Biscuit and I followed Billi and her dogs along some of the internal paths, away from most of the grass-covered hills and into the mini-forest of knobcone pine trees.

There were other people around, too—a few seniors being walked by their dogs, some teens texting as they strolled, and a young couple looking more into each other's eyes than at the uneven path, possibly foreboding a tripping disaster.

For a short while, Billi and I talked only about our dogs, the pets at Mountaintop Rescue, and how I'd give her some slightly aging treats when she left to bring to her beloved shelter.

Beloved by both her and me. That was why, before long, I realized that my momentary fizzle about continuing with my murder investigation meant nothing.

Not just my ability to host an adoption event at the Barkery was at stake. The lives of a lot of shelter animals would be on the line if the wrong person was sent to prison. No one could run Mountaintop Rescue as well as Billi did. And from what she said, the Knobcone Heights Police seemed to be zeroing in on her as their main suspect and were about to take her into custody.

"I get the impression, when I talk to Chief Loretta sometimes," she said, so softly I had to strain to hear her over the crunch of dried leaves beneath our feet, "that she and the others are bending over backward not to give me the benefit of any doubt just because I happen to be a City Councilwoman. Or maybe they have some kind of feud with City Council that I'm not aware of and they're taking it out on me. Or—well, maybe for some reason that they haven't revealed, they actually think I'm guilty."

She told me that she was now being interrogated nearly daily about her relationship with Jack, when she'd met Wanda, what she'd thought of her—all repetitious stuff, as if they hoped she would stumble and reveal a prior lie.

I'd considered Billi a bit too thin before, but now, even just a few days later, she looked nearly emaciated, her attractive face narrow, her red Mountaintop Rescue shirt and jeans baggy. I wanted to run back to Icing and grab some cookies or cupcakes and force-feed her—not that it would do any good.

"But I've told them everything," she said when we stopped as Fanny circled for an imminent squat. Billi's expression as she looked at me was both heartrending and frantic. "I thought I actually cared for Jack, but now I wish I'd never met him. I've told the detectives the former but not the latter, although I'm fairly sure they can interpret that from the way I talk about him now. I certainly didn't like the ideas Wanda conveyed, that she and Jack had a relationship at the same time he was working on one with me. But kill her? I guess I wished her out of our lives, but certainly not that way."

"I know that, Billi," I said softly. "But what makes you think they're about to arrest you?"

"They told me so. At least with Ted Culbert present, thanks to you. A lot of what I learn is when he's with me, making sure I don't say anything I shouldn't. But he isn't able to shut them up as they threaten me. The one who's making the most threats is Detective Bridget Morana. She talked to you, too, didn't she, when you were a murder suspect?"

"Yes." We started forward again once Billi had cleaned up after Fanny. "I've also been asked some questions since Wanda's murder, but they've all come from Wayne Crunoll. Maybe they think I like him better so I'll reveal more of what I've learned during my unofficial investigation. But I don't really know anything, and all I've told him about you is that you're innocent." I didn't want to get into the other things I'd discussed with Wayne. My suspicions about Jack, and of Harris and Elise as well, might give her inappropriate hope. "I'd be glad to talk to Ted about some more ideas I have, though."

"Oh, would you?" Billi sounded thrilled, as if I'd suddenly saved her.

"Of course, although I'm not sure how helpful they'll be."

"Even if they don't lead to anything, I'm sure they'll be helpful." She paused, then said, "I don't know what I'm going to do, Carrie. I'm innocent, of course, but if they arrest me … well, would you take over managing Mountaintop Rescue? I've got some assistants and volunteers who'd be helpful but they don't really know how to run a business, especially a non-profit like that. I'm so worried about our residents if I can't be there to take care of them."

So was I. I wouldn't be the ideal choice to take over the shelter, though. Taking on a third career would not be a good idea.

But I couldn't say no. "I'll do all I can to help," I promised her. I could only hope that kind of involvement would never become necessary.

All in all, our conversation continued to eradicate my brief idea about walking away from the murder investigation. I had to figure out who'd done it, and fast—not only for Billi's sake but for all the animals at Mountaintop Rescue.

It was a good thing I'd had that conversation with Billi before Biscuit and I headed to Reed's for dinner that night. He was bringing in roast chicken, he'd told me, and when we spoke on the phone that afternoon, he'd heard in my voice that I wanted to talk.

What I'd intended to tell him was how frustrated I'd become ever since he'd told me not to get involved in the first place, so I was considering backing away.

Now, though, as I sat across his kitchen table eating a chicken leg and some spinach on the side, I told him about my conversation with Billi.

"I need to get this figured out fast," I all but cried out.

"You need to let the cops figure it out fast," he contradicted me, but the expression on his handsome face appeared understanding despite his words. His dark brown eyes locked on mine, even as the corner of his mouth quirked up. "But we've gone through this before. You're going to keep at it no matter what I say. So let me repeat: be careful. And keep me informed. Maybe I can help in some way, too."

I leaned toward him over his oval, dark wood kitchen table to give him a kiss. My movement encouraged some scrabbling paws on the vinyl wood-grained floor beneath us. We'd given both Biscuit and Hugo some bone-free pieces of chicken as we started to eat, and they clearly thought that had just been an appetizer. My lips met Reed's briefly, and only then did I allow myself to laugh.

"Thanks." I sat back again. "For the kiss, and for the offer to help. I'll let you know if I think of anything you can do."

"I know a couple of things you can do to take your mind off what you're up to for a short while." His grin looked teasing, but I knew he wasn't.

"For one, you'd like me to come in for a shift at the clinic tomorrow?"

"You got it. Will you?"

"Sure," I said. I just hoped no hugely helpful idea came to me about finding Wanda's killer that I absolutely had to follow up on tomorrow afternoon.

Reed and I had kind of gotten into a routine for the nights that I either ate at his home or we wound up here after going out to dinner. We walked the dogs as soon as we were done eating. It was cool and dark and slightly drizzly by the time we went outside, but the streetlights in his neighborhood were abundant.

When we were done with our walk and Hugo and Biscuit seemed happy, we returned to the house, where Reed and I partook in some of our own kind of recreation—the second thing to temporarily get my mind off my murder investigation.

But Biscuit and I didn't stay late. As always, I had to get up early to start baking for my shops, so we soon headed home.

Neal's car was in the garage when I parked. He was awake, watching a rerun of a football game played the day before.

He put it on pause when Biscuit and I came in. "You okay, sis?"

Something apparently showed on my face: my determination. My earlier ambivalence that I'd had to slough off. Or maybe enjoyment of my time with Reed, although that wouldn't have garnered Neal's questions.

The answers I gave him, as he petted his Bug and observed me with concern, mostly involved my conversation with Billi.

"So you really thought you'd stop snooping into this killing?" he asked when I was done. "Sure, you've now got a good reason to continue, but I know you, sis. You'd have kept at it anyway."

"Maybe." Then I added with a huge grin, "Of course!"

He accompanied Biscuit and me outside for a final walk of the night, then returned to the living room while Biscuit and I started getting ready for bed.

I'd hoped to fall asleep fast that night, but instead I thought long and hard—and not for the first time—about what to do next to try to solve Wanda's murder. Talk to the VimPets execs when they got here, maybe? Be pushier with Jack? Something else?

Did I reach any conclusions?

Only that I was going to be tired tomorrow.

Surprise, surprise. I had a hard time getting out of bed the next day when my clock radio came on, but I managed to do so. Biscuit wouldn't have allowed me to sleep in anyway. She and I were soon at the shops and I started baking.

The morning progressed as usual. My two assistants for the day were Dinah, the first to arrive, and Janelle, who joined us a couple of hours later.

The shops were only moderately busy that day. I wondered if I'd been too optimistic in my conclusion about how well things were going. But most days we made a lot of sales, so I told myself not to get pessimistic about everything.

Including about solving Wanda's murder. I hadn't formed any great new idea about what to do next that would definitely result in a resolution.

Go see one of the detectives and act as if I knew something they didn't, to get them to trade secrets? I had kind of done that with Wayne, but I doubted he'd continue to play along.

Talk to Jack some more? Tell him I'd heard he was about to be arrested? Oops—or was it supposed to be Billi?

In actuality, I had no idea if either of them was that close to being taken into custody. It might just have been Billi's nerves. Or maybe the detectives were pulling an ace out of the hole so they could scare her into revealing all—whatever *all* might be.

Check in with Harris again? Elise? And ask them what?

The morning passed quickly despite not having a huge number of customers. Things perked up as lunchtime drew near, so I hung around to help out, but only till one o'clock. I'd promised Reed I would do a shift at the clinic, and when I called in, I learned when he had scheduled me.

As always, I brought Biscuit along to put into doggy daycare. Things at the clinic that afternoon were relatively tame—mostly regular patients in for checkups and shots, a dog with kennel cough, and not a whole lot else.

It was, as always, enjoyable to see Reed again. And to touch base with my dear friend and mentor Arvie.

Still, the day could be considered a bit boring—except I needed a boring day so I could keep my mind active and planning. Yet nothing particular came to mind.

Not until I was leaving the clinic. That was when I received a call from Jack. "Hi, Carrie," he said. "Do you have dinner plans? I'm not sure I can get you an invitation to join us, but you can at least show up at the resort and meet a couple of the VimPets executives. They're here now to talk to the police—and also to pay their respects, in their way, to Wanda."

"Of course!" I promised to be there at six o'clock. I'd have to get my assistants to close up shop, but that should work out fine.

As I hung up with Jack, my phone rang again. It was Neal. "I probably shouldn't be telling you this, Carrie, but—"

"But some VimPets executives are in town and staying at the resort. Right?"

"Are you psychic?" he asked, sounding surprised.

Oh, if only I was.

TWENTY-FOUR

FORTUNATELY, DINAH WAS NOT only reliable in getting things done at the shop, but she was also great at closing it up. As my only full-time assistant, she'd helped out that way before, and she was willing and able to do it that night, too.

As I drove Biscuit home—I didn't want to leave her at the shops nor take her along, since I had no idea how things might work out that evening—I once again thought of the possibility of granting raises to my helpers.

I also thought about the few hours today when the shops weren't particularly busy and recognized that the raise couldn't happen tomorrow.

But mostly, I thought about what awaited me. Would I get to eat dinner with Jack and his bosses and, hopefully, learn what they thought of their difficult, and now deceased, employee Wanda?

Was one of them Marv Langwell, who evidently had had a relationship with her—or at least she'd wanted him to?

Biscuit didn't seem to mind when I took her inside the house after a brief walk—maybe because I left her as she was eating dinner. I drove as quickly as I could to the resort.

Should I hope for psychic visions? Mind reading? I still wished I could do that, since I doubted, however things worked out that evening, that anyone would admit to having killed Wanda, even though I might in fact be in the company of her murderer.

Which still could be Jack.

The resort parking lot was nearly full, but I found a spot near the entry from the street. That gave me a short hike up to the main building, and time for my thoughts to keep churning.

Reed and I hadn't made dinner plans for that evening, which was a good thing. I didn't want to tell him what I was up to until it was over. I already knew what he'd say again anyway: be careful. And keep him informed. Both were fine with me.

When I entered the lobby, it looked a bit less crowded than I was used to seeing, which made it easier for me to slip off to the right toward the reception desk. Neal was speaking with a guest when I got there, so I just waved. He stopped briefly, and I had the impression he wanted me to wait, but I figured I could come back and talk to him later.

Right now, I hoped to find Jack—and the people he was with. The most likely place was the restaurant, since he'd mentioned dinner.

As I'd thought before, it was a good thing I liked the food at this place, in case I yet again wound up eating there while trying to accomplish my real goal of the evening: meeting the VimPets guys and subtly—or not—trying to learn anything they knew or suspected about Wanda and her demise.

Would they accuse their own employee, Jack? They just might, especially if one of them was the killer.

I peeked into the bar first thing but didn't see him. Maybe, if I stayed for dinner, I'd fortify myself with a glass of wine… but not in there.

I kept going, past the spa's entry and the door to the patio, then reached the restaurant. Although I liked this place a lot, I didn't like the fact that I could probably stride through it blindfolded.

Blindfolded. I recognized that as a good analogy for a couple of things: Wanda's murder, since I assume she hadn't been expecting any kind of attack. And now, here I was, figuratively blindfolded since I hadn't determined, and couldn't prove, what had happened to her.

For now, eyes wide open, I strode into the restaurant through the arched doorway, attempting to look in charge and confident so I'd give the VimPets men the right impression—that they should pay attention to me and answer my questions. Or at least buy a recipe or two from me, which was the original reason Jack had wanted me to have a relationship with their company.

My assumed confidence wavered almost immediately when, looking around, I didn't see Jack. Despite the resort's lobby being fairly empty, the bar had been busy, and this restaurant was, as usual, buzzing with activity. Still, I'd always been able to spot whoever I'd intended to meet fairly quickly when I'd come in here before.

Not this time.

I continued to stand there. The evening's hostess appeared busy, talking to someone near the kitchen. Might she know Jack? I couldn't recall her name, but I'd seen her here before. Maybe she knew some of the most frequent diners, but—

"Hi, Carrie." I turned to my left to see Gwen standing there. "Is anyone joining you? Do you want a table tonight? If so, hold on just a minute and I'll get you set up."

"I'm looking for Jack right now," I told her. "I think he's here having dinner with a couple of guys. Not sure if I'm joining them, but I want to say hi."

Gwen's eyebrows raised slightly, as if she was assessing my relationship with Jack again. I resisted the urge to tell her it was business, all about recipes, whatever … but she said, "He's on the patio out back. I can take you to him."

"No need," I said, "but thanks. Now that I know he's there I'll find him."

Jack and his party of two executives were at a table at the patio's rear, beneath one of the warming lights and overlooking the lake's shoreline and water below. Jack had probably wanted the best location for his bosses and had maybe even paid the hostess a little extra to find him such a good spot.

Once again I assumed the demeanor of a confident businessperson ready to negotiate terms for selling some dog treat recipes, if I so chose. Wending my way through occupied tables, I strode over to them and stopped beside Jack, who sat on the right side of the group.

"Hi," I said, then looked at his companions. "Gentlemen, good to see you."

All three men, clad in dark suits and serious demeanors, stood. "Hi, Carrie," Jack said. "I'd like you to meet Fitzgerald Jagit, our CEO, and Marv Langwell, our Products Vice President."

Marv. The guy Wanda had been had involved with. I held out my hand to him first. He looked like an executive, with a smoothly shaved face and smooth demeanor, too—the way he shot me a quick smile and curious gaze with narrowed blue eyes. "Ah, we meet at last, Carrie. Jack has been telling me about your dog treat bakery and your excellent, healthy recipes for months."

So, in addition to being high enough in the chain of command to have captured Wanda's attention, he was probably the one who'd expressed interest in VimPets buying one or more of those recipes.

After trading a firm handshake with Marv, I turned to Fitzgerald. He was older and stouter and not nearly as smooth. His silver mustache matched his wavy hair, which was now blowing in the slight breeze from the lake. But he shook hands just as firmly, and the way he examined my face suggested he wanted to peek inside and read my brain—maybe even extract some of my recipes that way.

"Are you joining us for dinner?" That was Jack, and when I glanced at him, I read, possibly mistakenly, a plea on his face. He'd looked stressed now and then recently, presumably because he was a murder suspect, but now the stress appeared to be etching lots of extra lines on a face that I'd considered much better looking before this last week or so.

"I guess I could." I glanced at the other men, trying to read how they felt about the idea. Fitzgerald glowered, but Marv had a large, welcoming smile on his face.

Did he consider me a possible successor to Wanda on his seduction list? Of course, that presumed he seduced *her*, or thought he did, rather than her being the seductress.

Either way, a motive to kill her might exist, although I wasn't certain what it was. The seduction angle? Because she might not have glommed solely onto him? And how had Jack fit into all this?

I was just reaching for answers.

"Then please join us." Marv stood and, by his expression, encouraged the others to rise too so he could rearrange the chairs.

I was soon seated beside Marv at the longer end of the table, facing the lake. Jack was on my right side, and Fitzgerald sat across the table from him.

I noticed that all three men had drinks in front of them, maybe scotch and sodas. When the server immediately came over—a guy I'd seen here before but never met—I ordered a glass of merlot.

I wondered if these gentlemen would pay for my meal—or, rather, VimPets would. I supposed that might depend on whether we talked business. I was willing to discuss recipes, but that remained far from the main reason I was there.

Before I could start on that subject, though, Neal came over to the table and stood behind Jack. "Hi, everyone. I'm Carrie's brother, and I work at the resort. I just wanted to say hi to her and to Jack, and also welcome the rest of you to the restaurant. You're staying at the resort, aren't you?" He looked at Marv and then at Fitzgerald. "I was the one who checked you in."

"That's right," Fitzgerald said. "Thank you for the welcome." He drew his shuttered gaze away from Neal and onto Jack, as if he had said all he intended to.

Not wanting to irritate the guy enough to make him unhappy even before I started delving into the topic of Wanda, I said, "Hi, Neal. Thanks for stopping over here. I'll talk to you later."

The order encompassed in my gaze apparently worked, since my brother said "Great" and walked away.

My wine arrived then, and I learned that the men had already given their dinner orders. I ordered one of my usuals, a Cobb salad.

I glanced around. The tables around us remained occupied. Even the patio was busy this evening.

So was my mind. I looked first at Fitzgerald and then at Marv. "I didn't know I would get this opportunity," I began, "but I would like to offer my condolences on the loss of your employee Wanda Addler. I met her here, and I'm sure the situation is very difficult for you."

The pleasant and, yes, seductive expression on Marv's face faded. Just because of the reminder of Wanda—or was he thinking something else? Something like he didn't want to discuss how he'd murdered her?

"Yes," Fitzgerald said from beside him, his tone serious but with a hint of drollness. "It's always difficult to lose an employee that way. They come and go, of course, but it's very rare that the reason for their departure is death rather than firing."

I felt my eyes widen as I looked at him, but his expression remained serious.

"Of course," I said. "I know she was eager to move up in your company. She and I talked about my possibly selling recipes to you, as Jack had suggested."

My gaze was now on Marv. He didn't respond at first, but as I continued looking at him, he said, "Yes, Wanda was an asset to our company and we looked forward to her growing within it. We'll miss her."

A very nice, very professional thing to say, I supposed. I wanted to ask Marv directly, *And how much will* you *miss her*? But I didn't.

After that, I wasn't sure how to keep pushing about Wanda other than to ask my tablemates which one killed her, but I didn't think that would go over well. Instead, all three seemed inclined to push me a bit about the recipes.

I described what Jack already knew about the ones I'd developed as a veterinary technician, how I'd told him I'd consider creating another recipe or two just for VimPets along the same lines, and that kind of thing.

By the time our food arrived, I was already tired of the conversation. I'd promised I'd still think about the possible recipe sale, then sat back while the three started talking among themselves. Some of it was about Jack and his prior and future travels on behalf of the company. He seemed to have relaxed, despite his stressed manner earlier. When the three men talked about other stuff, I started tuning them out.

At one point, though, Fitzgerald brought Wanda up again, and my attention once more perked up.

"We'll only be staying here through tomorrow, Jack," he said. "I assume you'll be back in LA soon. I know Wanda was acting more or less as your assistant and that you'll need someone else. Have you met again with that woman you mentioned a few weeks ago? I know you said she's from this area."

"I didn't want to bring up the job with her again until we'd discussed it internally," Jack responded. "She seemed interested, but I wanted to get your opinion on it before I followed up with her."

"Well, she's certainly one possibility," Fitzgerald said. "Maybe we could meet her in person before we leave town."

"I think you can meet her right now," Jack replied. "She works here, at this restaurant."

Really? Interesting. My brother probably knew her.

"Well, sure. Bring her over," Marv said.

Jack rose and headed to the restaurant door. In a few minutes, he returned.

Gwen was with him.

Skirting the other diners, she walked to the table with him, looking a little uncomfortable.

So she and Jack had talked about her going to work for VimPets?

That evening, Gwen was dressed as she often was, in a skirt and blouse and coppery pinecone necklace. She glanced at me, smiled slightly, and then looked away.

"Everyone, this is Gwen Orway. Gwen, these are some of the VimPets people I told you about before."

I'd thought Gwen liked her job at the resort. On the other hand, she might want something more exciting—and lucrative—than being a restaurant server forever. Plus, she'd broken off whatever she'd had with Neal partly because she had another romantic interest somewhere down the mountains. Maybe she wanted to live closer to him and this would be a good thing for her.

"Hello, Gwen," Marv said.

"Can you join us for a minute?" Fitzgerald turned his head as if looking for another chair.

"Sorry," Gwen said. "I'm on duty now. And... well, although I like the position and appreciate that Jack talked to me about coming to work for VimPets, I've been thinking about it, and I've decided I'd rather stay here, at least for now. Thanks for thinking of me, though." She aimed a small smile at Jack, who still stood beside her, and then toward each of the men at the table.

Gwen looked at me, too, gave a shrug, and sucked her mouth in a little, appearing even more embarrassed.

"I'm sure your server is taking good care of you, and I'd better get back to work," she continued. "Thanks again." She raised one hand in a wave and let it trail behind her as she left.

"Too bad," Jack said, watching after her. I wondered if Gwen had been one of the many women he flirted with. That might have inspired her to think about taking a job with his company. Or not.

In any event, I dug into my salad with a little more gusto so I could finish it quickly. The men, too, began eating and talking again—not really mentioning Gwen's departure.

And what about the potential guilt of either of these two executives in Wanda's murder?

I got a sudden inspiration as to what might help me figure it out. At a lull in their conversation, I said, "I know you're both aware of how Jack has come to Knobcone Heights frequently to promote VimPets products and discuss the recipes with me. He's brought other colleagues at various times, but I don't recall meeting either of you. Have you been to this area before?"

"I intended to come up sometime before this," Fitzgerald responded, taking a bite of his roast beef sandwich. "It sounded like an enjoyable place for sightseers. I'm sorry to say that the thing that finally brought me here was my promise to the local cops that I would come talk with them, and bring Marv as well."

"I've been here before," Marv said, and my attention perked up once more. "Quite a while ago, though. I wouldn't mind coming back to sightsee, maybe bring my dogs and give them some of your store's special biscuits."

Okay, so Marv had been here. He claimed it was long ago. How about last week?

But I couldn't easily ask him that. I merely said, "If you come to my Barkery tomorrow, I'll give you a sample for your pets. What kinds of dogs do you have?"

They were pit bull mixes, he said. He appreciated the offer.

And then I added, “What time of year were you here? When it was as chilly as this?”

“Yes,” he said. “It was around this time of year.” He nodded, smiling at me.

Which left me wondering, again, about where he was last week.

Too bad I hadn’t become skilled at mind reading.

TWENTY-FIVE

GENTLEMEN THAT THEY WERE, or at least appeared to be, the Vim-Pets execs did pay for my dinner. That earned them a point or two in my estimation but didn't remove them, or at least Marv, from my consideration as suspects in Wanda's murder.

Unfortunately, Jack remained on that list, too.

Fitzgerald—whom I didn't really suspect—handled the bill, and I hung out with the others inside, in the cash register area near the restaurant door.

Gwen stood nearby, taking orders at a table where half a dozen seniors sat. She noticed us and gave a small wave before appearing to concentrate again on their requests.

"I'll see you tomorrow at your Barkery," Marv said as we waited for Fitzgerald.

"Great," I said. "As I said, I'll be glad to give you a few sample treats for your dogs."

"Thanks. I'll buy some, too. I plan to come back to town soon, by the way. My appetite has been whetted, and not just for dog biscuits. I want to explore Knobcone Heights some more."

"Good idea," I said. "And if you like hiking, come with me right now. I'm going to talk to my brother before I leave, and he hosts tours of the area. He's going to lead one sometime this weekend, I think."

"Love the idea. He's the one who said hi to you before?"

"That's him. His hikes are great. You should definitely try one out when you're in town. I'm hoping to go on one of the upcoming ones."

Fitzgerald got his credit card and receipt, and we all walked out of the restaurant. We exchanged goodbyes and I told them I'd be in touch with Jack about the recipe idea soon.

"We'll wait for you in the bar," Fitzgerald said after Marv explained he wanted to talk to my brother about a hike.

Marv and I went to the registration desk. Though it was late, Neal still sat there, despite there being two other employees present. He might have been waiting to talk to me, but that needed to be put temporarily on hold; I explained that Marv wanted to discuss upcoming hikes with him.

Neal said he'd just decided that his next hike would be on Saturday morning, starting near the lake and going up into the adjoining mountains—one of the pre-Halloween adventures he'd been considering, since the holiday was a week later. Those who hiked with him then would not be trick-or-treating, as he'd decided his Halloween night followers could, but they'd get to see some amazing views of the area.

"Sounds like fun," I said.

"You want to come, too?" he asked. "You know you're always welcome, sis."

"Thanks. I'll try."

Neal proceeded to give Marv the details of the date, time, and cost while I continued to stand there. Were we being too nice to the person who'd killed Wanda?

Unfortunately, I still didn't know. But if nothing else, maybe the hike would somehow provide me with a way to find out.

I said goodbye to Marv, then told Neal I'd see him at home soon. He agreed, so he probably wasn't getting together with Janelle any more than I was seeing Reed that evening.

Before leaving, I headed to the restroom. The facility was a little crowded, but I found a stall quickly. As I finished and washed my hands, Gwen came in. She looked tired, but she seemed to perk up as she saw me.

She also looked around as if seeking someone who might be there, who I suspected was Elise, or perhaps her more direct supervisor at the restaurant. "I hope you understand that I was just considering my options and future and all, when I told Jack I might be interested in a job," she said. "And I don't really want word to get out about it."

"I'm sure Jack seduced you into it," I said with a smile, "like he tried to seduce me into selling him some dog treat recipes. Or at least that's what I'll say if anyone asks me, and I won't bring it up."

"Well ... yes, that's kind of how it was at the time. But—" She hesitated, then changed the subject, at least somewhat. "Did I hear right, that Neal's leading one of his hikes this weekend?"

"Yes. Are you interested?" I hoped she would interpret my question the right way: interested in the hikes, not Neal.

She headed toward an open stall. "Not sure. But thanks for asking."

"See you there," I called, "or here." Then I left.

I hurried home and was walking Biscuit in front of my house when Neal returned, too. He pulled his car down the driveway, opened the garage door with his remote button, and pulled in. In a few minutes, he'd closed the door and joined us.

"So how did your dinner go?" he asked. "I assume that was all about trying to determine another murder suspect, right?"

"They knew Wanda," I agreed, nodding. "She worked for them and, as you know, had apparently been trying to outshine Jack."

Biscuit finished her sniffing and we all headed toward the unlocked front door, the way my pup and I had exited the house.

"Did you learn anything?" Neal opened the door, and Biscuit and I walked inside.

"Not really. I was already aware that the younger guy, Marv, knew Wanda. The senior executive apparently did too, but maybe not as well. Marv has visited Knobcone Heights before, so he knows his way around, but I didn't hear anything that suggested he was here last week. That's not to say he wasn't, though."

We'd reached the kitchen and both got glasses of ice water from the refrigerator door, then adjourned to the living room, Biscuit at our feet. Neal turned on the television and found a news station, but put it on mute as we both sat on the sofa looking at each other.

"So what's next?" he asked. "I assume from what you've told me that the cops might actually be right this time. The killer is most likely to be Jack Loroco—or even Billi Matlock." He frowned a little, tilting his head. "Or do you still think it could be Harris or Elise?"

"I wish I knew," I said, shaking my head. "Jack seemed to know Wanda best of any of those people, and she was trying to get him fired. He'd been working hard, from what I gathered. He kept trying to get me to sell him some recipes with a veterinary technician's twist to them, but then Wanda butted in and tried to usurp my business relationship with him. Not that my treats were hugely special, or that he couldn't have found another vet tech somewhere who was also developing recipes for special treats."

"Hey, yours are extra special, sis." My nice-looking brother aimed a huge and contagious smile at me. "You've got the Barkery and its increasing business to prove it."

I could only smile back. "Thanks. I just wish I understood better what Jack was going through. I know Wanda was rough on him and that he could have wanted her ousted from the company. And—"

I suddenly stopped as a completely absurd new idea came to me.

Whoever killed Wanda might have wanted to silence her. I already had some suspects in mind, such as the VimPets exec who'd been seduced by Wanda and perhaps wanted to shut her up. Or maybe he hadn't yet given in and wanted to oust her before he succumbed. This meant that maybe one of the two men I'd just met had killed her. And there were potentially others in the company who could also have had reason to silence Wanda.

But one other person in particular came to mind at that moment, as ridiculous as it seemed.

Or not so ridiculous …

I'd need to talk to Jack about it, but in a way that wouldn't give away my silly idea to him. I didn't have to do it in a hurry, though. I could ponder what was the best approach to take, one that didn't tell him what I was thinking—I hoped.

"What's going on, Carrie?" Neal's inquiry sounded like a clap of thunder in my head, even though it hadn't been very loud. But it had definitely resounded in a way that disrupted my odd train of thought.

"Actually," I said, "I'm not really sure. But you know my imagination. I've got some strange ideas percolating, probably nothing particularly useful. But I need to—"

My phone rang, and I was relieved to take it out of my pocket. I didn't want to answer the questions Neal was clearly about to ask, judging by the frown he'd leveled on me just before opening his mouth to spit out whatever had come to him.

Fortunately, my caller was Reed.

Our conversation was brief. Since I'd promised to keep him informed about what I learned while snooping into Wanda's murder, I described my dinner with Jack and his bosses.

I told Reed that I still didn't know who'd killed her, but I hadn't eliminated any of the people I'd come to consider as suspects, some of whom I'd seen at resort that evening. Plus, there were others I wanted to find out more about.

I kept my latest suspicion to myself. After all, I had nothing really to base it on, except that I had an open mind as to suspects. And the list in my head kept expanding.

But maybe this would be the one murder in town lately that the cops would solve without my actually figuring it out. Which would be fine with me, even though I'd already spent so much time trying to solve it.

"Hey, if that's Reed, be sure to invite Hugo and him on my hike this Saturday," Neal called from the other end of the sofa. "You and Bug are coming, aren't you?"

Biscuit, hearing her special name, moved away from where she lay at my feet to grab some attention from her uncle as I complied with his order. "Neal's doing a hike on Saturday morning. Biscuit and I are going, and he wanted me to invite Hugo and you, too. Can you come?"

"I doubt it," Reed said. "I'm scheduled at the clinic that day."

"Oh, well." I was disappointed, but of course I understood.

If my brother hadn't been in the same room I'd have provided Reed with a sexier good night, maybe even thrown him a kiss over the phone. As it was, we just discussed that I'd have a shift at the clinic the following day, and also maybe on Friday. "See you tomorrow, then," I told him and said goodbye.

"So when are you staying the night with him again?" Neal asked, standing up to go to bed.

I wanted to say it wasn't really any of his business, but it actually was, since it would let him know when the house was free for him to invite Janelle. "Not sure, but I'll let you know as soon as we make plans."

"Good. So I probably won't see you till tomorrow night—maybe. Right? Unless I wake up before you leave tomorrow for work, which I hope I don't."

Since Neal seldom did, I didn't think he should be overly concerned.

Something occurred to me then. Yet another visit to the resort?

I had a potentially good reason for it.

"Can you join me for a quick coffee tomorrow morning at the resort restaurant?" I asked.

"Sure," he said, his brow sinking in a dubious expression. "But why?"

Without answering, I called Biscuit. "Time for our last visit outside," I told her. "Good night, Neal. I'll let you know tomorrow when I'm on my way, and also as soon as I know about my plans later in the day."

My day in the shops on Wednesday morning started out so busy that I considered postponing my coffee with Neal. But I knew my own compulsive nature, so I instead rallied my assistants—three of them that day, fortunately: Dinah, Frida, and Vicky. Once they were all there and the doors to the shops were about to open, I told them about my erratic schedule that included a meeting that morning plus a vet clinic shift that afternoon.

As always, they were wholly supportive and sweet and practically said they'd boot me out the door soon so I could meet up with my brother. Plus, they promised to take their usual loving care of Biscuit so I could leave her at the shops with no worries.

Once more, though, I struggled with how I'd supply all of them with raises. Was it possible, after this murder was solved, that I'd still be able to sell a new recipe or two to VimPets, get some kind of royalty on its use, and pass on the profits to my employees?

I hoped so. And that made it feel even more necessary for me not only to figure out who'd killed Wanda, but to do so quickly.

And so, at around nine that morning, I sat in the corner of the not especially busy resort restaurant with Neal, who assured me he had officially taken a permitted break.

"Yes," he told me as we waited for our server to come take our orders, "those two VimPets executives are still registered here as hotel guests, but they're now scheduled to leave tomorrow."

Would that still give me the time I needed to collect the information I was after? Surely it would.

And their leaving now wouldn't keep the cops from going after them if it turned out one of them was guilty.

Gwen came over to take our order. "Coffee and wheat toast for me," I said to her.

Neal ordered coffee, too, plus a cinnamon roll. The ones here at the resort weren't as good as the ones I made, but Chef Manfred Indor had provided the recipe before being dropped as head chef of this restaurant, so they were at least okay.

"Wait just a second, Gwen," I said once we'd both given our orders. I kept my voice low. "I gather that those executives from VimPets are still staying here. I know you said otherwise, but do you have any regrets about not pursuing the job? If so, this would be a good time to bring it up again."

"Like I said, I'm not interested anymore," she said quietly, leaning so that her head was between Neal's and mine.

"That's definitely good for the resort," I said. "And now I want to ask something else, and I'm sure you'll understand why. Wanda apparently had something going with that Marv guy, and possibly manipulated him as well as Jack. Maybe she had something similar with the big wheel, Fitzgerald, too. Did you ever hear either of those men discuss, with or without Jack, anything that Wanda had done to manipulate anyone?"

"Nothing specific, but I—well, I shouldn't say anything because they're still our guests." She turned to look at Neal, as if she expected him to tell her to stay quiet.

My brother may not have known exactly what I was up to, but he remained on my side. "It's okay. I won't say anything. Carrie's seeing if she can figure out evidence against those men. It would certainly be better for Knobcone Heights if one of them turned out to be the killer."

"Or if Jack did," Gwen said, still quietly. "He's not from around here either, and I thought he'd be the one the cops would decide had done it."

"Could be," I agreed. "Wanda clearly tried to manipulate Jack, in public and evidently in private, too. Did he tell you anything about it? Did you hear anything about her when you were looking into a possible job with the company?"

"Maybe. Well, I'm not sure."

"You said that the execs are scheduled to leave tomorrow," I said, looking at Neal, who nodded. "I thought Marv might stay to go on the hike on Saturday."

"All he said was that he'd like to come, but if he did, he'd have to come back up here since he's got to go back to LA first," Neal explained.

"Got it. They're not exactly rushing off, though. If one of them murdered Wanda, he must not think the cops are zeroing in on him. But Gwen, if you think of anything potentially helpful that either of them said, I hope you'll let me know. Oh, and the cops too, of course."

"Sure." Gwen moved, then, standing up and looking toward her right. "Look, I'd better get back to work. But—well, I'm sure you guessed that if I had to pick the killer from out of the air, I'd go for Jack, not necessarily his bosses. Can I provide the cops with anything to prove it? No. But I believe Jack and Wanda had a strange relationship for a while. Now, sorry, I'll go get your order, and I'd better take some others, too."

As she walked off, Neal looked at me. "I'm sorry too, sis. I know you don't want it to be Jack, but if I had to guess whodunit, he's the one I'd focus on. Unless, of course, you have something on those executive guys that you haven't told me."

"Maybe. Or maybe I'm considering another angle. Anyway, I hope Gwen hurries with our stuff. We both need to get back to work."

Neal and I didn't talk about the murder during the short time we enjoyed our coffee and snacks and conversation with each other. I paid our tab, thanked Gwen, and aimed a questioning smile toward her as I said again, "Hope you'll keep our conversation in mind and let me know if you think of anything helpful."

"I will," she said.

A few minutes later, as I walked Neal back to the registration desk, I promised I'd explain what all that had been about—eventually. But I had more to look into as a result.

"Thanks, bro," were my last words to him as I took off for my shops. "See you later."

TWENTY-SIX

At least I got one more shot at asking questions of one of the VimPets execs later that morning. Marv came into the Barkery, as promised, a while after I'd returned. He had to ask for me, since I was in the kitchen.

I didn't know who'd inquired about me till I headed into the shop. I wasn't entirely surprised to see who it was. After all, I'd promised him some sample treats.

"My dogs will be happy when I bring these home to them," he told me, half leaning on the glass-fronted display case. He'd clearly edged his way to the front of the store, since we had a fair-sized crowd there also looking at our treats. He had to raise his voice a bit to be heard over the conversations of our other customers, who stood around the area in groups, some with their dogs. Fortunately, Dinah was in the Barkery too, helping serve them.

Marv looked a little less smooth than when I'd seen him before, since he wore jeans and a VimPets sweatshirt instead of business wear. He nevertheless managed to look at me as if assessing me with his inquisitive blue eyes. He was taller than me, as he would have been with Wanda. He flirted with me, and apparently had with her, too.

Had he snuck up to Knobcone Heights and killed her?

Maybe, although he was now only one of the suspects on my list.

"What, you won't try them yourself to see if any of the recipes are worthy of VimPets attempting to buy them?" I smiled, since I was kind of teasing, although I was interested in his reaction.

"I just might." He grinned back. "And maybe then I'll be able to talk you into it. But I unfortunately don't think I'll be able to bring my dogs here this weekend for your brother's hike. Maybe for the Halloween one, though."

"That would be good." My mind raced to figure out questions to ask the guy now, during what might be my last opportunity to interrogate him—at least for nearly two weeks. "I wonder if Wanda's murder will be solved by Halloween. I know she grated on the nerves of a lot of people—Jack, you, and Fitzgerald, for example. Anyone else you can think of?"

"You're one nosy lady," he said, although his smile didn't waver. "Do you want a list of VimPets employees she worked with? Outside vendors and others I think she had contact with? I figure any one of them could have had reason to do away with our dear Wanda."

"Any rise above the rest as suspects?" I wasn't about to stop pushing. "Did you hear any particularly bad arguments? Or hear about any you weren't privy to?" *Or did you kill her*?

His eyes moved upward as if he was thinking. Then he looked back at me and responded to my spoken questions. "Not really. I've pretty much kept myself from speculating about what happened to Wanda, and I'm not about to tell you any ideas I have, not without any kind of proof. But I gather Wanda did rile at least one person by getting in that person's way… and now I'll shut up. Hey, could I get some of those great-looking biscuits shaped like dog bones?"

He pointed into the display case, and the rest of our conversation remained friendly and general and had nothing to do with what had happened to Wanda.

Marv clearly hadn't admitted to killing Wanda himself, and my suspicion of him wasn't the strongest anyway. Not that I was exonerating him, but his attitude suggested that he hadn't been that close to Wanda after all. I really didn't know what to think anymore, considering how she'd talked about him—and talked to him.

And in any case, he could be innocent of murdering her. Plus, he apparently had a suspect in his mind, someone who he wasn't naming.

Might it be someone I was thinking about, too?

I saw Reed that afternoon when I went to the clinic for my shift. I followed the usual routine and left Biscuit with the great folks at the facility's doggy daycare.

I went inside and changed, and my first assignment that day was to help Reed in an examination room with a large sheepdog mix with a small attention span. The dog was there just for a checkup and shots but still required more control than his middle-aged human mom could provide on her own.

The pup's exam turned out fine. So did my stamina, and his owner seemed most grateful.

"You might want to give him some very special treats," Reed said. "Have you tried any of the products at Barkery and Biscuits?" He aimed a wink at me.

Reed asked his patients' owners this once in a while, even though I'd told him I didn't expect it and didn't want them to think he was prescribing anything—even though I did consider all my treats to be healthful, especially since they'd been developed for the clinic's patients in the first place.

But I thought it was sweet and thoughtful of him to do it anyway, whenever he did.

This owner looked confused at first, and I quickly explained that the Barkery was one of my businesses and told her how I'd come up with the recipes.

"Wonderful!" the lady said. "I'll have to give it a try."

When she left, I thanked Reed. "It's especially nice that you help me to promote the Barkery, but you don't have to."

"Of course I don't. But I believe in what you do there, Carrie."

I shot him a warm grin—that grew cooler when he continued.

"Even though I can't say the same about your amateur sleuthing. How are things going, by the way?"

I could have given him a huge and sorrowful rundown on where I was—or wasn't—in looking into Wanda's murder. I kept it brief, though.

"I've got suspects besides Jack and Billi, of course. I'm still looking into all of them. And if you've got any suggestions—besides telling me to back off—please let me know."

"That's my biggest one," he said, sounding sad. "But I'll let you know if I think of anything else. Hey, I can't make dinner tonight, but how about tomorrow?"

"Sure," I said. That would be something to look forward to. So was Neal's hike this Saturday, even though Reed wouldn't be there.

I was also happy that I'd have another shift here at the clinic in two days. And that all seemed to be going well at my shops.

But despite having some new—and aging—ideas about solving Wanda Addler's murder, I wasn't sure what to do next.

———

The next few days passed without my doing anything regarding my investigation, just thinking about it. A lot.

I considered asking someone for advice—but the big question mark about that was *who*?

I knew I could use Neal as a sounding board. Reed, too, maybe—depending on his mood. He certainly was smart and intuitive enough to help me with ideas, but I felt sure any suggestions he had would be prefaced, or ended, with advice to back out or just tell the cops all my evidence-free ideas.

The good thing—maybe—was that I stayed away from the resort for several days. I didn't go to the Knob Hill Pet Emporium either, despite still considering Harris to be someone I might want to ask further questions of. Maybe he'd interacted with some of my other highest-up suspects—one in particular. But I was still pondering whether to talk to him again, and, if so, what I'd say.

I had no interest in speaking with Elise, despite her remaining a potential suspect in my mind.

Notwithstanding my concerns about it, I considered running my ideas by Reed when we got together for dinner at my house. I decided against it, though. Despite my mind darting off to my stalled investigation now and then, I didn't bring up Wanda's murder at all, and neither did Reed.

Earlier on Thursday, my only foray away from the stores had been to dash off to Mountaintop Rescue for an hour or so. My excuse was to bring some leftover treats for the dog residents. My real goal was to talk to Billi, and I succeeded. I even discussed with her my latest visits to the resort and who I'd seen and talked to and questioned. She said she'd never met the VimPets execs but felt bad for Jack, not only because of his having to work so hard to keep his job but also because he, like her, was a murder suspect.

Speaking of suspicions, that led me to believe even more that she still cared a lot about Jack and had hoped for some kind of real relationship with him.

Would she still want that if both of them were finally cleared as persons of interest because the real killer was found?

The person I now was considering with particular interest wouldn't be an obstacle between them. At least I didn't think so.

But I still believed my own suspicion to be so weird and off-base that I tried not to think about it much, except to figure out what to do next. And so far, I hadn't decided.

Friday passed fairly normally, with my spending most of my day at the shops, interrupted only by a short shift at the vet clinic.

And on Saturday, I asked all four of my assistants to plan on working for a while. I wanted to go on Neal's pre-Halloween hike, partly to clear my head and partly to ponder even more what to do next.

An internal conflict? Absolutely.

Around eight a.m., after starting the baking and being there to open the shops at seven, I left Dinah in charge, with Frida also present. Janelle and Vicky would arrive in an hour or so. Loading Biscuit in the car, I drove to the place Neal picked to meet up with those taking his latest hike—the parking lot for the Knobcone House of Celebration, a very special, architecturally unique modern venue for very special events in this very special town. It was south of the resort, fronting on the lake, and at the foot of a small but gorgeous mountain range.

Neal was already there. He'd forgiven me for putting Janelle to work that day, but swore he wouldn't if I made her hang out in the shops on Halloween weekend. He had taken both days off from his job at the resort.

My brother looked good in his new black sweatshirt decorated with the name of his new website that advertised and described his hikes: KeepUpWithKennersly.com. As always on his hikes, he wore a backpack that contained various useful supplies. He also carried the baton he used to make sure his group knew where he was. He'd dubbed the baton his "staff," since it was also his assistant in leading folks on trails, particularly up and down hills, and he used it as a walking stick in flat areas. It was four feet long with a crook at the top, and was colored a bright and glossy red.

At the moment, Neal stood at the edge of the nearly empty parking lot with the staff over his head, ensuring that his followers knew where to go. Biscuit and I headed in that direction. I, too, wore a sweatshirt, since the air was nippy. Mine promoted my entrepreneurial enterprises as well, since it contained the names of both Barkery and Biscuits and Icing on the Cake.

Neal had warned me that a couple of cops were likely to be on the hike. He'd been getting more interest lately from members of the local force, and several had joined him on his outings recently. He wasn't sure who might be coming, since the police department apparently would book several reservations for the hikes and then decide which cops would be able to take advantage of them. But he had at least wanted to let me know.

Which was fine. I could ignore the cops or be friendly, but resolved not to discuss the most recent murder at all with them.

Unless I thought it would be helpful…

As I drew closer, I was surprised to note that the crowd of maybe fifteen people so far included someone I'd not anticipated coming along: Reed. He had Hugo with him, and when Neal lifted his staff even higher to greet me, Reed turned to smile at me.

"Hey," I said as Biscuit and I caught up with them. "What are you doing here?"

"Just wanted to keep an eye on you," he said. "In case you thought you'd be stalking a murder suspect on this hike."

I punched his arm gently as I laughed. "Yeah, of course I am."

"I was able to take the day off after all," he added. Which made me smile.

I glanced down. Biscuit, at the end of her leash, was trading nose sniffs with Hugo. There was a big difference in their sizes, but they'd always been friendly with one another.

Which was fortunate, since Reed and I continued to become friendlier with one another, too.

I didn't recognize most of the others waiting for the hike to begin, which wasn't surprising, since many of them were undoubtedly guests at the resort whom Neal had encouraged to sign up for his hike—this was completely permitted by his bosses, he'd assured me. It was a good and fun thing for Knobcone Heights Resort guests to do while in town, after all.

I did recognize the cops among the soon-to-be hikers, though. One was Sergeant Himura. I'd met him several months before, when he was my contact when I'd expressed concern about issues involving dogs in and around our town. He hadn't impressed me as being particularly interested in dogs, nor in being a particularly good cop. Maybe he'd be a better hiker.

The other cop on the hike surprised me even more: Chief Loretta Jonas, boss to Sergeant Himura, Detective Wayne Crunoll,

Detective Bridget Morana, and many more—like, the entire Knobcone Heights police force. She had her dog Jellybean, a schnauzer mix, with her.

Neither Loretta nor Himura was dressed in cop gear. They looked as if they were trying to fit in with civilians.

I gave them a small smile of greeting without getting close to them. Not now, at least.

I turned to Reed, who stood beside me watching Neal for any signals. "Did you tell Neal not to let me know you were coming?"

"Would I do a thing like that?" he asked, which gave me my answer. "I figured I'd surprise you just for fun, without any hidden motive."

"Of course."

A couple of other people in sweatshirts and boots were now clustered around Neal with the rest of us. It was time to go.

"Okay, everyone," my brother said. "Here's what we're going to do." He turned to point at the path at the far side of the parking lot from the House of Celebration. It quickly disappeared into a forest of trees that decorated a steeply sloping mountainside behind it. "We're starting there and making our way upward. This is going to be a fairly short hike, just around an hour and a half, but you're going to see some pretty spectacular vistas, including the lake and rocky overlooks from which you can view the town below and more of the mountains around here. Everyone ready?"

A low roar of yeses chorused around us.

"Then let's go!" Neal waved his staff in the air. "Follow me."

Everyone obeyed. In minutes we were well ensconced on the dirt path and moving quickly forward—well, as quickly as is possible on a narrow trail where no more than a couple of people could walk side by side.

Reed and I kept up with the rest of the group of around twenty, now, even preceding most of them. We both started pointing out things to see, such as a hawk flying up above and lizards on the ground skittering to get out of the way.

After a while, Reed said, "Remind me again. How many of Neal's hikes have you taken?"

Both Hugo and Biscuit pulled gently ahead of us on their leashes as the dirt path wound beneath some tall knobcone pines. The air was cool and breezy, and branches waved above us. We were near the front of the group, partly since I wanted to stay as close to my brother as possible.

"Probably half a dozen," I replied. "Some were just hikes around the lake, and there were a couple where Neal took groups to see some of the more interesting residential areas in and near Knobcone Heights. I've taken this one a couple of times, too."

"Is it all Neal described that it'd be?"

"Definitely. Wait till you see some of those vistas he's described."

Previously, I'd looked back to see who was behind us, and it appeared a group of tourists was following. Nevertheless, I now heard a female voice say, "I've done this hike before but without your brother, Carrie." I turned slightly. Chief Loretta, dressed in her warm civilian wear, followed us closely now, preceded by Jellybean. They must have maneuvered around some of the crowd. "This is one of my favorite trails, so I decided to give Neal's guidance here a try and asked for one of the slots the department booked."

"He's a great tour leader," I said, hoping all went well on this outing. The latest murder was unlikely to be mentioned, and no one who was a suspect was with us—or at least no one I knew about.

"So I heard from a few of my officers," the chief said.

Neal stopped us in several clearings, mostly overlooking mountain vistas, and waved for the group to cluster around him. He described where we were and what we were seeing.

At the fourth such stop the three dogs all started acting odd, pulling toward the cliff's craggy edge. "No, Biscuit!" I commanded, and Reed and Chief Loretta did the same with their pups.

They all began barking, though—and then I heard it. The sound of a fourth dog yipping. Could it be something wild, a coyote or wolf or some other kind of canine?

I didn't see it, though it sounded as if it came from the edge of the cliff but below us. I needed to find out what was going on, and so I moved away from the crowd, which included Reed. I told Biscuit "Sit!" and as she obeyed, I hooked my end of her leash up to a substantial-looking bush nearby. I moved forward to the rocky outcropping, walking carefully but determined to see downward. I pulled out my phone, ready to take a picture with my extended arm if I couldn't maneuver the rest of my body at an angle to see.

As I drew slowly closer, my feet started sliding on the slick rock surface. I screamed, even as I noticed that I wasn't the only one sliding. Neal and Sergeant Himura were, too. We were all heading toward the cliff's edge, and there was nothing close by to stop us.

Were we all going to die?

TWENTY-SEVEN

THE ANSWER, FORTUNATELY, WAS no.

As I scrambled wildly to try to find something to grab onto, or some other way to stop, I heard Reed yell, "Neal! Your hook!"

I saw my brother scrambling, too. He must have understood what Reed meant, for instead of trying to stab his staff into the unyielding rock surface, he turned and held it out, hook side backward. From the corner of my eye I saw Reed seize that end. He wasn't sliding, so he must still be on solid, non-oily ground.

"Carrie," he yelled then. "Sergeant. Grab on."

I somehow changed the way I was sliding to aim myself in that direction and I did, in fact, clutch onto Neal's staff. He still held the straight end, and Sergeant Himura stuck his hand out to take hold, too.

I then saw that along with Reed, a bunch of the other hikers were holding the staff tightly, anchoring it. As we all clung to it, they pulled us back off the terrible oily surface.

Soon we were safe. I saw that one of the other hikers held Hugo's leash, and Chief Loretta held not only Jellybean's but Biscuit's, too —a good thing, since my little girl was straining to get closer to me.

Plus, I still heard that yappy little dog voice from over the cliff. What was that about?

I wasn't the only one concerned. "Glad you're all okay," Chief Loretta said, "but I think a dog needs help."

"I think we can check from down below," Neal said, and after telling most of the hikers to stay where they were—but away from the edge—he quickly led a bunch of us down the path we'd hiked up.

I was panting like an overheated dog, more from fear and stress than warmth in this brisk air, but no way was I going to ignore that yapping.

Sure enough, from a sideways angle, looking up, we could see what appeared to be a little Yorkie jumping around on a narrow ledge. He was still yapping, and sounded and appeared frenzied.

How had he avoided falling? "We have to help him," I cried out quietly.

My sweet and skilled brother pulled a rope from his backpack, turned one end into a noose, and tossed the looped end until he hooked it onto a large bush that grew from the cliffside near where the dog was.

"No, Neal!" I yelled to him as, holding the rope, he began to pull himself upward. Sure, it looked as if the end was tied fairly securely onto that bush—but "fairly" didn't mean tightly enough.

Plus, who knew how strong that bush actually was?

But Neal kept going.

Fortunately, there was a rough surface below the area where my brother climbed, and he was able to swing himself slightly sideways—enough to grab onto the dog.

Soon, amazingly, both of them were back safely on the ground near where I stood shaking.

"Hey, dog-lady sis. You want this little guy?"

"You saved him!" I rushed forward to take the Yorkie and hug my brother. "You're a hero, Neal."

The hike was over. Neal was exhausted, as were the rest of us.

Reed and I walked slowly toward the rear of the group as Neal led us all back down to the parking area. Chief Loretta and Sergeant Himura hung back with us, too. We talked about the little Yorkie, now held by Reed. He believed the pup was okay, just scratched here and there, but he would dash off to the clinic with him to perform a checkup.

I'd head there too, a little later, once I checked on the shops. But right now we were talking with the cops about the situation and how they were going to attempt to find out how the dog had gotten onto the ledge.

I had some ideas and voiced them, at least somewhat. It didn't look like the poor pup could have gotten there all by herself. She didn't have a collar, but maybe she was microchipped. Where was her owner? Surely the owner wouldn't have done such a heinous thing.

We finished our conversation in the parking lot. Neal said goodbye to those who'd paid to hike with him, promising them a big discount next time—and also a different location.

I headed toward the far side of the lot toward my car, allowing Biscuit to sniff on the way. I pushed the button to unlock my elderly white Toyota, then hesitated before getting in, but Biscuit jumped right onto the passenger seat so I followed her.

"You're such a good girl," I told her. "I know you're looking out for me."

We soon reached the parking lot behind my shops. "Wish we could close early today," I told Biscuit as I pulled my car into a vacant spot. "I'm pooped—er, tired. Not the way you think of poop."

I wanted to check in with my assistants, of course. But I'd no intention of going home early. I would, however, take an hour or so to drive to the vet clinic to see how that little Yorkie was doing.

As soon as I opened my car door to get out, though, Biscuit started barking.

And no wonder. Someone had come up to my car and was standing right there.

Someone with a gun at her side, as if to try to hide it in case anyone from the neighboring shops happened to be looking in our direction.

Someone I'd kind of figured I'd be confronted by—although not here and now.

"Hi, Gwen," I said.

She climbed into the backseat of my car and was now arranging herself into a slump so that her head was probably not visible through any of the windows. That angle might make it hard for her to shoot me—but I didn't want to take any chances.

I held Biscuit on my lap, though my little dog kept trying to leap out of my arms and into the back. Did she just want to say hi to Gwen? I didn't think so. She was acting uncharacteristically stressed, and I figured it was at least partly because she sensed my fear and worry.

I figured Gwen would instruct me to drive somewhere. That could be the end of me. And Biscuit.

I wasn't going to let that happen.

I had to at least try to distract her.

The first thing on my mind probably shouldn't have been the first, but I had to ask. "You obviously knew I was on Neal's hike. Did you have anything to do with endangering that little dog that was trapped on a ledge?"

I gritted my teeth as I heard her bark of a laugh. "Of course. I also spread some oil on the ground since I figured you'd be the first one to try to help the creature. But obviously you didn't slide off the cliff like I'd hoped."

"You endangered other people," I said angrily. "Not to mention that poor dog." But she clearly knew me well. Of course I would attempt to save a dog who was in danger.

"I saw you all get away from there, unfortunately," she responded offhandedly. "I stayed in the area to watch."

So she wanted to see me die, and maybe the dog, too. Any other hikers who were injured would be collateral damage, I supposed.

I might become furious with people, but this was one of the few times I would have liked to inflict on her what she'd hoped to accomplish with me.

"Now," she said, "I think it's time for us to go. You need to start driving."

"Not yet," I said quickly. "I have some more questions. And if you just shoot me right now, you'll make noise people will hear and you'll have to get out of the car to run, or drive away."

"Yeah, it would have been a whole lot easier if you'd just fallen off the damned cliff. But we're getting away from here—or I'll shoot your dog first."

I hugged Biscuit even closer to me, trying to shield her in case this clearly insane woman decided to act immediately. Even so, I attempted to maintain a calm demeanor.

Reed had told me to only talk one-on-one with the person I believed to be the killer if I was in public and safe.

He'd also said I couldn't always choose the time and place to talk, and that certainly was the situation now—despite my wishes otherwise.

"No shooting necessary," I told Gwen. "I'll do what you want—soon. But before we go anywhere, I'd really like to know why you killed Wanda in the first place. I mean, she wasn't very likeable and other people might applaud that you got rid of her. But why? Was it because you like Jack? Or was it something about VimPets?"

"VimPets," she spat. "And it wasn't Jack I liked but your miserable brother."

Interesting, I thought. Maybe she'd intended for Neal to fall off the mountain, too.

"But I thought you told him you had a guy who lived somewhere else." I glanced out the windshield, seeking a means of escape if it became necessary. I'd pulled straight into the space, so I only saw the wall of the building. I supposed I could start the engine again and drive into it, in the hopes the collision would harm Gwen, but Biscuit and I were likely to get hurt first.

"I lied, to try to get him interested in winning me away from another guy. But then he met Janelle and obviously liked her more than me, so I pretended not to care. And when Jack started flirting with me, well, I played along, thinking I could get him to find me a new job with VimPets far away from this hokey town, get me a job that really counted with a good company. And Jack agreed. I was waiting for him to come up here again and take me back with him, even just for a short visit while I met the VimPets people and interviewed for the job we'd talked about as his assistant. It sounded so good. But instead of just coming up here to see Billi and you, he brought Wanda with him. And when I took him aside to ask about our plans, she butted in. Laughed at me. Said I was just some crummy little waitress in a crummy little town and that was that. There'd be nothing at VimPets for me."

Gwen must really have wanted that job. Killing someone for preventing it seemed way beyond rationality.

Of course, murdering someone at all wasn't exactly rational.

"I can understand how upsetting that must have been. But—why use a poop scooper? And I gather you somehow made it into a weapon?"

"Yeah, wasn't that clever? I snuck one out of Mountaintop Rescue while pretending to be looking for a new pet. I wore different clothes and a hat and all, so no one would recognize me."

"Is that where you got the little dog you stuck on the mountain?" I tried to sound conversational even though I was seething.

"No, that one belongs to a guest at the resort. A simple dognapping while the owner was away. Aren't you going to ask me how I turned the poop scooper into a weapon?"

"Well, sure. How did you?" I figured, from the little I'd heard about how Wanda had been stabbed, that the killer must have carved at least one of the wooden ends of the crossed sticks into a point, and that's in fact what Gwen described.

"Wow. You really thought this through," I said, trying to sound impressed.

"Plus," Gwen added, "I did it all wearing gloves so any fingerprints the cops found wouldn't be mine."

"Wow," I said again. It had clearly been a premeditated murder. I would never have thought—before—that the quiet restaurant server would do such a heinous thing.

But Gwen must have been hiding who she really was inside as she took people's orders, served them what they wanted, and acted friendly for tips.

And now?

She must have thought she'd get away with it, or why come after me?

Why come after me? my mind repeated. I asked it aloud.

"Because you were meddling, damn you!" Gwen spat it out as if she were facing me head-on and aiming the gun at my chest. "I knew you'd solved those other murders. I figured you'd nose your way into this one, too. That's why I made sure there were plenty of reasons and clues around so the cops would go after Jack. He deserved it, after all. He's the one who turned his back on me. I wanted to leave this horrible town. I wanted that damned job, and that damned Wanda was preventing it. She had to go."

I heard a thumping nearly at my side as Biscuit barked again, and I hugged her even more as I realized what the noise was. Gwen was shaking. Banging the gun against the seat. She probably had her finger on the trigger.

She might shoot us even without intending to.

But her rant continued. "I was glad they were seriously considering another suspect, Billi Matlock. But you just wouldn't let that alone. Oh, no. You kept asking questions even when your own boyfriend and brother told you to butt out. I heard some of that, during all those times you were at the resort. I wanted to discourage you, too, but couldn't do much without giving myself away. And still you asked questions. Butted in. I knew if things went on as they had been you'd figure out it was me. And so I had to stop you. I'll stop you now, for sure. Right now. It's time. Start the engine and drive where I tell you."

"Oh, I don't think so, Gwen," I said softly, finally seeing a movement beyond the passenger side window. "You see, you're right that I'd figured out it was you. In fact, I mentioned this little insight to Chief Loretta and Sergeant Himura when we hiked back down the mountain a little while ago, and I gave them my reasons. They bought into it, so much so that I just happen to be wearing a bug right now. They wanted to eavesdrop if you showed up. Which you did."

Hearing her special name, Biscuit/Bug squirmed again, but I held her tightly.

"What!" Gwen screamed, just as figures began to appear outside all the windows.

They were in fact cops—including Chief Loretta and Sergeant Himura. They all held guns trained on Gwen.

I quickly drew Biscuit down onto the seat with me, in case some of those guns went off.

But, thank heavens, my part in all this was over.

TWENTY-EIGHT

It was exactly a week later—the day before Halloween. I had decorated my shops with jack-o'-lanterns and also baked people treats shaped like pumpkins and ghosts.

As soon as the doors opened that morning, Billi arrived at the Barkery with some of her assistants and volunteers from Mountaintop Rescue. She brought rescued animals, too—mostly dogs, although a couple of adorable cats had been brought in crates.

We were holding one of those miraculous adoption events.

Within an hour of opening, wonderful chaos swirled on the tile floor. I stood with Billi near the door, watching it with probably the hugest grin that had ever appeared on my face. About eight of the volunteers held the leashes of dogs of all sizes and breed combos, from Chihuahua mixes to pit bulls to collie mixes, and the public eagerly checked them out. Cute young receptionist Mimi was there, her white shirt with a golden retriever face on it reading *Adopt today. Love forever.*

Biscuit and Go were in the large fenced crate at the side of the room, to keep them from getting in the way—or to prevent people from attempting to adopt them. Both seemed highly interested in what was going on, watching and trading nose sniffs with the rescue dogs who got close enough. Of the dozen dogs that Mountaintop Rescue had brought to the event, four had been adopted already.

"This is so wonderful," I told our City Councilwoman. Billi appeared a whole lot prettier and more relaxed than she'd been last week and the days before.

And why not? She'd been cleared as a murder suspect.

"*You're* so wonderful," Billi countered, holding out her hands to grasp mine. Her brown eyes were glowing, her posture perfect beneath her Mountaintop Rescue T-shirt and black jeans, and her smile most likely matched mine. "In fact, Jack—"

"Jack what?" interrupted a voice behind us, which sounded a whole lot like that very guy. I turned.

Jack was in fact there, dressed as the businessman that he was. He, too, was smiling—and his smile was aimed at Billi.

She seemed to flush a little as she looked at him, and I figured that whatever their differences were before, they might be an item once again.

"Jack's welcome here," I finished for her.

"In case I haven't told you often enough before," Jack said, looking at me, "Jack is very grateful."

I laughed. "He's also innocent," I said. "You both were."

"Of course," Jack said. "But that doesn't mean we weren't in danger of being arrested."

"Amen." Billi turned to me. "You know they'll never admit it to you, Carrie, but the cops are starting to respect your murder-solving abilities."

"Yeah, right."

"No, I mean it," Billi said. "In fact—wait a minute. Someone's coming in who should hear this."

I knew who must be entering the shop and turned to see Reed come in.

"Hey, I took an hour off at the clinic. I wanted to see this." He came up and put his arm around me.

If we hadn't been in public, I'd have kissed him. But being in public didn't matter to him. He bent down and kissed me, so I of course had to kiss him back.

"Now, Reed, you should hear what I'm about to say." Billi was speaking, but Jack had taken the opportunity, given my closeness with Reed, to snuggle up to her. In all fairness, the shop was so crowded that all the humans seemed to be close to one another, but still…

"Hear what?" Reed looked particularly handsome that day in his blue Knobcone Veterinary Clinic sweatshirt, with his angular, smiling face beneath messy dark hair. Oh, heck. He always looked handsome to me.

"I made a point of talking to Chief Loretta a couple of days ago—as a City Councilwoman, not just to express my relief at being cleared of the murder. Despite my concerns about how the case was initially handled, she was very nice and gracious and made a comment something like, 'this police department is highly skilled in ensuring justice is done, and we appreciate and respect our citizens' assistance.'"

"That sounds familiar," Jack said. "Was it the same quote she gave to local media?"

"Could be," Billi said. Her arm was around his back, as his was around hers, and I felt really happy for them.

"You did a good job, Carrie." Reed sounded reluctant. "I'd never deny that. But when that woman was caught holding a gun on you, after trying to make you fall down the mountainside—"

"Yeah. Even though the cops were listening, I wasn't exactly safe. I know it. And I was scared. You were right. I should be more careful." I looked up at him solemnly, to find him watching me with a caring and worried expression.

"So even if a dozen more murders occur in this town, you'll stay out of trying to solve them?"

I pursed my lips. "I never wanted to get involved in the first place, but given the circumstances and the people involved … "

"I get it." Reed shook his head. "You can't say no."

"Well, I didn't say I would do it again, either. In fact, no. I won't ever solve a murder again."

"That makes me very glad." He bent to kiss me again.

"Hey, you two."

When I pulled away, I saw Neal entering the store—and Janelle making her way toward him from behind the glass display counter. They, too, traded kisses.

My other assistants were in Icing, which was busy, too, with people who'd come to see the dogs and left wanting treats of their own. I definitely had to work out how to give some raises around here. Since I'd finally made up my mind to sell one recipe to Vim-Pets and Jack, my idea to use at least some of the proceeds for raises sounded more logical than ever. And depending on how that first sale went, I might even sell them some more later.

I noticed then that Neal hadn't come in alone. A short, thin lady in a fussy blouse and long skirt followed him. And in her arms was a small Yorkie mix—maybe the dog who'd been rescued on the hike.

Any doubt I had was immediately dispelled. "You're Carrie. I'm Hilda, Witchy's owner. I can't believe what happened when I was only away for one day! I hope Neal's told you how much I appreciate what you did to help save Witchy from that ledge." She got closer and used her arm that was not holding her little dog—Witchy—to hug me.

"Neal was the real hero," I told her. I'd already heard from Reed that little Witchy was fine after her exam and was back with her owner.

"I know he is. But I've heard the whole story now and I really appreciate you and everyone else here. In fact, I think Witchy needs a friend. If there are any small dogs available for adoption today, I want to meet them."

Billi had clearly been eavesdropping. "I want to introduce you to Honey, then. She's a Chihuahua mix, about Witchy's size." She gestured for Hilda to follow her.

"I think it's time to pass out more sample treats that people can bring home to their pets—and that the dogs here can taste, too," I said to Janelle. She grinned, and we both made our way behind the display case.

When we emerged, we each held a paper plate filled mostly with small carob biscuits shaped like bones. We started passing them out.

And I was thrilled, a minute later, to hear a cheer go up from the Mountaintop Rescue volunteers. A lab mix named Singsing was about to be adopted. The would-be owner had already filled out the form, which Billi approved pending a later follow-up.

And then it was Honey's turn. Hilda did in fact want to adopt her as Witchy's friend, and Billi approved her paperwork, too.

I joined in the cheers and applause.

And felt really, really good. Just over a week ago I'd feared we would never be able to hold another event like this again, since Billi might be arrested at any minute.

Now, the right person was behind bars for Wanda Addler's murder, and some wonderful, needy dogs were finding new homes. Apparently the cats were, too.

Plus, Halloween was tomorrow, and my brother would hold his next hike then. All was well.

I smiled yet again, and as I did so, I met Reed's gaze.

"Care to join Hugo and me for dinner at our place tonight?" he asked, and I liked the suggestive expression on his face.

"Oh, yes. Biscuit and I will definitely be there." I took a step closer to him and held his hand as another potential adopter started filling out the paperwork for a pit bull.

THE END

BARKERY AND BISCUITS DOG TREAT RECIPE

Pumpkin Peanut Butter Bites

2½ cups whole wheat flour
2 large eggs
2 Tbsp honey (local is best)
¼ cup pureed pumpkin
3 Tbsp peanut butter (creamy)
¼ tsp salt
½ tsp cinnamon
Water

Preheat oven to 350°F.

Whisk together the flour, eggs, honey, pumpkin, peanut butter, salt, and cinnamon. Dough should be dry and stiff, but workable. Add tiny amounts of water if needed. Roll the dough until it's about ½ inch thick. Cut into small bits, about an inch. (Cut into squares, triangles, hearts, even bone shapes with cutter—any small shape you would like).

Bake in a preheated oven until hard. About 35 minutes. (Ovens vary.) Store in airtight container.

ICING ON THE CAKE PEOPLE TREAT RECIPE

Pumpkin Snickerdoodle Cookies

1½ cups granulated sugar
½ cup butter
½ cup vegetable shortening (i.e. Crisco butter flavor baking stick)
2 large eggs
¾ cup canned pumpkin puree
2¾ cup all-purpose flour
2 tsp cream of tartar
1 tsp baking soda
¼ tsp salt
¼ cup sugar for topping
2 tsp ground cinnamon for topping

Cream together sugar, butter, and shortening. Add in eggs and mix well. Sift together flour, cream of tartar, baking soda, and salt. Slowly add dry ingredients to the sugar/butter mixture. Stir in pumpkin puree. Place dough in freezer to chill for at least 2 hours, but overnight is best. Dough must be chilled for cookies to turn out right.

Preheat oven to 350°F. In a small bowl combine ¼ cup sugar with 2 tsp ground cinnamon. Measure tablespoon of cookie dough and use your hands to roll into a ball. Roll ball around in the cinnamon sugar mixture. (Can make smaller cookies, if desired.) Place the balls of cookie dough on baking sheets lined with parchment paper.

Bake for about 12–13 minutes. Remove from oven just when the edges of the cookies start to brown.

ACKNOWLEDGMENTS

Again no surprises: thanks to my amazing agent Paige Wheeler. Thanks also to the wonderful people at Midnight Ink who work with me: acquisitions editor Terri Bischoff, production editor Sandy Sullivan, and publicist Katie Mickschl.

And yes, I again want to express my appreciation to a couple of friends for the recipes at the back of the book. Lisa Kelley once more gave me a wonderful dog treat recipe, Pumpkin Peanut Butter Bites—my pups ate these quickly and then barked for more. And Paula Riggin provided the recipe for the people treat, Pumpkin Snickerdoodle Cookies, which my husband Fred and I loved and shared with others. Lots of tasty pumpkin this time. Thanks to both of you!

ABOUT THE AUTHOR

Linda O. Johnston (Los Angeles, CA) has published forty-five romance and mystery novels, including the Pet Rescue Mystery series and the Pet-Sitter Mystery series for Berkley Prime Crime. With Midnight Ink, she's published *Lost Under a Ladder*, *Knock on Wood,* and *Unlucky Charms* in the Superstition Mystery series, along with the first two Barkery & Biscuits Mysteries, *Bite the Biscuit* and *To Catch a Treat.*